TO STEAL A DUKE

The Sisterhood of Independent Ladies
Book One

by Maeve Greyson

ARE YOU SIGNED UP FOR DRAGONBLADE'S BLOG?

You'll get the latest news and information on exclusive giveaways, exclusive excerpts, coming releases, sales, free books, cover reveals and more.

Check out our complete list of authors, too!

No spam, no junk. That's a promise!

Sign Up Here

www.dragonbladepublishing.com

Dearest Reader;

Thank you for your support of a small press. At Dragonblade Publishing, we strive to bring you the highest quality Historical Romance from some of the best authors in the business. Without your support, there is no 'us', so we sincerely hope you adore these stories and find some new favorite authors along the way.

Happy Reading!

CEO, Dragonblade Publishing

Additional Dragonblade books by Author Maeve Greyson

The Sisterhood of Independent Ladies Series
To Steal a Duke (Book 1)

Once Upon a Scot Series
A Scot of Her Own (Book 1)
A Scot to Have and to Hold (Book 2)
A Scot To Love and Protect (Book 3)

Time to Love a Highlander Series
Loving Her Highland Thief (Book 1)
Taming Her Highland Legend (Book 2)
Winning Her Highland Warrior (Book 3)
Capturing Her Highland Keeper (Book 4)
Saving Her Highland Traitor (Book 5)
Loving Her Lonely Highlander (Book 6)
Delighting Her Highland Devil (Book 7)
When the Midnight Bell Tolls (Novella)

Highland Heroes Series
The Guardian (Book 1)
The Warrior (Book 2)
The Judge (Book 3)
The Dreamer (Book 4)
The Bard (Book 5)
The Ghost (Book 6)
A Yuletide Yearning (Novella)
Love's Charity (Novella)

Also from Maeve Greyson
Guardian of Midnight Manor (Novella)

CHAPTER ONE

Bening Manor
East of Emden, Germany
March 1815

LADY CECELIA TUTTCLIFFE, Celia to a dearest few, ran her finger down the line of numbers for the third time, smearing them in the process. "Oh, for heaven's sake, Celia, stop!" She slammed the ledger shut and shoved it to the corner of her desk. It was time to compose herself. Losing all sense of reason simply would not do.

She eyed the long-handled bell waiting close at hand on its small, round silver salver. "Blast it all!" She snatched it up and shook it, half tempted to lob it across the room.

Friedrich, the loyal footman who guarded them better than any soldier, governess, or highly trained mastiff, opened the library door before the jingling faded. "My lady?"

"He is still in there?"

The sandy-haired giant whom she felt sure was close to her age of three and twenty offered a sympathetic nod. "Yes, my lady. The physician is still with Her Grace."

Celia was keenly aware that servants possessed a dangerously intimate knowledge of what went on in a manor. Keeping secrets from them was next to impossible. Winning their loyalty and rewarding them for their silence was a much wiser course of action—especially for her and Mama. "Berta has heard nothing through the door?"

Friedrich avoided her gaze and resettled his footing, squaring his broad shoulders as though bracing himself. Celia almost smiled. The footman always did that when he found a question uncomfortable. "Friedrich, I am well aware that Berta has the uncanny ability to hear a mouse squeak in the next province. What has she heard through that door?"

The man's shoulders slumped, and he stared at the floor. "Berta will not tell me, my lady. She cannot speak for weeping."

Celia swallowed hard but failed to rid herself of the lump of emotions choking her. She cleared her throat and fought to maintain a calm exterior. "Weeping?"

"Yes, my lady. I am sorry."

"Thank you, Friedrich. You may go." Celia pushed away from the desk and went to the window, blinking furiously against tears she refused to shed. Mama would not die. Not yet. Not from this infuriating fatigue that none of these ridiculous doctors appeared able to diagnose or treat. Bloody quacks. The lot of them.

She fisted her hands against her middle and channeled her fears into a determined rage. Mama would live. The inimitable Thea Tuttcliffe, Dowager Duchess of Hasterton, was not but a few years past twoscore years of age. A young widow by many accounts. She would live. Celia would consider nothing less.

"My lady?" Friedrich quietly called from the doorway. "Her Grace asks that you join her now."

Prepared to hear the same ineptness all the other physicians had spouted, Celia exited the library, pausing only long enough to select the correct key on her chatelaine and lock the door behind her. She had not secured the ledgers nor properly reviewed the most recent business correspondence on her desk. While she didn't question the loyalties of most of the staff, she never set caution aside. "Friedrich, please let Mrs. Thacker know I have locked the library. I shall let her know when she can open it for the maids to see to its tidying."

"Yes, my lady."

Celia hurried up the stairs, noting that Berta, her mother's lady's maid, no longer waited outside the double doors to Mama's suite. She pushed through them to find the elegant dowager duchess reclining on her favorite velvet lounge in front of the sunny expanse of windows overlooking her gardens.

The noted physician summoned from Austria stood at a nearby table rummaging through his black leather satchel. The man's wild gray brows knotted in a furious scowl. He glanced up when Celia entered and squinted at her over the tops of his spectacles. "There is nothing to be done, my lady. Your brother should consider returning to Emden." The doctor shrugged on his stark black greatcoat, then spared a stern glance for Duchess Thea. "His Grace should return sooner, rather than later. That is my recommendation."

"Did you not say your coach was waiting, Dr. Mendelson?" The duchess countered his stern glare with a tight-jawed look of her own. "Forgive us for not offering you tea, but I would never wish to cause you to miss your connection in Bremen."

The man snorted a disgruntled huff, then presented a curt bow. "I strongly recommend you take my advice to heart, Your Grace. For your own good and that of your family. Good day." He gave Celia a snapping nod, then headed for the door.

Celia followed and closed the doors behind him with a rude bang. "What a waste of time. Godspeed, you priggish little man."

"Now, Celia—to let another control your behavior is a sign of weakness. Never relinquish your control, dear girl." Her mother smiled and waved her closer. "Come. We have decisions to make."

"I shall cast a wider net, Mama. There are other medical experts to be found." Celia yanked on the bellpull. They needed tea. Or more aptly, something stronger. Mama's favorite pear brandy would not be amiss.

"Celia, come here now." Her mother's tone held more than its usual weariness. It echoed with resignation and heartbreaking finality.

Celia pulled a small, cushioned footstool over and sat beside her mother. Taking Mama's hands in hers, she leaned in close. "You must not give up. The doctors I have found so far are nothing more than charlatans adept at fleecing the hopeful. I shall find another. And then another, if necessary, until I find the ultimate medical professional to help you." She scowled at the closed doors. "Where is Berta? She never takes this long when you ring."

"The doctor sent her to give Cook a recipe for a special calves' foot jelly and some other concoction to build my blood." Duchess Thea wrinkled her nose. "I am sure it will be dreadful, and if I am to die anyway, why should I waste any of my precious few moments on anything dreadful?"

"Mama! Do not say that." Celia rushed to the bellpull and yanked on it again and again.

Mrs. Thacker, their generously proportioned housekeeper, trundled into the room, clutching her chest and gasping for air. "Your Grace. Lady Cecilia. I am here."

"Mrs. Thacker, please sit and catch your breath." The dowager waved the red-faced woman to the nearest chair, then fixed a chiding look on Celia. "And do forgive Lady Cecilia. It seems her impatience knows no bounds today."

Celia helped the poor woman to the seat. "I am sorry, Mrs. Thacker. That useless doctor has me distraught about Mama, and both of us need something stronger than calves' foot jelly, barley broth, or tea."

The housekeeper waved away the words as her hard breathing slowed to her usual huffing and puffing. "I feared as much about that man." She shook a chubby finger high in the air. "That one had a dodgy look about him. Saw it in his eyes from the moment he stepped through the front door."

The double doors swung open wider, and Berta entered, bearing a tray filled with cold meats, cheeses, and fruit. Friedrich followed close behind. His tray held a teapot, teacups, and a round-bellied decanter of golden pear brandy.

Mrs. Thacker pushed herself to her feet and offered both Celia and the duchess a kindly smile. "Forgive me for being so bold, but I thought this might be warranted after that dreadful man overstayed his welcome."

"Thank you, Mrs. Thacker." Celia blinked hard against those irritatingly persistent tears while scolding herself for being such an emotional ninny. Now was not the time. She had to be strong and convince Mama to persevere. "All of you take such good care of us." She turned to include Berta and Friedrich in the praise. Their loyalty and support meant everything. "We appreciate you more than you know."

Berta dipped a quick curtsy. Her bottom lip quivered, and she swiped at her red-rimmed eyes. "We are thankful to be here, my lady. You do so much to help our families."

Friedrich cleared his throat and bowed his head. "We are proud to serve this house, my lady. Proud indeed."

Dabbing at her eyes with a handkerchief, Mrs. Thacker trundled forward and supervised the footman while he set the table. After an approving nod, she turned to the duchess. "Does Your Grace wish to take her tea while enjoying the sunshine at the window? I can prepare a small lap tray."

"No, Mrs. Thacker. Thank you." Celia's mother slowly pushed herself up from the lounge, moved to the table, and, with Friedrich's help, settled into a chair. "I feel it is important to keep moving. Thank you. You may all go now."

The trio left and closed the doors with a quiet click.

Celia poured their tea, then added a gentle splash of brandy to their cups. She paused with the decanter over her mother's cup. "More?" Mama's pallor worried her. She had seemed much healthier before that fool physician's visit.

Duchess Thea delicately waved the bottle away. "That is enough for now, thank you." She took a sip, closed her eyes, and smiled. "Excellent. This was your father's favorite brandy."

Whenever Mama spoke about Father, she was melancholy

indeed. While the two had never been in love, they had enjoyed an agreeable friendship during their brief marriage. Their union had lasted less than two years before he was killed in a carriage accident, leaving Mama alone, heavy with child, and praying for the babe to be a son to become the sixth Duke of Hasterton. Instead, Celia was born, and Mama, in her desperation, had launched a most remarkable endeavor to protect what the world would deny her child just because she was a daughter rather than a son.

"This afternoon, I shall write to that Italian physician I read about earlier this week," Celia said. "Remember the one? I showed you the article." She sipped her tea, then added more brandy when Mama remained silent. "Remember?" she prodded. "His results are reported to be quite exceptional."

"Celia." Mama didn't look up from the delicate, gold-rimmed teacup in front of her. She gazed down into it with a faint smile, as if watching her last days unfold. "It is time we accept what is and decide what we shall do with the time I have remaining." She leaned back in the chair and rested her hands on the padded armrests. "There are three things I wish to accomplish before I find my eternal rest. The first of which is seeing my beloved London again and enjoying this year's Season. Easter came early this year, but we can still reach Town in time to enjoy a good portion of the season's offerings."

"You wish to travel to London?" Celia could not believe her ears. London was not safe. They could be discovered. "And enjoy the Season? To submit yourself to all those marriage-minded mothers wishing to match their daughters with your son, the duke, who is really your daughter—the one not considered suitable to inherit the title, even though she has built the Hasterton dukedom into quite an impressive empire?" Celia shook her head. "Out of the question. We simply cannot, Mama. It is difficult enough to protect our extremely complicated venture from here in Germany. Need I remind you that Mrs. Thacker had to dismiss the two newest maids and a footman because they took too great an interest in why my imaginary twin never visited us here at the manor?"

"Are you quite finished?" Mama arched a sleek, dark brow.

Celia folded her hands in her lap and proffered an apologetic nod. "Forgive me. You wish to enjoy this year's Season. What are your other wishes? You spoke of three."

"I wish to see you happily married to a good man of my choosing."

"Mama."

"None of the three are unreasonable or extravagant. Do you not agree?" Mama lifted her cup for another sip, her sharp gaze pinned on Celia all the while.

"And your third wish?" Celia preferred to know every detail before engaging in battle—especially with Mama.

"I told you."

"You did not." Celia added more tea and milk to both their cups. Battling with her mother required a sober mind. "You stated your wish to go to London and your silly desire for me to marry a man of your choosing."

"And you happy," her mother added with a subtle tip of her head. "Your happiness is my third, yet greatest desire."

"You know I can never be presented in London, and you cannot travel alone." Celia applauded herself for countering request number one and number two effectively. "And I am happy." She offered a genuine smile. "As long as you fight to remain alive and well, I am happy."

"You are not happy. You have become an old curmudgeon— a most soured, miserly sort of person who is interested in nothing but business." Mama leaned forward and thumped her delicate fist on the table, her mouth pressed in a hard, flat line. "There is more to life than adding to our coffers, starting new business ventures, and buying more land."

"I am not miserly." How could Mama say such a thing? "When have I ever refused a purchase or an expense you requested? And might I also remind you that several of our businesses have set up a great many women in their own shops, so they might feed their families and earn a proper living without demeaning or endangering themselves?"

"It is time you helped yourself, my child. There is no shame in that. You are young, Celia, and trust me, this exciting time of your life is fleeting." Regret filled her mother's eyes and lent a lonely echo to her voice. "You should be dancing, courting, enjoying your friends." Mama shuddered as if finding the entire subject too exasperating to bear. "At three and twenty, you should be a silly, carefree girl dreaming of the perfect husband. In fact, you should already be married and providing me with grandchildren. You are too serious for your age. It pains me to see how terribly I have failed you."

"I have friends," Celia argued. "I wrote to Sophie and Frannie just the other day." Her defense sounded childish even to her.

"Friends other than those of the Sisterhood." The gentleness of Mama's reprimand gained a sharper edge, cutting like well-honed steel. "You should also have acquaintances oblivious to our subterfuge. Friends not operating as we do to keep from losing what they have. Emmeline, Lavinia, and I created the Sisterhood of Independent Ladies when we all became widowed early, then bore daughters rather than sons. It is a support system, Celia. Not a permanent prison for you, Sophie, and Frannie. I intend to meet with our solicitor while in London. It is time you were freed of this terrible farce I was foolish enough to create."

"Freed? And lose everything we worked for? People depend on us, Mama. We cannot lose our businesses, and I cannot believe you wish to let the title go extinct. I couldn't bear to see our entailments revert to the Crown until some undeserving lout worms them away by fawning all over Prinny." Celia struggled not to raise her voice even though frustration at the unfairness of it all made her want to scream. But she wouldn't shout. Not at Mama. "Your brilliance laid the groundwork for all I have done in the years since I took over. How can you be so ready to toss it all away?"

"It is time to find a *legal* way to see you cared for and happy." Mama sat taller, reclaiming the persona of the strong, fearless woman Celia had always known and loved—the woman Mama had been before she became plagued with days of unrelenting fatigue and pain. "This is not your decision, Celia. It is mine, and I will see it done."

Celia pushed away from the table and rose, unable to sit any longer. Her mind raced through everything that could go wrong, even the terrible possibility that both of them could face numerous charges of fraud for impersonating a peer. Well, they hadn't actually impersonated Charles. Mama had merely invented him to keep what should rightly be theirs. But she doubted very much if that would grant them any leniency with the prosecuting courts.

"Surely, you do not expect to go to London and present me to the *ton* without anyone questioning us about Charles or why we never visit any of our properties in England. And I realize we can have our London townhouse fully staffed with individuals our Bow Street Runner investigated, but will they not expect the duke to accompany us? Rumors about us will set the scandal sheets ablaze." She spun to face her mother and threw her hands in the air. "And then I'm sure the courts will get involved. The ladies of the *ton* will not allow their husbands to ignore the mysteriousness of our situation!"

The dowager frowned, peering at Celia as though unable to recognize her. "When did you become so dramatic?"

"When everything I have ever been taught is suddenly considered irrelevant. A whim. A way to get by until I could be carted off like prime breeding stock and matched with the best stallion." Celia pointed at her mother. "I refuse to sign off on that exorbitant dowry you suggested, and you have never been able to imitate my *Charles* signature."

Mama rolled her eyes. "I said nothing about presenting you for the Season. I know that is not possible under our rather delicate circumstances. It could draw the wrong people too close." She laced her thin fingers together and rested her clasped hands in her lap. "I want to go to London for the Season. See you married. Know that you are happy and protected. Those three things. Simple as that."

Celia massaged her suddenly throbbing temples. These headaches usually only came after hours of wading through ledgers and contracts requiring her signature—or Charles's signature, to put a finer point on it. "And what shall we tell everyone about Charles? Why is he not traveling with us or attending the Season in search of a wife?"

"He is on the Continent investigating the most promising business deals of his life." The duchess twitched a dismissive shrug. "And as your twin, Charles is but three and twenty. He has plenty of time to marry."

Celia rolled her eyes. "And how do you explain not presenting his sister, who is actually past the age for coming out and surely must be frantically in need of a husband?"

"His sister remained in Germany because of her frail health. Sadly, she is not able to attend this year's Season."

"You cannot travel alone."

"I do not intend to."

"Mama—"

"You are quickly reaching the point of being unreasonable." The dowager directed Celia back to her chair. "Sit and calm yourself. You are usually so much more creative than this. Are you unwell?"

"I am quite well." Celia hovered behind the chair and clutched the curved wood of its back, digging her nails into the voluptuous upholstery of the cushions. "I am simply beside myself because I cannot seem to make you see sense."

"You will accompany me as my companion, Miss Celia Bening, since my daughter's ill health and my son's urgent business ventures prevent them from attending to their ailing mother's wish to see her beloved London one last time."

"My, don't we sound like a pair of ungrateful, self-centered children?"

Her mother smiled as she poured them both a bit more brandy. "Well, you know how children can be. Once they are grown, they often have no use for their parents. Sit down, Cecilia."

Celia took her seat. When Mama used her given name rather than the usual endearment of Celia, that meant she had endured all her patience could bear. And heaven help Celia if Mama used all the names of her christening. A curtly snapped *Cecilia Elizabeth Madeline Rose Bening* had once meant being sent to bed without her supper. Now it was worse. It meant Mama was so angry that she would not allow Celia back in her presence until her temper had cooled. And sometimes that cooling took more than a day.

After a delicate sip, Celia risked meeting her mother's gaze and couldn't help but smile. A healthy rosiness bloomed across Mama's cheeks and vigor flashed in her eyes. The excitement of a trip to London and the delicious prospect of deceiving the *ton* had benefited Duchess Thea more than any amount of specially prepared calves' foot jelly. Mama had always loved a challenge, and admittedly, so did Celia.

She lifted her teacup in a toast. "To London and the excitement of the Season."

Mama gently touched her porcelain cup to Celia's and smiled. "To happiness, a good man, and love."

"Mama."

Duchess Thea kept her cup against Celia's and waited with a parental look that refused to be ignored.

"Fine." With an indulgent sigh, Celia dutifully repeated, "To happiness, a good man, and love."

CHAPTER TWO

Law Office of Parkerton, Hodgely, and Kane
London, England
April 1815

L ORD ELIAS RAINES, younger brother to the Duke of Almsbury and newest partner in the law office of Parkerton, Hodgely, and Kane, marked his place in the current year's Hasterton records. He propped it open with a notebook, set it aside, then selected the previous year's ledger and compared the two.

"Impossible," he muttered, then flipped through a few more pages while shaking his head. "Impossibly brilliant," he amended. In the span of twelve short months, the Duke of Hasterton had more than doubled his vast holdings—almost tripled them. "The man is an utter genius."

No wonder Hasterton had always been a favorite client of Master Hodgely's—God rest his mentor's eccentric soul. Elias sorted through a few more documents from the prior years, then frowned. The duke's signature differed on this contract. Dramatically so. The dowager duchess must have signed for her son, since he would have been within a few months of legal age at that time. Highly irregular for her to sign his name. She should have had His Grace sign in front of witnesses, then initialed it when they purchased that parcel of land.

Elias vaguely remembered Master Hodgely remarking on a few other peculiarities about the Hasterton files over the years—

such as the regular transfer of assets from Hasterton accounts to those of an account under the name of Bening, the dowager duchess's maiden name, that was overseen by a solicitor in Germany. His mentor had also mentioned that the fifth Duke of Hasterton had died before the current duke and his twin sister were born. Rather than return to London with her children, Duchess Thea had elected to remain at her family's estate, Bening Manor, in Germany. However, by that time, she had no family left alive to assist her. Only servants. The dowager had even seen that the young duke received his education abroad.

Reportedly, the man had never set foot in London. He, like his mother, retained the office of Parkerton, Hodgely, and Kane to assist with most legalities and business dealings while retaining the German solicitor primarily for the Bening holdings. It was quite an odd situation, indeed. While Elias's mentor had never expressed an issue about not meeting the current duke, Master Hodgely had bemoaned on more than one occasion how he truly wished he could once again see the duke's lovely mother—a dear lady for which he had always held a great fondness. Of course, whenever Elias pressed the man for more details, Master Hodgely always changed the subject. Strange behavior, indeed. Now that Master Hodgely had passed and Elias had taken his place, this esteemed client was now his responsibility.

After assuming the new position at the firm, Elias had introduced himself to each of his new clients. All were of London's most elite, and he felt it important to meet with them face to face and assure them that even though Master Hodgely no longer looked after them, they were still in quite capable hands. He had successfully met with everyone except for the Duke of Hasterton. That meeting had proven to be somewhat of a challenge, since His Grace never came to London. Of course, Elias could not merely show up at Bening Manor in Germany uninvited. To do so would be the height of rudeness. But as yet, every correspondence he had sent that gently and respectfully requested an introductory meeting had gone unanswered.

"Most frustrating," Elias said as he leaned back in his leather chair. The sixth Duke of Hasterton was obviously ignoring him, and there was nothing he could do except wait. A light knock on his office door pulled him from his fuming. "Enter."

"Messengers just left these, my lord." Young Thomas, the office runner, strode in, deposited several missives into the basket on Elias's desk, then left just as quickly after a respectful dip of his chin.

The letter on top bore an interesting wax seal with which Elias was quite familiar. Could it possibly be? He snatched it up, turned it to a proper angle, and smiled. It *was* the Hasterton crest. But this letter hardly appeared worn enough to have traveled all the way from Germany.

He hurried to open it and devoured the brief note, hoping it held an invitation. It did. But he would not be going to Germany. He reread it, slower this time. The Dowager Duchess of Hasterton requested he call upon her at her London townhouse today. She would receive between the hours of three and six. If he was unable to comply with this request, a reply with a more agreeable appointment date and time would be most appreciated.

If he was unable to comply? Elias allowed himself an amused snort. He would clear his schedule immediately for a meeting with the dowager duchess. Perhaps the duke would also be in attendance. After all, if his mother had decided to partake in the London Season, surely the duke and his sister would as well. In fact, this Season might be the sister's debut. What better reason to show up in London after all these years?

He checked his timepiece, then vainly assessed his attire. Dear old Mrs. Camp had dutifully brushed his coat and hat within an inch of their lives and had her son polish his boots. As she had presented his breakfast, she had also blessed him with her daily wish for a prosperous day. "Well done, Mrs. Camp," he said under his breath. Perhaps the grandmotherly lady's wish had resulted in the dowager's note.

He refolded the paper and tucked it into the inside pocket of his jacket, then nervously brushed imagined lint and crumbs from his buff-colored pantaloons. "Remember who you are, Elias," he quietly admonished himself as he placed a selection of the Hasterton files into the fine leather satchel his brother had presented him upon completion of his education. He donned his hat and gloves, took up the satchel, and headed out.

"I am meeting a client," he informed one of the young men apprenticing in the office. "Please inform Parkerton and Kane I am unsure when I shall return."

"Yes, my lord," the young man said, his tone filled with envy.

Elias understood completely. He had once been in that lad's position. He made a mental note to be more approachable and helpful, as Master Hodgely had been with him.

"Shall I get you a hackney, Lord Raines?" Thomas asked while holding the door.

"That would be most appreciated," Elias said. The Hasterton townhouse was not within reasonable walking distance.

The helpful lad soon had a coach ready, and Elias embarked on the meeting he had sought for months. Or, at least, he hoped the duke would also be present, since he couldn't in good conscience question the dowager about business details.

As the coach came to a stop in front of the residence, Elias checked his watch again. Perhaps he had been a bit overzealous, since it was not yet three. He stepped down from the coach and eyed the place as though about to descend upon Napoleon's camp.

"Should I wait, sir?" the driver called down from his perch.

Elias had no idea and hated feeling as if he were some inexperienced lad. Good heavens, he was a respected solicitor, the son of a duke, and an esteemed member of the *ton*—although as a *second* son, the esteem he commanded was debatable. However, he never had a problem attracting the ladies, much to the consternation of their mothers. "Yes. Do wait, good sir," he instructed the driver while adding enough to the fare to make it worth the man's while.

The driver's smile widened as he thumbed through the coinage in his palm. He doffed his hat. "Thank you much, sir. I shall wait here as long as you like."

After a decisive nod, Elias strode up the steps and reached for the gleaming brass door knocker in the shape of a lion's head with a ring in its mouth. He rapped three times for luck.

The door quickly swung open, revealing the stern countenance of a tall, older man still muscular enough to oust any unwanted visitor with an easy flick of his thick wrist. His scowling demeanor suggested he was quite the protective butler. "May I help you, sir?"

"Lord Elias Raines from Parkerton, Hodgely, and Kane. Her Grace is expecting me."

"Welcome, my lord." The butler stepped back and held the door open wide enough for Elias to pass, then quickly closed it. "Her Grace informed me you would arrive during receiving hours."

Elias almost smiled at the merest hint of rebuke in the gruff man's voice. "Yes, I am early," he admitted as he handed over his hat and gloves. "I do hope Her Grace will forgive me."

The butler's expression remained unchanged. He merely responded, "Your bag, my lord?"

Elias tucked the satchel under his arm. "I shall keep this with me, thank you."

The door to their immediate left popped open, revealing a lovely young woman with an even more furious scowl than the butler. She huffed an errant ebony curl out of her eyes while shuffling through an armload of books and papers. "Gransdon, are you quite certain all the trunks have been placed in the proper rooms? I am missing at least three ledgers that are most important."

"I will check again, *Miss Bening.*" The butler cleared his throat as if trying to warn the lady they had company.

The exquisite beauty's head jerked up, and her pale, green-eyed gaze homed in on Elias. "I beg your pardon, my lord," she said with a hurried curtsy. "I was not aware of the time." Her eyes narrowed as though she couldn't decide whether to welcome him or have Gransdon escort him out. "Lord Raines, I presume? Her Grace mentioned she had sent for you."

"Yes, Lord Elias Raines at your service, Miss Bening."

What a breathtaking woman she was with her tousled curls of gleaming black framing her high cheekbones. And the unusual shade of her eyes—a pale yet brilliant green, like those of a fierce kitten sizing him up as prey. From the butler's manner toward her, this woman was no servant.

Elias politely tipped his head, determined to become better acquainted with the delightful Miss Bening. "Forgive me for calling before three."

She responded with a slight humming noise that reminded him of a soft growl and piqued his interest even more. Then she gifted him with a polite yet detached smile. "You will find Her Grace very forgiving," she said. "If you would be so kind as to follow Gransdon down to the parlor, I shall let Her Grace know you are here."

"Thank you, Miss Bening." Elias found himself entranced, watching her glide up the stairs with the fluid grace of a hawk soaring into the heavens. Her muslin gown, a soft green that brought out her eyes, swirled around her, offering a teasing glimpse of her tempting curves.

Gransdon cleared his throat twice. When Elias turned his way, the butler directed him to follow down the hallway to a set of double doors on the right. "The parlor, my lord."

"Thank you." Elias strolled through the doors, taking in the room's tasteful opulence. The furnishings whispered of elegance in gentle mauves and delicate blue and green florals. Small, round mahogany tables adorned with petite vases of flowers were situated among the perfect number of chairs and sofas. Not too cluttered nor too sparse. Rich draperies of the deepest burgundy framed the wall of windows, and the panes between were shielded with sheer lace panels to assure a modicum of privacy. A decidedly feminine room. As a duchess's parlor should be.

Elias caught the butler before he exited. "Gransdon—is His Grace in today?"

The man's jaw flexed, as though hardening at the impertinence of the question. "We do not expect His Grace today, my lord." With a proper bow, he retreated and closed the double doors behind him before Elias could ask anything more.

"Not expected *today*?" Elias repeated under his breath, frustrated at the subtle insinuation that perhaps they did not expect His Grace's arrival ever. He scowled at the doors, willing them to provide more information. Surely, the duke had not allowed his mother and sister to travel unprotected all the way from Germany. Perhaps the man had seen them settled in at the townhouse, then gone to the club to update himself about London. Yes, that had to be the case.

The double doors opened once more, and Elias almost forgot his manners. With a delayed start, he stood and offered a proper bow. "Your Grace." The elderly dowager he had expected did not exist. The Duchess of Hasterton was a regal beauty. Older, yes, but still the sort of woman that made a man take a second and even a third glance.

"Lord Raines." She kindly directed him to a different chair. "Thank you so much for responding to my request so promptly. I know we are not your only client." She gracefully motioned for Miss Bening to come closer. "I understand you have already met my Celia—Miss Celia Bening. She is my delightful companion on this visit to London."

Companion? Elias politely smiled while sorting through the whirlwind of inferences clamoring in his head. He offered a less dramatic nod to Miss Bening. "Yes, I had the pleasure of meeting her earlier," he said, while noting that the resemblance between the two women was remarkable. Then he remembered that *Bening* Manor was Her Grace's family home in Germany. Perhaps Miss Bening was not only a companion but a relation. Odd, since according to all the information in his files, the Hasterton/Bening line had all but died out. The duke, the dowager, and the duke's sister were the sole living members of the two families.

"Lord Raines?" Miss Bening said, her louder tone tinged with a hint of irritation.

"I beg your pardon." Elias bowed to them both again, then settled into his chair. While he had stood there sorting through this puzzlement like a foolhardy schoolboy, both ladies had seated themselves. "Do forgive me, but the two of you share quite a lovely resemblance." He tried to soften his boldness with a laugh as he turned to the duchess. "I recall Bening was your family name before marriage, Your Grace. Is Miss Bening a long-lost cousin, perhaps?"

"You, my lord, are very impertinent," Miss Bening interjected before the dowager could answer. "It is truly a pity our trusted Master Hodgely is not still with us."

"Celia!" The dowager lightly patted her foot in Miss Bening's direction before turning to Elias with an indulgent, albeit somewhat weary, smile. "Do forgive her, my lord. We only arrived in London late yesterday, and I fear my dear Miss Bening does not travel well at all."

"Think nothing of it, Your Grace." Elias stored away the lovely Celia's reaction for further rumination later. "Miss Bening is quite right. My rudeness is inexcusable, and I assure you it will not happen again." He returned Her Grace's indulgent smile, then also offered one to Miss Bening. "I too wish Master Hodgely was still with us. He was not only my mentor, but much like a father to me. He is greatly missed."

The duchess hitched in a sharp sniff, then bowed her head as though struggling for composure. "Raymond was a dear friend. News of his passing brought us great sorrow."

"Indeed." Elias bowed his head out of respect for his mentor. After allowing a quiet moment, he glanced over at the satchel he had placed in another chair. "I took the liberty of bringing your files today. I thought His Grace might like to review them once I attended to the matters for which you invited me."

"His Grace is still abroad," Miss Bening said a little too curtly. "And Lady Cecilia remained in Germany as well. Unfortunately, her health is even more fragile than Her Grace's."

Elias sensed Miss Bening did not like him at all and was also hiding something. Something important. He prided himself on his ability to read a person and figure them out—discover the truths they didn't wish to share. Master Hodgely had often remarked that that was one of Elias's most exemplary talents. He looked forward to discovering the *real* Miss Bening.

"I am truly sorry to hear of Lady Cecilia's poor health," he politely responded. He would make no more remarks of a personal nature until he had completed further research on this unusual situation. He turned to the dowager. "How can I be of service to Your Grace?"

"I require a last will and testament. Immediately."

It was then that Elias noticed a frailness plaguing the lady. Shadows of unusual weariness settled beneath her pale green eyes, making them appear almost sunken. A hollowness accentuated her high cheekbones. She was still a lovely woman, but struggling to remain so, and was entirely too thin. She possessed an almost fragile translucence—like the finest porcelain. Elias knew without a doubt that Her Grace was dying. He had watched his beloved aunt fade from this world in much the same way.

"I can absolutely see to your will immediately, Your Grace. In fact, if you would like, I shall return tomorrow well before receiving hours so as not to hinder any of your social engagements."

"That will not be necessary, Lord Raines." The duchess appeared to be struggling with her composure as she turned to Miss Bening. "My list, Celia? Do be kind enough to fetch it."

"Of course, Your Grace." Miss Bening rose and hurried from the room.

"I feel I understand the need for expediency, Your Grace, but are you quite certain you wish to do this today?" Elias wondered if the ailing lady might need a rest. Her extreme fatigue had become even more apparent during their short visit. "After all, you said you arrived late yesterday. I am sure traveling from Germany is quite arduous."

The duchess's rueful smile didn't soften the resentment in her eyes. "Do I appear so frail as to offend you, my lord?"

"You could never offend me, Your Grace." He could tell the duchess hated that her life was being stolen from her, and he didn't blame her. "You are a beautiful woman whom fate has treated quite unfairly. I wish it were not so."

She fixed him with a piercing stare that seemed almost calculating. "How much did Master Hodgely tell you about the Hasterton line?"

Elias sensed she was asking him a great deal more than if he was familiar with their files. "He always spoke of Your Grace and your children with much fondness and admiration when informing me of the appropriate condition of the estate, and how it should be managed." He paused, watching her closely. "Master Hodgely gave me the impression that he considered your account the most important of all his clients."

Before the duchess could respond, Miss Bening returned to the room. "Forgive me for the delay, Your Grace," she said as she handed the duchess a long, narrow envelope bearing the Hasterton seal. "It appears the maids attended to the library and moved it. I shall speak to Mrs. Harcourt immediately regarding how the servants will address a door locked by one of us."

What an unusual thing to say. Elias also noted the high coloring on Miss Bening's cheeks. The lady was frustrated to no end, and as fiercely protective of the dowager as a lioness protecting her young.

"It is all right, Celia," the duchess said after examining the envelope. "The seal is still intact. Do not be too hard on them. Remember, we are new to them."

Miss Bening cleared her throat with a nervous cough, then turned to Elias. "Would you care for tea, my lord? Forgive me for being so remiss. I should have offered it earlier."

"That would be most lovely, Miss Bening, and no apology is necessary. As Her Grace pointed out, the two of you have barely had sufficient time to settle into your household here in London—since arriving late last night." He wondered if she would pick up on his speaking of the household as though it belonged to her as well as the duchess.

She did.

"*Her Grace's* household," Miss Bening gently corrected him, with the slightest hint of displeasure creasing her brow. She excused herself with a subtle nod, then stepped into the hall and spoke quietly to Gransdon.

A deep, rumbling "At once, my lady, and I do apologize most heartily" came from that direction, but Elias couldn't pick up on Miss Bening's response. He did, however, find Gransdon's reference to her as *my lady* quite interesting indeed.

"Here is my list, Lord Raines," the dowager announced in a loud voice while waving the envelope at him. "The terms I require in my will. I trust you will put everything in order and bring it here for my signature by tomorrow?"

"By tomorrow, Your Grace?" Elias hefted the envelope in one hand. It obviously contained several pages.

"Yes. Tomorrow." The duchess's eyes gleamed with iron-willed determination. "I want nothing left to chance. No loose ends. The crossing from Germany made me quite aware of my mortality, and those things over which I have no control."

"Tea will be here shortly," Miss Bening said as she rejoined them. Her gaze settled on the envelope Elias held. "If you would like to review the list while we wait, that would be most acceptable. After all, there might be items you wish to clarify."

He found it interesting that a lady's companion would make such a statement about something that had absolutely nothing to do with her. But he didn't comment on Miss Bening's unusual behavior. Instead, he turned back to the duchess. "Do you wish me to do so, Your Grace? Review the list here and now?"

After a quick glance at Miss Bening, the dowager nodded. "Yes. I agree it would be best."

Elias carefully opened the packet and scanned the sheets of instructions, finding all the terms quite unusual. The dowager duchess's Bening holdings appeared quite impressive—if this account was accurate. He would have to confirm the figures with the records back at his office.

The solicitor in Germany, Erwin Von Gaelinson, was listed as the individual overseeing the duchess's original provision account that was set up when she married the duke. Elias remembered that name appearing on the transfers from the Hasterton accounts to the Bening account he had handled. The man's contact information was listed, and he wished to receive a witnessed copy of the will upon its completion. Nothing unusual there.

However, Elias had always found their need for an additional solicitor quite surprising, since Her Grace had expressed such trust and affection for Master Hodgely. Their office could have easily and efficiently handled all of her accounts.

When he reached the final page of the document, he came up short and read it twice. The duchess wished for everything to be placed in a trust for Miss Bening. Not a single item mentioned her daughter or her son. Most surprising, indeed. He lifted his gaze from the documents and looked straight into the duchess's sharp-eyed stare. "This is most unusual, Your Grace, and I must caution that your son and daughter could successfully contest such a will."

Before the duchess could respond, Miss Bening huffed a very unladylike snort. "It is my understanding, my lord, that the Hasterton holdings will not be affected. After all, we have already settled everything that belonged to the fifth Duke of Hasterton upon the sixth, including provisions for a generous dowry for Lady Cecilia. Is that not so?"

"That is my understanding," Elias said while attempting to ignore a growing uneasiness in his gut. Instinct told him there was so much more going on here of which he was not aware. He returned his attention to the duchess. "But this still raises the question. Do you wish nothing to go to your daughter? Not even your jewelry?"

"She has jewelry of her own, and her brother will see to her until such time as she marries." The duchess suddenly became cold and detached. She lifted her chin in defiance. "And of course, once she marries, everything becomes her husband's property. Correct?"

"Yes, Your Grace. That is the usual way of it. Except for what is stipulated in the marriage contract to be saved for her and any future children, should she become widowed."

"Yes." The duchess spat out the word as though it tasted foul. "Thank heavens for a proper marriage contract to protect those deemed irrelevant by England's legal system."

Bitterness and resentment thickened the air of the parlor like a dense London fog. Elias rose from his seat. "Perhaps I should take my leave and get to work on your documents." He carefully tucked the papers back into their envelope, then stowed them safely inside his satchel. A strange storm brewed in this residence, and he wanted no part of it until armed with more information. He offered both ladies a proper bow.

"No tea, then, my lord?" Miss Bening asked in a decidedly victorious tone.

"Thank you, no. Perhaps another time." He paused and unabashedly studied her. Was this mysterious beauty as cunningly avaricious as the dowager's request portrayed her to be?

"You are staring, my lord," she said. "Is there something else you wish to say?"

"Not at this particular time." Elias squared his shoulders, suddenly looking forward to a battle of wits with this lovely lady. And with any luck, so much more. He didn't sense greed from her. More like a subtle leeriness tinged with desperation—but why?

"I promise you, though," he said, "you and I shall have much to discuss in the future."

CHAPTER THREE

CELIA PEEPED THROUGH the side window framing the door. The handsome yet infuriating Lord Raines strode to the awaiting hackney with the same powerful grace of the restless panther that had entranced her at the menagerie in Germany. The man was dangerous to their cause, yet something about him made her ache to know him better. She yearned to see him again and apologize for behaving like an overly protective, bitter shrew. Her despondent sigh fogged the window. How else could she behave? She dared not let anyone too close or share too much information. She allowed the lacy sheer to fall back in place and returned to the parlor.

"That did not go well at all," she said to her mother as she returned to her seat. "The man suspects something and is sure to go digging. I am certain of it."

"I agree." Her mother released a weary sigh. "We must become better at portraying ourselves as a dowager and her companion rather than mother and daughter. I fear we failed miserably with Lord Raines."

They both went silent as Gransdon entered, followed by Friedrich, their loyal footman from Germany, and Reginald, the new English footman. Both bore trays with every item required for a proper tea.

"That will be all, gentlemen." Gransdon dismissed the footmen with a curt nod. "I shall serve Her Grace and Miss Bening."

Friedrich and Reginald bowed, then hurried out.

Gransdon served the duchess, then Celia, without commenting on the missing Lord Raines.

"Thank you, Gransdon," Duchess Thea said. "That will be all."

"Yes, Your Grace." He gave a respectful bow, then strode out and closed the doors as if understanding their unspoken need for privacy.

"And that is another issue." Celia hated the feeling of their orderly game crumbling. Her inability to control every nuance suffocated her. "*Your* Mr. Elkin assured us that his Bow Street Runners had thoroughly assessed each of the servants and guaranteed their loyalty. Earlier, Gransdon addressed me as *my lady*, and I am most certain that Lord Raines couldn't help but overhear that man's loud, booming voice."

"I am sure he heard it because I did. And by the way, Mr. Elkin is not *mine*." The duchess rolled her eyes, then took another sip of her tea. She returned the delicate porcelain cup to its saucer, then shot Celia an accusing look. "Mr. Elkin guaranteed their loyalty. Not their ability to play this complicated charade as well as we do—which, I might reiterate, we failed at miserably today." She shuddered as though thoroughly disgusted. "And you must stop being so defensive. Has it ever occurred to you that if you feed Lord Raines's sense of self-importance and throw a flirtatious compliment or two his way, he would overlook a multitude of sins while proudly preening his feathers? You must handle men a certain way, Celia. Use your beauty to your advantage."

"I am sorry, but I do not like him. He is too..." Celia paused, searching for an appropriate and also acceptable description for the frustrating Lord Raines. He had caught her off guard in the hallway when he arrived, and she hated being put at a disadvantage. And it wasn't that she didn't like him, really. Or wouldn't. Blast! Blast! Blast!

"He is too what?" her mother curtly prompted. "Too intelligent and inquisitive for our own good?" She set her tea on the table and fisted her hands in her lap. "That is exactly the sort of solicitor we require. Has he not handled our accounts as efficiently as Raymond?"

"Impertinent," Celia snapped, ignoring her mother's affectionate reference to Master Hodgely. "Lord Raines is entirely too impertinent, and you can tell by his behavior that he thinks far too highly of himself."

"There is nothing wrong with a man having a good opinion of himself," her mother said. "He did not give me an inflated perception of his own worth, merely good self-esteem. I could accuse you of possessing that same trait, you know." The duchess's eyes narrowed. "Or do you dislike him because he obviously appears interested in you?"

"His only interest in me is proving me to be a fraud. I read it in his eyes."

"They were quite intense, those blue eyes of his."

"Topaz, Mama. Those dark golden eyes of his reminded me of that large panther in the menagerie we visited in Hamburg."

Her mother's sly smile revealed Celia had just stepped into a snare. But surprisingly, the duchess didn't indulge in an immediate moment of gloating; instead, she nodded at the teapot and lifted her cup. "Be a dear, Celia. I fear this tea has already gone cold."

Celia clenched her teeth, bracing herself for the next comment regarding Lord Raines. With a forced smile, she took the half-empty cup to the table and replaced it with the one meant for the irritating solicitor. "A shame we didn't request they stock any pear brandy here." She filled the extra cup with tea and added a dollop of milk and a drizzle of honey.

"Indeed." Her mother accepted her fresh tea with a smug tilt of her head. "And now, shall we address how you should behave toward the golden-eyed Lord Raines in the future?"

"We shall not discuss—"

Thankfully, the parlor doors opened and Gransdon announced, "The Dowager Marchioness of Ardsmere and Lady Ardsmere, as well as the Dowager Countess of Rydleshire and Lady Sophie, are here to call on Your Grace and Lady Ceci—Miss Bening." He flinched as though struck by an unseen force and bowed his head. "Forgive me, Miss Bening. I shall endeavor to do better."

"Thank you, Gransdon. Please do try to remember." Celia tried not to be too harsh with the poor man. For whatever reason, Mama had chosen to reveal Celia's true identity, and she prayed that decision would not be their downfall. "And please show the ladies in. We were expecting them."

He bowed again, then quickly retreated from the deluge of Sophie and Frannie's joyful shrieks as they burst into the room without waiting for his escort.

"Celia!" Frannie squealed, her dark blonde ringlets fluttering wildly. She came up short and offered a quick curtsy to the duchess. "Your Grace!"

"My Celia!" Sophie shouted with even shriller effervescence. "I have missed you so very much!" She aimed a running curtsy at the duchess. "Your Grace! It is so good to see you too."

"Sophie! Frannie!" Celia vaulted into their arms and hugged them both tightly. She could be honest with these dear souls and not fear retribution, because they too played the game of stealing the life denied them because they were born female. "I have missed both of you so very much. Letters simply do not do our friendship justice."

"Our sisterhood," Frannie corrected her, with an arm around Celia and the other around Sophie. She hugged them both closer. "You two are my sisters, and I shall not hear you addressed as anything less."

"My goodness, girls," exclaimed the Dowager Marchioness of Ardsmere as she swept in behind them. "All of London surely heard that entrance." Before the young ladies could defend themselves, the marchioness beamed a teary-eyed smile at Celia's mother. "Thea, my dearest Thea." She hurried over, scooped up both of the duchess's hands, and lost the battle to hold back tears.

The duchess teetered on the verge of tears as well. "It is so good to see you, Emmie."

"I took the liberty of ordering more tea and whatever brandy you have on hand," announced the Dowager Countess of Rydleshire as she strode into the room like a war hero. Her thin face softened with a sad smile as she rushed to take one of the duchess's hands away from the marchioness. "Share, Emmie. I have missed her as much as you have." She leaned in and pecked a quick kiss on each of the duchess's cheeks. "Darling Thea. You should have sent for us sooner. We could have just as easily come to you in Germany."

"Oh, Nia… I needed to see my beloved London one last time. And all of you here with me. Where we began our friendship." The duchess bowed her head and gave way to her sorrow. The countess and marchioness knelt on either side of her and hugged in close, clinging to her as they all sobbed unashamedly.

Celia blinked furiously and turned away from the heart-wrenching sight. Mama never openly wept. Never.

Sophie caught hold of her arm and gently whispered, "Is there a drawing room where we might go?"

"Good idea." Frannie glanced back at their mothers. "They need their privacy, as we need ours."

Not trusting herself to speak, Celia waved for them to follow her. The library would do. Especially since she wished to eventually go over a few of the ledgers with Frannie and benefit from the girl's brilliance about some business projections. Sophie could offer advice regarding the Bow Street Runner's reports on the servants and perhaps even help with the infuriating Lord Raines. Sophie's expertise lay in stealth, tactical planning, and defense.

If Celia's heart didn't ache so much for her precious mother, she would laugh. Rather than excel at needlework, painting, or the pianoforte, Frannie, Sophie, and she had magnificently conquered the successful running of businesses, the making of promising investments, and spy warfare with a feminine touch.

Gransdon met them halfway down the hall. "Might I be of service, Miss Bening?"

"A tea for the three of us in the library would be much appreciated, Gransdon." Celia offered the gray-haired giant a sympathetic smile. It was more than a little obvious that he still berated himself for his earlier slip of the tongue.

"Right away, miss." He bowed, then disappeared down an adjoining hallway.

"Did you bring your servants from Germany?" Sophie asked as they continued on to the library.

"Only a few. I wish we had brought more, since they are more accustomed to keeping our secrets safe from the light of day." Celia ushered them into the disheveled library of books, papers, and partially unpacked trunks. "Mr. Elkin validated these London servants, but I still find them questionable."

"If Mr. Elkin scrutinized their backgrounds, they *should* suit." Sophie's auburn brows drew together in a frown that resembled more of a studious pout. She twiddled with a coppery red curl, wrapping it around her finger. "Elkin is a senior member of the Bow Street Runners. Mama and I have worked with him frequently and found him to be quite infallible."

"I fear their suitability is not the sole issue here." Celia cleared stacks of books off the chairs, then allowed herself a heavy sigh as she motioned for her friends to sit. "For our ruse to be convincing, the servants must be accomplished actors as well."

"And as fiercely loyal and protective as trained hounds." Frannie perched on her seat as though ready to spring to her feet at a moment's notice. Her nervous trait of jiggling her leg made her skirts quiver. "Whenever Mama and I travel from Belgium, the entire household comes with us."

"But how do you keep your properties tended to when they're empty?" Celia assumed the very unladylike position of propping back against the edge of her desk and crossing her feet at the ankles. That was the beauty of Frannie and Sophie's company. She could behave any way she liked. These sisters by choice loved her unconditionally. "Do you merely keep the houses closed until you intend to use them?"

"Absolutely." Frannie's sapphire-blue eyes flashed beneath her fair brows, and she twitched her leg faster. "It is much more cost-effective to only open properties whenever we are here in London. Our trips have become more frequent of late, but not so much as to warrant employing more staff to see to the residence while we are home in Belgium."

"Back to the most important matter at hand," Sophie said. "Your letter was most alarming. I can see your mother is unwell, but from your report, I expected her to be too weak to leave her bed, much less travel from Germany to London."

Celia hugged herself and stared down at the floor. "She has her good days and bad—and the bad days are becoming more frequent than the good, I fear." She lifted her head and fixed her dear friends with a despondent look. "But you know how our mothers are when they set their minds on something. She refused to be deterred. Not even by illness. She insisted on coming to London."

"There is more troubling you than your mother's mortality," Frannie said, with the cutting bluntness that made her advice indispensable when reviewing contracts.

"Frannie!" Sophie swatted the girl's arm. "This is not some future investment we are discussing. Could you possibly show a modicum of empathy for our dear Celia?"

"Celia knows I love her and would do anything to help her avoid what we all know cannot be changed." Frannie snorted like an irritated horse, then shifted her focus back to Celia. "Out with it. You cannot hide anything from us, and nor should you have to, or even try."

"Frannie is right about that," Sophie said with a curt nod that set her cascade of coppery ringlets aquiver.

"I fear we are soon to be discovered." Celia pulled in a deep breath, preparing to explain, then jerked and pushed off the desk as Gransdon quietly knocked, then entered the library with their tea. The man set her on edge for absolutely no reason whatsoever. Or perhaps she was just on edge because they were in London, and she very much doubted Mama would ever be able to make the return trip to Germany.

What would she do then? How would she explain the absence of the Duke of Hasterton and his sister, Lady Cecilia, when they didn't appear for the funeral? Or would she simply need to transport Mama back to Germany and lay her to rest there with little or no ceremony? She could always claim Mama wished to be buried beside Father, and for once, that would be the truth.

She massaged her throbbing temples. This was not as simple as faking a birth announcement or claiming one twin was ill while having the other christened, and then playing the ruse all over again a week later so everyone thought that both she and her brother had been duly baptized in the church. God bless Nanny Hildegarde for helping with the complicated charade throughout Celia's childhood—or at least until the imaginary Charles reached the age of attending boarding schools and then expanded his schooling to a foreign university.

"Will there be anything else?" Gransdon asked, interrupting her turmoil. He hovered over the table of tea and cakes, looking at Celia with his bushy brows arched like a hound perking its ears.

"This is quite perfect, Gransdon. Thank you." Celia forced a smile as the man bowed, then left the room. As soon as he closed the door behind him, she sagged back against the edge of the desk.

"Why do you fear you're soon to be discovered?" Sophie rose and poured the tea, serving Celia first. "Is it a matter of security? I can help with guards."

"And I can help with a few discreet inquiries," Frannie volunteered as she accepted a cup from Sophie, then scooted back deeper into her chair. "We are not without resources."

"What do you know about Lord Elias Raines of Parkerton, Hodgely, and Kane?" Celia sipped her tea, then recalled the liquor cabinet she had discovered built into the shelves behind the desk. As she went in search of spirits suitable for mixing with tea, she cast a glance back at her friends. "He ascended to the position of partner upon the death of our Master Hodgely, a solicitor we trusted for many years." She pulled a decanter from the cabinet and sniffed the contents. Brandy. Not pear, but it would do. She offered it to Frannie and Sophie. They both held out their cups for a soothing dram. "In fact, I am positive that Master Hodgely held a great fondness for Mama, and she for him. Unfortunately, their union would not only have made them social outcasts but also cost Master Hodgely his London clientele. So, she married my father." Celia sighed, regretting her mother's many sacrifices over the years—all in the name of acceptability and keeping everyone happy but herself.

"Lord Elias Raines," Sophie repeated, as though sorting through her thoughts. "Isn't he the younger brother of the Duke of Almsbury?"

Frannie went still with her teacup partway to her mouth and narrowed her eyes. "I remember him. We sometimes use Parkerton at that same office. Lord Raines came with Parkerton to assist him when we required different wording in a contract, and they refused to make the change until we met with them." She beamed with a proud smile. "They think I am the Marchioness of Ardsmere, and that my husband trusts me implicitly to operate in his stead, since his mother, the dowager marchioness, so often lauds my astuteness."

"And Lord Raines?" Celia prompted, hoping for helpful information.

Frannie gave her a tight-lipped look. "Deucedly clever and stubborn to the point of being dangerous as an adder. Once he gets the scent, Parkerton said nothing will veer him from the hunt."

"Is he the one with whom Lady Castledown had that rather indiscreet affair?" Sophie asked.

"No." Frannie made a face. "That was his brother. Are you

having an off day, Sophie? Even from your villa in France, you normally have your fingertip on the pulse of the *ton's* gossip."

With an irritated huff, Sophie rolled her eyes and took another sip of her tea.

"What else do you know about Lord Raines other than his clever stubbornness?" Celia added more brandy to all their cups, then wondered if she should have stayed her hand. Keeping Sophie and Frannie on topic could sometimes be as difficult as herding wild rabbits.

"Quite handsome, as I remember. Dark, curly hair cut in the latest fashion. Broad shoulders. Narrow waist. Impressively muscular and quite stunning in buff-colored pantaloons that show off his powerful legs." Frannie frowned as she took a heartier sip of her brandy-laced tea while gazing off into the distance. "And the most unusual eyes. Like rare tiger eye gemstones from South Africa. A golden, honeyed richness."

"I believe you have had enough brandy," Celia said while offering a plate of cakes to Frannie. "Best offset it by eating."

"It sounds to me as if she has had enough of virginity," Sophie said with a very unladylike snort. "Isn't it so lovely to be able to say whatever we wish with each other without fear of retribution?" She offered Celia a teasing smile. "What are *your* thoughts on the beguiling Lord Raines?"

"He is not beguiling. He is infuriating, impertinent, and the most worrisome risk Mama and I have ever taken."

Sophie straightened and immediately became serious. "What risk?"

Celia braced herself, knowing that Sophie and Frannie would both fuss about not being consulted regarding her mother's will. And she completely agreed, but Mama had adamantly refused, stating they would do it as she wished and would brook no argument. "Mama requested Lord Raines draw up a will that places all of her personal assets and unentailed properties into a trust for me, her companion, Miss Bening—leaving nothing to her son or her daughter. Not even her jewelry."

"Oh, Celia," Frannie and Sophie groaned in unison.

"You are now the fox and Lord Raines is the relentless hound," Frannie said.

"I fear you are correct." Celia set her tea on the desk beside her, closed her eyes, and massaged her temples that no longer throbbed but pounded. "And I have no idea what to do about it. If he finds out that Charles is nothing more than an imaginary means to an end…"

"He could have you both charged with fraud." Sophie's ominous tone made Celia's head hurt even more. "They do not look kindly on pretending to be a peer."

"We are not pretending to be one," Celia said, knowing the argument was ridiculous. "We created one."

"You have signed his name ever since you took over running the estate," Frannie said. "At the very least, they could imprison you and your mother for forgery, proclaim the title extinct, and revert everything you and your mother have worked so very hard for to the Crown to either be kept or doled out to Prinny's favorites."

"You have systematically transferred monies and lands from Hasterton holdings to your mother's Bening accounts that her marriage contract set aside should she become widowed, correct?" Sophie groaned and shook her head. "Lord Raines could very well presume that you and your mother are attempting to fleece the Duke of Hasterton of his wealth. Why in heaven's name did you choose to pose as Miss *Bening* rather than Miss *Name-No-One-Knows?*"

"Lord Raines is sure to notice." Frannie rose, set her tea aside, and wrapped an arm around Celia's shoulders. "You never make such careless mistakes. Not ever." She gave Celia a gentle, sympathetic shake. "Your terror of losing your mother has you at your wits' end."

"Would you not be the same?" Celia couldn't remain brave and stoic any longer. She covered her face and sobbed. "I cannot imagine doing all *this* without her. It has always been just the two of us, united against the world. And now I am so afraid *that man* and his rummaging about is going to make her demise come even faster.”

“Dearest Celia,” Frannie cried, hugging her as Sophie rushed in to hug them both.

“I know the course to take.” Sophie pushed away and took hold of Celia by the shoulders. Excitement shone on her face. “Seduce him.”

Celia stared at Sophie. “Have you gone mad, or is it merely the brandy talking?”

“Think about it.” Sophie gave her a gentle shake. “If the man becomes besotted with you, he will protect you. Do you not think Master Hodgely knew the truth all those years and yet said nothing?”

Sophie’s observation did possess merit. Celia chewed on the corner of her lip. “I am not certain if Master Hodgely knew the extent of our endeavors or not, but I do know he loved Mama.” She lowered her voice even though it was just them in the room. “I accidentally read one of his correspondences to her.”

“And how exactly do you *accidentally* read someone else’s correspondence?” Frannie asked with a coy tilt of her head.

Celia haughtily drew herself up even though she still felt a twinge of guilt about what she had done. “I saw it was from the law office and thought it to be business.” She wrinkled her nose and sheepishly admitted, “And once I started reading it, I could not seem to stop.” Her heart still ached whenever she remembered Master Hodgely’s loving prose, and she wondered what it would be like to have someone feel such a depth of affection for her. A wistful sigh escaped before she could stop it.

“If that sigh is any indication of the love Master Hodgely felt for your mother,” Frannie said, “then I would wager he knew the truth about your family. Sophie is right. Seduce Lord Raines to either distract him completely or force him to become so infatuated with you that he would never reveal your secrets.” She twitched a shrug. “You have your mother’s beauty. Mama said when she and Sophie's mother presented at court, all eyes followed your mother." Frannie offered a generous smile. "The only reason they didn't hate her was because of her sweet nature and how she helped Mama hide the torn hem of her petticoat so no one else would know."

"I have no idea how to seduce a man," Celia said through clenched teeth. Even the thought of attempting such a thing made her palms go all damp and unpleasant. She gave Sophie a dubious look. "How do *you* do it?"

Sophie's rich brown eyes widened. "I have never done it."

"You suggested it," Celia insisted.

"That does not mean I've done it." Sophie turned to Frannie. "What about you? Your mother wrote to mine about how everyone's attention was on you at Lady…" She frowned. "I don't recall her name, but she was one of Belgium's most esteemed peers. You were the center of attention at her gala."

Frannie's fair cheeks flushed an alarming shade of red. "Mama embellished my popularity at the ball to mask her mortification. I was the center of attention because my heel snagged in the braided trim of some drapery, and I unknowingly almost yanked it off the wall when I started across the dance floor."

Celia covered her mouth to keep from gaping at her poor friend. "Oh, Frannie, how awful." She hurried to defend her dear sister. "That was not your fault. They should not have had the draperies arranged so that someone might trip over them. I say they owe you a very public apology."

Frannie emerged from her embarrassment with a lopsided grin. "It all worked out. The woman's hideous son had been making unwelcome advances all night. After I ruined his mother's ball, she kept him at bay with the determination of a very devoted herd dog."

Celia joined the girls in a fit of giggling, then sadly quieted once again. If only a bit of poorly hung drapery could solve all their problems. She slowly shook her head. "I cannot imagine how I am going to seduce Lord Raines. It will be utterly impossible."

"Nonsense!" Frannie gave her a stern scowl. "It's not as if he is repulsive, and you are exceptional. Both our mothers said so—did they not, Sophie?"

"Absolutely." Sophie dramatically pressed the back of her hand to her forehead, as if overcome by such exquisiteness. "A raven-haired beauty with eyes as bewitching and rare as green sapphires."

"If either of you thinks this behavior is helpful—you are wrong." Celia lifted her chin and folded her arms tightly across her middle. "There is more to seduction than looks." A disgruntled huff escaped her. "Or so I have been told. Even Mama somewhat suggested what you two propose. Although she phrased it as being nice to the man and playing to his ego."

Both Frannie and Sophie threw up their hands and cheered as though they had just won at whist.

"You can do this," Frannie assured her.

"Most definitely," Sophie agreed.

"Whether or not I can remains to be seen." Celia returned to massaging her poor, throbbing temples. "Please tell me the two of you plan to remain in London for the Season?"

"Oh, absolutely." Frannie turned and arched a brow at Sophie.

"Certainly." Sophie handed them each their teacups, refreshed them with brandy, then held hers high for a toast. "To a successful Season of subterfuge and seduction."

"Success," Frannie echoed wholeheartedly.

"Success," Celia said, feeling more doubt than enthusiasm.

Chapter Four

Thomas stuck his head inside Elias's office. "Mr. Portney here to see you, my lord."

"Send him in." Elias set aside the Duchess of Hasterton's papers and rubbed his eyes, which were gritty and overtired from poring over the entire Hasterton files and trying to solve the mystery of their strange situation.

"Good day, my lord." Mr. Jack Portney, the Bow Street Runner Elias always consulted, approached the desk.

The unmistakably disappointed sag to the man's shoulders frustrated Elias. "I take it you found nothing on Miss Celia Bening?"

"Nothing, my lord." Jack removed his hat. "Some good news about that, though. At least there are no records of arrest." The man worried the brim, slowly turning his topper in his hands. "The only information I found regarding a Bening was when Lady Thea Bening married Edmond Tuttcliffe, the fifth Duke of Hasterton. And of course, the report of the duke's death in that carriage accident while they were abroad." He tipped his head to the side and pursed his lips. "Lady Thea was the daughter of a German nobleman and an English mother whose father was a baronet. That would explain the lack of records on the Bening name here in London."

Elias rubbed the back of his neck, trying to work out the tension from this thoroughly frustrating matter. "Thank you,

Jack. I know you did your best." He pulled a payment voucher out of his center desk drawer, filled it out, and gave it to the fellow. "Take this to James, and your strictest confidence is appreciated, as always."

"Thank you, my lord. I wish I could have found more." Jack took the slip, offered a respectful tip of his head, then left the room.

Elias stared down at the dowager's folder while going back over every nuance of yesterday's meeting with her and the mysterious yet enticing Miss Bening. The two beauties had to be related. Such a remarkable resemblance would be an extreme rarity any other way.

He snorted with a soft laugh. Of course, they had neither denied nor confirmed a shared bloodline when he had asked. Miss Bening had merely accused him of impertinence.

He checked his timepiece, then scowled down at the newly drawn last will and testament of the Duchess of Hasterton. All the documents needed were the lady's signature, those of the witnesses, and a seal. But he preferred to wait until he received a response from the solicitor in Germany and the duke himself. Unfortunately, that could take weeks—or, with the duke's tendency to ignore his correspondence, forever.

Time to call upon the duchess and attempt to buy himself more time. He hated delaying because of her failing health, but felt duty-bound to protect *all* his clients. Namely, the current duke and his sister.

Elias rose, tucked the pertinent paperwork into a protective sleeve, then placed the packet into his satchel. "Thomas!" he called while securing the bag's leather straps and buckles.

The young man popped in as though he was waiting on the other side of the door. "Yes, my lord?"

"A hackney, if you please."

"Right away, my lord."

Smiling to himself, Elias looked forward to another enjoyable confrontation with the inimitable Miss Bening. He tucked his satchel under his arm and hurried out to the waiting hackney. Upon arriving at the Hasterton townhouse, he again paid the driver to wait. After all, Miss Bening could very well have him tossed out on his ear when he tried his own bit of subterfuge to counter the many inconsistencies of the Hasterton household.

The front door opened before he banged the lion's brass ring against its plate.

"Miss Bening is expecting you, my lord," Gransdon said with a proper bow.

"Miss Bening and the dowager duchess?"

"No, my lord. Her Grace is not receiving today." The butler closed the front door and directed Elias down the hall to a room on the left. "Miss Bening requested you join her in the library."

"In the library?" Elias repeated, hoping to draw more information from the stoic servant before entering the delightfully ferocious feline's den. "Alone?"

Gransdon's stony expression hardened even more. He came to a halt in front of the partially opened door and held out his hand. "I presume you will keep your bag on your person as before, my lord?"

Elias handed over his hat and gloves. "You presume correctly, Gransdon. Thank you."

The butler offered another aloof yet respectful nod, then turned and left without a word.

"Do come in, Lord Raines," Miss Bening called from within. "And leave the door open, if you would."

"I am yours to command, Miss Bening." Elias entered cautiously, admiring the multiple levels of a room that could only be described as a book lover's heaven on earth. Shelves of tomes covered every wall from floor to ceiling on the first level, and from what he could see of the second floor, those walls held more of the same. At the far end of the room, a cheery fire crackled in a modest hearth framed by a pair of generously cushioned chairs perfect for reading.

Miss Bening rose from behind a large mahogany desk at the

end of the room closest to him and offered not only a graceful curtsy but an unusually beguiling smile to go along with it. She wore another deep green confection of muslin that brought out her eyes, but this one was embroidered with strands of ivy that accentuated her lovely curves—not that they needed accentuating. Her shapely form caught a man's eye and turned his thoughts to all sorts of delicious, forbidden possibilities.

"A pleasure to see you again, my lord," she said in a sultry tone that made him swallow hard.

"Is it really?" He moved closer, unable to keep himself from grinning. "Yesterday, you wished to order me ousted."

"I did not." Her eyes flashed with the admirable defensiveness of their first meeting.

He couldn't help but chuckle. "Your eyes do not match your denial, Miss Bening."

She coyly lowered her gaze while moving closer. "I must beg your forgiveness, then, for an ill temper brought on by the weariness of travel." She met his appreciative stare and treated him to a fetching smile that made the tempting bow of her mouth appear even more kissable. "Might you find it possible to allow us to start our acquaintance over? Clear the slate, so to speak, and start anew?"

"Indeed." Elias sealed the tempting agreement with a polite nod, but his guard immediately sharpened. The leery yet fearless lioness of yesterday had become a seductive minx, and the role did not suit her. He found the change in her demeanor a bloody shame. He liked the green-eyed lioness better. Perhaps he could coax the exciting feline back with a few well-placed questions. "Might I ask after Her Grace? I fully expected to meet with her today."

Miss Bening's come-hither smile faltered. "Her Grace is resting today. She will not be joining us."

"I was very sorry to learn about Her Grace's failing health." And Elias meant that sentiment. Whether a relative or merely a companion, it was more than a little obvious that Miss Bening's fondness for the duchess ran deep. He turned to leave. "I should call at another time. Please ask Her Grace to send for me when she feels well enough to receive company."

"Her Grace asked that I review the will. If I find it suitable, she will sign it immediately. I can deliver it to her in her rooms, then return it to you after she signs." The wily minx subtly arched her back as though ensuring she offered the mouthwatering fullness of her perfect breasts at the best possible angle.

Damn. He could appreciate those breasts at any angle. Elias cleared his throat and forced his mind back to the matter at hand. "The document must also be witnessed, Miss Bening." Before she could counter his statement, he added, "And please understand that I intend no rudeness, but a will is a very personal matter. I insist on reviewing it with Her Grace. Alone." He tried to soften the warning with a gentler tone. "After all, with you as the beneficiary, your review of the will would be most inappropriate."

He patted the satchel still tucked under his arm. "Besides, I fear I have yet to complete the document as Her Grace wished. I am waiting for an answer from the solicitor in Germany as well as a response from her son, the duke."

A transformation came over Miss Bening. She moved even closer, as though he had suddenly become her prey. His senses thrilled at the return of the fearless lioness.

"Her Grace requested everything be finalized by today," she said. "What portion of that request was unclear?" The lady glaring at him as though ready to unleash her fury mesmerized him to the point of silence. "I bid you answer, my lord, so I might assist you in the resolution of any confusion."

"The confusion, Miss Bening," he said softly, moving to stand close enough to indulge in the sensual sweetness of her delicate jasmine scent, "is that Her Grace named you as her sole beneficiary and completely left out her children. Especially her daughter—whom one might consider as the rightful heir of the Bening accounts that were set aside in Her Grace's marriage contract. It is highly irregular, and I can almost guarantee that her children will challenge it."

"I assure you Her Grace's children are well set for the future." She didn't smile, and her earlier coyness had disappeared. "And they will not fight the will when the time comes."

Elias was glad her sham of false coyness had dropped away. He wanted nothing but the truth from this exquisite lady. "While I would like nothing more than to take your assurances to heart, I fear I cannot."

"And why is that?" Her chin jutted higher. She was ready to do battle, and he found it exhilarating.

"Because the duke, the dowager duchess, and Lady Cecilia are my clients," he said, "and you, Miss Bening, are not."

She blinked faster, as though fighting back tears. In fact, the pale green of her eyes gleamed overly bright beneath the many candles lighting the room. Was the beauty frustrated at being thwarted from her riches, or was it something else? "Her Grace could very well die before you hear from Germany," she said. "Would you have her leave this world frustrated that her last requests were denied?"

The faint tremor in her voice took hold of his heart. It bespoke of protectiveness and sorrow for the dowager rather than a hunger for wealth and possessions. He lowered his gaze as she turned away to compose herself. She moved to a portion of the bookcase directly behind the desk.

"Might I offer you a glass of wine, my lord?" She spoke so quietly, he wasn't certain he had heard her correctly.

"I beg your pardon?" He stepped closer, took a stand between the pair of chairs in front of the desk, and set his satchel in one of them.

She still didn't turn, merely stood taller, as though trying to remain the perfect hostess while recovering from her overset state. "Wine, my lord," she said louder without facing him. "Would you care for some?"

"That would be most kind, thank you." Elias found her unexplainable suffering most intolerable. "I can help you, Miss Bening, if only you will allow it. Please tell me how I might make things easier."

"I am quite capable of pouring two glasses of wine without aid from either you or a servant, but I thank you." She turned from the liquor cabinet built into the shelves and offered him a glass. "I fear all we have at this time is Madeira. The brandy has yet to be replenished. Shall I ring for tea instead?" She attempted a smile and failed. "It would be no trouble," she said with a great deal of difficulty as she stared downward and waited for him to take the wineglass from her.

He purposely took hold of the goblet so that his fingers covered hers with a protective intimacy. The warm silkiness of her bare fingers stirred him more than he thought possible. "I can help you," he repeated softly. "You need but tell me how."

Their fingers still touching, she lifted her gaze and locked eyes with him for the span of several heartbeats, long enough to lift his hopes. Then she glanced downward again and released the glass, pulling her touch from his. "You can help me by fulfilling Her Grace's request." She primly clasped her hands in front of her waist. "It is of the utmost importance to me she not be overset or put upon during what I feel are most certainly her last days."

"You love her as if she were your mother." The observation came out before he could stop it.

She nodded while staring down at her untouched glass on the desk. "I do," she whispered. "I have known her all my life."

"Then you must know the duke and Lady Cecilia as well."

She lifted her head and returned her chin to its stubborn angle. "Yes. I know them both quite well."

"Then you also must realize they will fight this will no matter what you believe at this moment." He had no idea if the two would fight it or not, but he felt an irrational need to keep this lady talking in the hopes that she might accidentally reveal her troubles.

Her smile turned bitter and defiant. "I can promise you, Lord

Raines, they will not fight this will. There is no doubt regarding that."

"Celia! You did not tell me Lord Raines had arrived." The dowager duchess stood in the doorway, pale yet lovely in her morning walking dress of a cambric print with tiny yellow flowers and a matching Spanish robe of jonquil muslin. Today, she carried a gleaming black cane, its golden handle decorated with inlays of colored glass. Even though she steadied herself with the stylish walking stick, she moved forward with the flawless grace of a swan gliding across a pond. "Lord Raines. So good of you to accede to my wishes for expediency regarding my documents."

Miss Bening cocked a brow and turned away with an almost gleeful air, leaving him to his own devices. "Would you like some Madeira, Your Grace?" she asked the duchess.

"Madeira?" The dowager frowned. "Have you not ordered tea?" She glanced around as though suddenly realizing where she was. "And why ever in the world would you receive Lord Raines in the library? And alone?" Her loveliness puckered with a furious scowl. "We shall discuss this matter later, Celia."

"Yes, Your Grace." Miss Bening dutifully guided the duchess to a chair. "But with you here now, I am no longer alone with Lord Raines, the most infamous rakehell, risking my reputation even with doors propped wide open and servants filling the halls. I shall order tea immediately."

As Miss Bening left the room, the dowager eyed him. Her gaze became a cutting stare, as if she was sorting through his mind to find the thought she wanted. "You did not complete my will as I requested."

Shocked at her astuteness, Elias flared his eyes wide despite his best efforts to remain unreadable. There was naught to do now but bow his head and beg forgiveness. The lady might be unwell, but she was far from confused, or the least bit foggy-minded. "I did not complete it, Your Grace. However, everything is ready to proceed as soon as I receive a response from your solicitor in Germany—and your son."

"And who, might I ask, instructed you to contact either of them?" Her glare became as cold as the Thames in the dead of winter.

"As solicitor over the Hasterton estate, it is my duty to protect the interests of all my clients. A last will and testament that fails to benefit all of you, namely the duke and Lady Cecilia, must be thoroughly investigated before it is finalized."

"You do realize that correspondence from Germany could take weeks and quite possibly months?" She clutched the ornate handle of her cane with both her petite hands, as if trying to control the urge to beat him with it. "I am dying, Lord Raines. I have no time for an unlicked cub whose sole concern is padding his self-importance by tattling to a vainglorious duke rather than acceding to a mere old woman's wishes. Complete the document or I shall find another solicitor who will."

Elias realized his jaw had dropped, and promptly closed his mouth. He was torn between begging for forgiveness or applauding the woman for the impressive dressing-down she had just delivered. Perhaps the dowager was healthier than she realized.

He bowed his head. "I am quite clear now on Your Grace's requirements, and I do beg your pardon."

The duchess huffed and looked away, as if still too angry to tolerate the sight of him.

Miss Bening returned and motioned to the chair next to the duchess. "Do be seated, my lord. Gransdon shall have the tea for us shortly."

With a sense of self-preservation solidly in place, Elias moved to stand in front of another chair that placed him well out of reach of the dowager's cane—just in case. He made a flourishing wave at the chair Miss Bening had recommended. "After you, Miss Bening."

She appeared to be trying not to smile, but an amused twinkle in her lovely eyes betrayed her. After a faintly mocking nod, she seated herself next to the duchess. With them seated side by side, he could not ignore their uncanny resemblance. After a pint too many one evening, Master Hodgely had once described the Duchess of Hasterton as an incomparable beauty. The man was sorely mistaken. Miss Bening's loveliness demanded the same adoration.

"Your Grace, again, I do apologize for failing to finalize your documents," Elias said. "As recompense, might I offer a rejuvenating ride through Hyde Park? My barouche can be readied at a moment's notice, and I believe you would find it quite comfortable on a day as glorious as today." The open carriage would suit the duchess much better than a tiring walk to announce her presence in London. Such an outing would also buy him some time and offer yet another opportunity to become better acquainted with the enchanting Miss Bening.

The regal matron studied him as though plotting the most efficient way of disposing of him after clubbing him senseless with her cane. She shifted, propped the fashionable walking stick against the arm of her chair, then folded her hands in her lap. "I fear I must beg off, since I have committed to attending Lady Bournebridge's ball tomorrow evening." Her expression hardened. "As I noted earlier, my health does not permit a crowded schedule of activities." With a sly glance Miss Bening's way, she smiled. "However, I do not wish to hold Miss Bening prisoner in this stuffy house on what you describe as such a *glorious* day. If Lady Sophie or Lady Ardsmere is available to join her, she may go while I fortify myself for tomorrow's outing."

"Lady Sophie?" he repeated, not familiar with the name.

"Lady Sophie is the daughter of the Dowager Countess of Rydleshire," Miss Bening explained. "And I believe you met Lady Ardsmere on a prior occasion. Your partner, Lord Parkerton, is her husband's solicitor."

"Yes, I have made Lady Ardsmere's acquaintance, but I have not yet had the pleasure of meeting Lord Ardsmere." Elias felt the fool for not knowing Lady Sophie—or at least not hearing about her in passing conversation. He prided himself on keeping an ear to the talk of the *ton* and staying informed about those in London for the Season. It was just good business to do so. He offered Miss Bening a hopeful smile. "After tea, I would be delighted to have my vehicle and coachman readied for an afternoon outing. Would that be acceptable to you, Miss Bening?"

"You have a barouche and employ a coachman, yet you travel from your office in a hackney?" Miss Bening arched a brow, challenging him to explain.

"Celia!" the duchess said. "Such rudeness is unacceptable."

Elias lifted a hand to belay the scolding. "Actually, it is a valid question, Your Grace. After all, I am in your employ, and you have the right to know everything about your solicitor."

The dowager huffed and kept a hard look trained on Miss Bening.

Gransdon entered the room and stepped aside, supervising the pair of footmen following him. Each of them carried a large silver tray. One tray held a fine china tea set, the teapot, cups, and saucers decorated with pale pink roses centered between bands of deep blue bordered in gold. The other bore matching plates and delightful platters of finger sandwiches and seedcakes.

"Shall I serve, Your Grace?" Gransdon asked.

"Thank you, no, Gransdon. Miss Bening will serve while Lord Raines regales us with the story of his barouche and coachman." The duchess's acerbic tone left no doubt that she considered today a complete and utter failure.

"Very good, Your Grace." Gransdon tipped a subtle nod that shooed both footmen out ahead of him. He softly pulled the door almost closed but did not latch it.

Miss Bening moved to serve them, allowing Elias yet another opportunity to admire her beauty. Her delicate features were unspoiled by pots of rouge or powder. The gleaming lushness of her ebony braid pinned into a simple chignon made him wonder what she would look like with her tresses freed and tumbling down her back—or across his pillows.

"Well, Lord Raines?" she said as she poured. "Your amusing story about your barouche and coachman?"

Elias laughed. "It is doubtful my story will amuse you. My brother gifted the coach to me upon my acceptance as partner at Parkerton, Hodgely, and Kane. It was terribly difficult to enjoy the company of several guests whenever I drove through the park, so I employed a coachman."

"Your brother?" Miss Bening left the question open-ended, but Elias understood exactly what she asked.

"The Duke of Almsbury," he said, adopting a feigned tone of warning. "Beware of him, Miss Bening. He is quite the scapegrace—but of course, I say that with all the affection my only brother is due."

Miss Bening, the fearless lioness he was determined to know so much better, gifted him with an almost teasing smile. "And would he say the same of you, my lord?"

"Doubtful," Elias said, and it wasn't *quite* a lie. He couldn't hold a candle to Monty's escapades. And more importantly, he was not about to admit that he had no troubles when it came to finding a lady to warm his bed. That topic simply wasn't brought up in polite company. "I was always the studious lad. More into books than mischief."

The dowager used her cane to push herself to her feet and ambled to the door. She opened it as wide as it would go, then turned and looked back at them. "I am tired and do not possess the energy to pretend otherwise." Her unsmiling focus centered on Miss Bening. "Enjoy your tea, enjoy the park, and leave this door as I have placed it." She shifted her sharp-eyed scowl to Elias. "I want that will ready for my signature before I depart for Lady Bournebridge's ball tomorrow evening. Are we quite clear on that, Lord Raines?"

"Yes, Your Grace." Knowing word would never arrive from Germany by tomorrow, Elias reluctantly and silently admitted defeat on delaying the document's finalization any longer. "I shall bring it for your signature tomorrow. You have my word."

"Very good." The duchess's weary attention turned back to Miss Bening. "Door open. Understand?"

"Yes, Your Grace." Miss Bening gave the woman a deep, respectful curtsy.

After a look of dubious approval, the dowager left them to their tea.

"Should you help her reach her rooms?" Elias asked, keeping his voice down.

Miss Bening jerked and stared at him as if she had forgotten he was there. "No, my lord. She prefers for her maid to attend to that when we are here at home."

Elias found the lady's nervousness concerning—as if the two of them had just become bait for the duchess's snare. He almost smiled. As a second son, he had never had to worry about a lady leg-shackling him by using a compromising situation. He was safe from the Marriage Mart. The lovely lioness's unease had to be from something else. "Miss Bening, are you unwell?"

"I am not." Her sharp gaze softened, turning almost thoughtful. "Forgive my bluntness, but your concern about Her Grace surprised me."

Elias found himself more than a little insulted. "Have you found my behavior wanting toward Her Grace or yourself? Have I been so rudely cold and callous?"

Genuine remorse shone on the lady's lovely face. With an apologetic tip of her head, she served him his tea. "Forgive me, my lord." A hint of a smile played across the tempting suppleness of her lips. "You have been impertinent and frustrating at times, but I have sensed no vicious intent from you."

"And you never will." Elias purposely touched her bare fingers again as he accepted the cup and saucer. "My intentions are nothing but the best for you, Miss Bening."

The half-smile that so delightfully plumped her cheeks returned. "Do not push too hard, my lord. I fear you may overwhelm me."

The sarcasm in her voice made him chuckle. "I doubt very

much that anything could overwhelm you, my lady."

"Miss Bening," she gently corrected him, then glanced at the open door. "Or Celia, when we find ourselves indulged with a bit of loosely chaperoned privacy, as we are now."

"Celia," he repeated. Her name tasted sweet, and he knew without a doubt that she would taste even sweeter. "Please call me Elias."

"Elias," she repeated, thrilling him to no end. "A form of Elijah that means *the Lord is my God.*" She seated herself, took a sip of her tea, then smiled. "Lady Sophie and Lady Ardsmere are staying here with us. I believe you would survive Lady Sophie on a carriage ride much easier than Lady Ardsmere." Her glance at him over the rim of her teacup was filled with mirth. "You will like her."

"I like you, Celia," he said, then blazed ahead as though such blunt honesty was entirely appropriate. "You are as intoxicating as the finest of wines." At her slightly shocked reaction, he attempted to reassure her he was not a buck of the first head. "Please take no insult, Celia, for I mean none. As a second son, I am rarely fortunate enough to meet such an admirable woman who is more fitting to my station than that of my brother, the duke." As soon as he said the words, he regretted them, because she stiffened and the room turned cold. Damn his foolish tongue!

"Ah, yes. More fitting," she repeated. "Heaven forbid I should consider myself worthy of a duke's status."

"Again, Celia. I meant no insult. Please know that."

Her jaw tightened, and her mouth went hard. "I am not insulted at you, my lord. I am insulted by…circumstances."

"Elias." Although he knew it to be forward, he reached across the space between them and barely touched the back of her bare hand. So soft. So silky. So in need of his protection and care. "You are an intriguing woman, Celia. I wish us to be—"

"What?" she said, cutting him off with a trembling whisper. Her green-eyed gaze enchanted him, making him willing to promise her anything to gain not only her trust but her affection.

"What do you wish for *us*, Elias? Tell me."

"Everything." It was the only word he could intelligently form at the moment.

"Perhaps you should fetch your barouche, while I fetch Lady Sophie." Celia rose and stepped away from him, making him hunger for her even more. After a graceful curtsy and a knowing smile, she left him there in the middle of the library, staring after her.

Suddenly, he recognized the clever snare he had earlier sensed. The dowager didn't fear leaving Celia in his company because she knew exactly what his fellow solicitors and the *ton* would think if he formed a slightly too convenient attachment to the beneficiary of her will—the will he had drawn up for the duchess.

"Damn," he said under his breath. The lady had effortlessly boxed him into a corner. He snorted and rolled his shoulders the same way he did when training at No. 13 Bond Street with Gentleman Jackson to box away his frustrations. "Do not count your winnings yet, Your Grace," he quietly warned as he stepped into the hall and looked up and down it for Gransdon to recover his hat and gloves. "I am a worthy opponent."

CHAPTER FIVE

"YOU CERTAINLY ARE playing the part of modest companion." Sophie perched on the chair in front of the dressing table, eying Celia as she donned her plainest bonnet, selected a pair of gloves, then retrieved an unadorned parasol and modest reticule. "You are not even going to change your dress?"

"I am not." Celia glanced down at her favorite ivy-embroidered muslin that had quite successfully caught Lord Raines's—no, not Lord Raines's, but Elias's—eye during tea. She smiled at the memory and grudgingly realized that perhaps he wasn't such an odious gentleman after all. In fact, she rather liked him. Probably much more than she should.

She gave a teasing wiggle of her shoulders. "The man seemed to appreciate my appearance well enough earlier. Why should he not continue?"

Sophie rose and circled Celia. "I suppose you are right. The trailing ivy does guide the eye to the qualities a man admires most. Or at least, so I have read." She interrupted herself with a wicked giggle. "Are you certain Frannie wouldn't be a more appropriate chaperone? After all, she is posing as a married woman."

"Frannie and her mother have an appointment with their favorite modiste today. The woman is highly sought after. I would hate to cause them to lose this opportunity while they are in London."

"I see." Sophie went to the window overlooking the street and parted the sheer panels of lace hanging between the draperies. "My, my, and what a fine barouche Lord Raines has."

"He is here already?" Celia shoved in and had a look for herself. A coachman stood beside the carriage's black horses. The beasts shone like a pair of highly polished onyx jewels, making them perfectly suited for the stylish barouche. It was painted a gleaming black with gold detailing, and the folds of its retracted top shone in the sun like the finest satin. "Lord Raines and his brother must be quite close to warrant such a gift."

"According to my contacts," Sophie said, "he and the duke are all that remains of their family. Much like me and Maman."

"Like all of us," Celia said while still peeping out the window. She swallowed hard against the sudden knot of dread tightening her throat. Soon, she would have no one. An emotionally charged huff escaped her. Of course, if Mama got her wish and married her off before losing the battle with the illness…

Celia dismissed that idea with a determined hiss. That particular wish would not come true. She refused to marry for anything other than love. Mama had never hidden the fact that her union with Father had been nothing more than a friendly business arrangement, so he might secure an heir, and she might improve her family's social standing. Mama had loved Master Hodgely—and lost him by doing what her family wanted rather than what her heart desired.

"Stop huffing and hissing. You sound like a stray cat spoiling for a fight." Sophie plucked a fresh sprig of greenery from her own bonnet and secured it to Celia's. "For luck, dear sister. And it matches your dress."

"I fear I shall need it." Celia fidgeted with her gloves. She hated the things but couldn't be seen on an outing without them. Determined to improve her own mood, she twitched her nose at Sophie, then winked. "He did ask me to call him Elias rather than *my lord.*"

"Very impressive." Sophie rewarded her with a proud smile,

then nudged her. "You did nothing improper to make such progress with the handsome Lord Raines, did you?"

Celia dramatically fanned herself. "I allowed him to touch my fingers when I handed him a glass of wine, and then later, I let him touch the back of my bare hand."

"Celia!" Sophie attempted to appear shocked before giving in to a fit of snorting giggles.

A knock at the door interrupted them. "Lady Sophie? Miss Bening?" one of the newest maids called without opening the door. "Mr. Gransdon says Lord Raines has arrived with his carriage."

Sophie rocked an auburn brow to an inquisitive height. "Are we ready?"

A sudden excited fluttering in Celia's middle caught her off guard. For heaven's sake, how ridiculous. She cleared her throat and swallowed hard to dispel the unreasonable feeling but failed. The finger sandwich she had eaten after leaving Lord Raines in the library must not have sat well. "I suppose I am as ready as I shall ever be."

"You've gone quite pink in the cheeks, and I know you never go near a pot of rouge. Are you all right? Shall I send him away?" With a concerned frown, Sophie removed her glove and pressed the backs of her fingers to Celia's forehead. "You don't appear to be overly warm."

"No," Celia said, inwardly chiding herself. "I appear to be overly silly." She led the way out into the hall and paused at her mother's door. A peek inside revealed Berta in the small sitting room quietly mending. The maid looked up and pressed a finger to her lips, then offered a sad smile. Celia nodded, closed the door, and continued on.

"Her Grace is sleeping?" Sophie whispered.

"Yes." Celia left it at that. To speak of it in any more depth would reduce her to tears and foil an opportunity to further seduce the rakishly handsome, yet entirely too curious, Lord Raines. As she descended the stairs, a pang of guilt about toying with the genuinely nice man not only surprised her but sent her stomach fluttering even more. She pressed a hand to her middle and silently ordered it to stop. It had to be those few bites of sandwich causing her such unusual distress. The meat paste must have surely turned. She would speak to Mrs. Harcourt after the outing.

Lord Raines—*Elias*, she gently reminded herself—waited in the hall, watching her as she traipsed down the stairs. The man possessed such an irresistible smile, with the faintest dimple in his left cheek. How had she not noticed it before? Probably because she found the rest of him just as irresistible and breathtaking, even though she shouldn't. The stylish, short curls of his thick, dark hair were as sleek as the golden-eyed panther that had entranced her at the menagerie. He held his hat curled in the crook of his arm, looking as relaxed as could be.

The finger sandwiches in her middle twirled at an alarming rate, making her catch her breath.

"Steady, Celia," Sophie warned from behind her. "Do not immerse yourself too deeply in the game."

Celia smiled and held her head higher. Sophie was right. The first rule of subterfuge: do not embrace the act so tightly as to trick yourself into believing it is real. "Thank you, dear sister," she said for Sophie's ears alone.

"We have a glorious day to enjoy, ladies." Elias bowed to them as they joined him in the hall.

That he persisted in bowing to her rather than offering a polite tip of his head concerned Celia, but she feared reminding him would make him study the Hasterton household even closer. She chose to ignore it for now. Instead, she turned to her ally. "Lady Sophie Redwell, allow me to present Lord Elias Raines."

Sophie maintained a knowing half-smile as she curtsied. "My lord."

Elias bowed again. "Lady Sophie." He made a sweeping gesture toward the front door as the butler swung it open. "To the carriage, dear ladies. Hyde Park awaits."

Celia and Sophie led the way. The coachman opened the carriage door and offered his hand to steady them as they climbed in and took their seats. Celia sat facing front and assumed Sophie would sit beside her with Elias on the seat behind the driver, facing them. When Sophie made herself quite comfortable on the seat behind the driver, Celia cleared her throat and flared her eyes as wide as she could. Sophie shot back a smile and shook her head, wiggling like a hen settling into a comfortable nest.

Before Celia could move to the spot beside Sophie, Elias climbed in and sat beside her. He nodded to the driver, then leaned back and smiled at them both. "My brother will be beside himself when I tell him of the outing he missed today."

"I suppose you could have invited him." Celia opened her parasol for some protective shade. "After all, Lady Sophie is as yet unattached." Her dear friend deserved that warning shot after creating such an intimate seating arrangement.

"And soon to return to France," Sophie reminded her, with a slight narrowing of her lovely brown eyes. She opened her frilly-edged parasol and twirled it as if to say, *En garde, sister.*

"I am a selfish man." Elias unleashed the smile that made Celia's strange indigestion flutter at an alarming speed. "An afternoon outing with not one, but two lovely ladies is something I refuse to share."

"You are too kind, my lord." Sophie pulled a small fan from her reticule and slowly twirled it in her right hand, signaling she loved another.

Elias turned as if about to say something else to Celia, then paused and seemed concerned. "Forgive me for such a personal inquiry, but are you too warm, Miss Bening?"

Good heavens. No, she was not warm. Well, yes, she was, but not because of the weather. It was the muscular length of his long leg occasionally pressing against hers whenever the carriage swayed. She could not allow him to win at this game. Her cheeks must be red again. The fairness of her skin was indeed a curse in times such as these.

"I'm not overly warm at all, my lord. The ride is exhilarating, and I fear my fair skin betrays my excitement about the outing." She retrieved her fan from her reticule and opened it wide, daring him to read the subtle signal of *wait for me*.

"I see," he said, then looked away as if to disguise subtly shifting even closer.

Sophie's eyes danced with mirth above the edge of her fan that failed to hide her soft snort of laughter. She coughed to explain away the sound. "Dear me, I seem to have choked on something."

"Take care, Sophie," Celia said while inwardly scolding herself without mercy. She had to regain control and be done with all this silliness. Yes, his nearness felt very nice, but that was no reason to behave like a complete ninny.

As they turned into Hyde Park, he leaned closer still, then feigned an expression of mild shock. "I beg your pardon for crowding you, Miss Bening. Do forgive me." But he made no effort to move and place more space between them.

Two could up the stakes of this game as long as they did so out of view of the others enjoying the park. Safely hidden by the sides of the carriage, she reached over and boldly patted his knee. "You, Lord Raines, appear to believe it is easier to ask forgiveness than permission."

His smile captivated her, but not nearly so soundly as his eyes—and the intentions turning them an even sultrier shade of golden brown. "It *is* easier to ask forgiveness," he said, locking his gaze with hers. "Do you not agree?"

"In some cases," she brazenly answered.

"Lady Bournebridge and her poisonous pair approach, *mon amie*." Sophie tipped a nod to bring Celia's attention to the spiteful marchioness and the two like-minded ladies accompanying her.

Celia adjusted the tilt of her parasol to shield herself from the directness of their stares as they passed. But that didn't prevent the judgmental three from turning in their seats and craning their necks to peer at them. "Ahh…the ruling triumvirate of gossip," Celia said. "According to Duchess Thea, Lady Bournebridge never steps out her door without Lady Essendon and Lady Mardlebon in tow."

"Pleasant day to you, ladies," Elias called out to the three with a polite tip of his hat. While still smiling, he lowered his voice for Celia and Sophie's pleasure alone. "Both the marchionesses and the countess are clients of mine. Or rather, their husbands are." He chuckled, a warm, friendly sound that sent a far-too-enjoyable shiver through Celia. "Or they were," he added while still smiling. "We shall see if I hear from them about today. I have quickly discovered that if the wives of my clients are unhappy, then so am I."

"Oh, I am sure they will remain your clients," Celia teased. "After all, it is my understanding that this Season is the debut for each of their daughters. I am also told their presentation at court did not go as well as they had hoped."

"As a second son, I am quite safe," Elias said with a grin.

"But your brother is not," Sophie reminded him before Celia could.

"Yes, and they will not wish to upset your brother by severing ties with you." It was Celia's turn to appear smug. "You should at least continue to have the pleasure of their patronage until your brother either marries or flees London to escape the Marriage Mart."

Elias grimaced as if suddenly tasting something very tart. "Lovely."

Celia laughed, and poor Sophie snorted her amusement and didn't attempt to cover it this time with coughing.

"I believe you two ladies can be quite wicked," Elias teased.

That made them laugh again, so much so that they both, for propriety's sake, hid behind their fans.

"This is such fun," Celia said, meaning it more than he would ever know. "Thank you so much for suggesting it." She hadn't felt this energized and carefree in—well, ever. The realization sobered her and trounced the desire to revel in the enjoyment further. The stark realization that this situation was not genuine hit her. Nor could she hope for it to last.

"Celia?" Concern echoed in Elias's deep voice as he gently tipped the shield of her fan away from her face.

"Miss Bening," she corrected him with a pointed glance in Sophie's direction. "We are not close enough for anything else, my lord."

He reacted with a somewhat injured demeanor. "Of course, Miss Bening. Forgive me."

Sophie scowled at her, leaned forward as though to say something, then, apparently, thought better of it and sat back. "It is a lovely day and an even lovelier ride, Lord Raines," she said without taking her narrow-eyed glare from Celia. "A much-needed escape from the sadness currently overshadowing Hasterton House."

Elias's injured demeanor immediately disappeared, replaced with his earlier concern. He boldly took Celia's fan, placed it on the seat between them, then took her hands in his. "There is no shame in seeking a brief respite from trials in order to better survive them."

She fought against sinking into his golden-eyed gaze. This was not how it was supposed to be. It was she who should ensnare him. Not the other way around. "You do not know," she started to explain, then went quiet, struggling for composure. "You cannot possibly understand." And she could never explain it to him.

He held her hands tighter and leaned in so close she could almost taste him. And she realized she wanted to—so very badly.

"Make me understand, Celia," he said as though the park held no one in it but them. "Help me help you."

Sophie snapped her fan and broke the spell. "The poisonous trio near us once again, my dears. I highly recommend a more appropriate posture. Especially since Celia is to accompany Her Grace to Lady Bournebridge's ball."

Celia reluctantly pulled her hands free, picked up her fan, and once again took refuge behind it. She turned her face away from Elias and made a point of fixing her gaze on anything but him, even going so far as to shift her parasol so it almost separated them.

As Sophie had warned, the ladies whom the *ton* hated—but hung on their every word—slowly passed, returning from their earlier direction. The three vicious women graced them with aloof smiles and regal nods. Celia remembered Mama describing how much she had detested Lady Bournebridge and her loyal followers, who had debuted the same year as those of the Sisterhood and been just as unpleasant then as now. She almost said so aloud but caught herself before it was too late. Her near-slip jolted her to an almost painful awareness of how precarious life had become—and how lonely.

"Celia!" Sophie hissed sharply.

Celia met her trusted friend's gaze and knew Sophie understood she had nearly toppled the game.

Elias gave the side of the carriage a hard thump, then turned to her. His dark brows drew together over his entirely-too-perceptive eyes. "Forgive me, Miss Bening, but you are causing me great concern."

The coachman eased the vehicle over to one side of the path and halted before turning to face him. "Yes, m'lord?"

"Return us to Hasterton House, Jamison." Elias continued studying Celia with a scrutiny that made her shift uncomfortably. "I fear the sun has become too strong for the ladies."

"No," Celia countered, determined to regain control and rise above her emotions. "Please do not cut this delight short because of my silliness. Might we find a shady place to sit or stroll for a while? After all," she said with what she hoped was a convincing smile, "I have a ball to attend tomorrow evening and must have fodder for Her Grace to share with the other ladies."

The driver shifted his focus back to Elias and waited.

Elias studied her a moment longer, then agreed. "As the lady wishes."

"There's a fair bit of shade by the lake," Jamison said before putting the carriage back in motion. "Should be nice walking there, if you don't mind my saying so."

"I would love a closer look at the Serpentine," Celia said. "Her Grace says it is quite lovely this time of year with spring-time's awakening."

"So be it." Elias gave a tip of his head, and the carriage smoothly rolled onward.

Sophie relaxed back in the seat and offered Celia a subtle nod of approval.

"I do hope we see some bugs or frogs." Celia tucked her fan back into her reticule, looking forward to the easily managed distractions a walk beside the lake promised. "Dragonflies especially. They are my favorite. So graceful with their shimmer-ing wings that put stained-glass windows to shame."

Elias eyed her as though she had sprouted a second head. "You *like* bugs? And frogs?" He shifted in the seat and continued looking at her with an incredulous stare. "Might I ask how you feel about snakes?"

"Venomous or benign?"

"Venomous," he said as though issuing a dare.

She sat taller, stretching to see if the lake's conditions would be conducive to frogs, bugs, and, with any luck, dragonflies, although it might yet be too early in the season. "I treat adders and vipers with the utmost respect, of course, but I do enjoy watching grass snakes when I happen to find them in the garden."

"You are an amazing woman, Miss Bening." Elias slowly shook his head.

"Why? Because I enjoy studying something other than em-broidery stitches?" She softened her sarcasm with a coy smile. "The world outside my parlor is full of many wonders waiting to be discovered. I need only lift my head and look around." She closed her parasol and tucked it into the corner beside the seat. With all the lovely shade, she wouldn't need it and didn't wish to be bothered with carrying it.

Elias opened his mouth to comment, but the carriage rolled to a stop and interrupted him. Jamison unlatched the carriage door, then moved to tend to the horses. After alighting with a nimble hop, Elias turned and helped Lady Sophie step to the ground. As he turned and offered his hand to Celia, he gave her a look that made her catch her breath.

"Your world and its wonders await to be discovered, Miss Bening," he said for her alone, leaving Celia with the distinct impression that he was *not* referring to bugs.

Determined to snare him just as effectively as he was ensnaring her, Celia leaned in closer than necessary and held tightly to his hand while stepping down from the carriage. "I am ready to discover everything," she said just as softly, then remembered to tease the tip of her tongue across her lip as Frannie had recommended. For what reason, neither of them knew, but the forbidden novel Frannie had found in her mother's bedside table drawer had recommended it. Unfortunately, they could not read it in its entirety because Frannie had to put it back before her mother discovered it was missing.

Elias's jaw flexed, and he held her hand even tighter though she now stood quite solidly on the ground. "I fear..." he said quietly, then his words trailed off as he slowly stroked his thumb back and forth across the back of her gloved hand.

"You fear what, Lord Raines?" she asked just as quietly.

His eyes narrowed and his smile became more self-assured. "I fear you play a dangerous game, Celia. Take care."

"Miss Bening," she gently corrected him, while easing her hand out of his. She cast a teasing glance back at him, then hurried to join Sophie.

"Indeed." He proffered a most gentlemanly nod. "Miss Bening."

"Admirable recovery," Sophie whispered to Celia before Elias fell in step beside them.

Celia thanked her with a smile, then turned her attention to the mirrorlike surface of the lake, which was only disturbed by a pair of regal swans gliding across it. "They are so lovely—and peaceful."

"And devoted to one another," Elias said. "They mate for life."

"Oh, to be a swan." Celia ambled along the waterside, her gaze fixed on the snowy-white birds.

Elias strolled next to her while Sophie diplomatically slowed and fell a few steps behind, feigning interest in the fluffy band of clouds floating just above the tree line.

"So, you do wish to marry someday?" Elias asked.

Celia didn't answer right away. It was essential she word her response carefully.

"Miss Bening?" he prompted, seeming impatient to hear her reply.

"Only for love," she finally said. "I will not subject myself to a union that is more of a business arrangement for breeding an heir or climbing Society's fickle ladder. Marriage should be a true joining of two loving souls." Before he could comment, she hastily added, "Of course, as a gentle-born woman of no title, I need not worry about becoming a sought-after item at the peerage's breeding market." She shifted her gaze from the swans to him. "What about you, Lord Raines? As a second son of a duke and a renowned solicitor who is already a partner in his firm, will you marry for prestige and riches to continue your elevation in Polite Society, or will you marry for love?"

"You insult me, Miss Bening. Do you truly think me so avaricious?"

She tossed a shrug his way. "I simply state the obvious. Gentlemen, even second sons, are trained from birth that it is quite acceptable to do whatever it takes to make one's mark in this world. Gain land, riches, and prestige." She fixed him with a look that dared him to deny it. "Tell me your father and mother taught you to marry for love, and I shall heartily beg your pardon."

"My mother died when I was born, and my father hated me

for it because he already had his heir. So, I fear I can neither deny nor confirm the parental guidance you suggest."

Celia came to a halt, ashamed for allowing a lifetime of bitterness to convict Elias of heartlessness when he had given her no reason to believe he was such a man. Staring down at the tips of her shoes, she fisted her hands against her middle. "I do beg your pardon, Lord Raines. I should not have spoken in such a cruel manner. I am sorry. Truly. I completely understand if you wish to return me to Hasterton House and be done with my company immediately."

"I do not wish to be done with your company, my dearest Celia. Not ever." He blew out a heavy sigh while turning to stare at the lake as if it held the answers he sought. "That is the dilemma with which I struggle." He faced her once more, squinting as though in pain. "And I beg that you call me Elias even with Lady Sophie present. I long to hear you say my name as though you enjoy being with me as much as I enjoy being with you."

He glanced back at Sophie where she dawdled a few steps behind them, then faced Celia once more with a look that made her catch her breath. "Who are you, Celia Bening? The truth, if you please. Who are you to the Duchess of Hasterton to make her care for you so much that she omitted both her children from her will? Do you not understand that the Duke of Hasterton will not stand for it? The man is ruthless about his vast holdings, and I feel certain that Lady Cecilia will join him in the courts— especially since the transfers from the Hasterton accounts to those of the Bening files have become more frequent of late. The duke has no idea what the dowager intends, but I know he will not allow it. Tell me, Celia. Tell me the truth about yourself, so I might spare you the pain and protect you from what could lie ahead."

Heart-wrenching disappointment and a healthy portion of fear replaced the guilt and shame she had felt for her earlier poor choice of words regarding his upbringing. Not trusting herself to speak, she turned and caught hold of her skirts, marching back toward the carriage path at a very unladylike pace.

"Celia!" Sophie called out as she hurried to catch her. "Celia! Whatever is wrong?"

"Miss Bening!" Elias rounded on them both and blocked the way. "Hear me out."

"I have heard quite enough from you, Lord Raines. You will return us to Hasterton House immediately." Celia had underestimated the man, been foolish enough to allow his mesmerizing smile and winning charm to blind her. That would not happen again.

"I meant no insult, and even you should agree that my questions are valid." The caring in his eyes made her want to slap him and then throw herself in his arms and weep for what she could never have. "I can help you, Celia. Please—let me."

"The only help I require from you, Lord Raines, is transport back to Hasterton House. Now." She drew herself up and clenched her teeth, forcing her composure to remain intact.

He bowed his head and slowly shook it, his mouth tight as though he clenched his teeth too.

"The carriage, Lord Raines," Sophie repeated while hugging an arm around Celia.

Elias curled his finger and thumb to his mouth and blew a sharp whistle that split the air. In an instant, the stylish barouche and its fine pair of black horses came to a stop in front of them.

Too irritated and embarrassed with herself to worry about social convention, Celia yanked open the door before the coachman or Elias could reach it. She clambered up into the vehicle, took her seat, and snapped open her parasol. "Sophie, you will seat yourself beside me, please."

"Of course." Sophie slid into the seat beside her and squeezed her arm in a silent message of sympathy.

"Take them to Hasterton House," Elias ordered the coachman.

"Then return for you, m'lord?" Jamison asked.

When he didn't answer, Celia peeped out from behind her parasol to see why. Her heart ached at the sight of Elias disappearing into the woods.

"Seduction is for naught," she said as the carriage took off at a brisk pace. "The hound only wishes to kill the fox."

"You underestimate yourself, sister." Sophie lightly squeezed her arm. "I believe he cares and is trying to protect you."

Celia blinked faster against the infuriating tears that refused to go away. "I will protect myself and Mama. Like always."

CHAPTER SIX

"MR. ELKIN STRONGLY recommended I tread lightly regarding the Dowager Duchess of Hasterton and her companion, my lord."

Elias eyed Jack, knowing the Bow Street Runner had never backed away from an investigation in all the years he had known him. "Did Mr. Elkin threaten your position if you continued looking into this matter for me?"

"He made it clear things would not go well for me if I caused the lady any trouble." Jack ambled closer to the desk and gave an emphatic dip of his chin. "He spoke as if she was his friend—or had once been more. I've seen that look in a man's eyes before."

"As have I." Elias remembered Master Hodgely's fondness for the dowager. Apparently, in her youth, the lady had gained several loyal admirers. Much as he had come to *admire* Celia and yearned to protect her. "I appreciate the information about the duke's background." He handed the man another voucher, doubling the payment this time. "Let it rest for now to get Elkin off the scent and keep your post intact. You have a wife and children to feed, and I do not want your loss of wages on my conscience."

"I can still keep an ear to the ground without old Elkin knowing. If I hear more, you'll know." Jack bobbed his head. "Good day to you, my lord."

"Good day, Jack." Elias watched the man leave, then leaned

back in his chair and thought over what the Bow Street Runner had reported about the duke. Nothing new, really. Elias was already aware that not a soul in London could remember meeting the man. They all recalled his father, the fifth Duke of Hasterton, but the sixth was only known by his signature and his astoundingly lucrative trading at the Stock Exchange by a representative who refused to speak to anyone. The duke had to have made that man rich as Croesus to secure such loyalty. The duke was also known as a ruthless businessman. *Ruthless.* Was the man cruel, also? Was he the one who put the fear and leeriness in Celia's eyes? Elias's blood boiled at the thought of anyone mistreating her. Renewed determination to protect her surged through him.

He thought back over every conversation with her, scrutinizing every word. Not once had Celia ever exhibited any apprehension about the duke—or commented about Lady Cecilia, other than mentioning the lady's poor health. And she had spoken as if she knew them both intimately.

A dangerous feeling of something much stronger than mere loyalty to a client stirred within his heart. He cared about Celia and wanted her with a relentlessness he'd never known. A need to protect the wondrous green-eyed goddess became stronger every day.

A heavy sigh escaped him. He had most assuredly estranged her in the park because of his determination to shield her from what would surely be a very public stripping away of everything the Duchess of Hasterton intended to leave to her. If Celia would just trust him, he could save her from such a scandalous humiliation.

"Blast and damn it all!"

A rap on the door and a curt "Carriage here, m'lord" interrupted his fuming. He pulled his watch from his pocket and glanced at it even though he knew the time. It couldn't be helped. He had waited as late as he dared. The duchess would surely be wondering why he had yet to arrive with the documents he had promised would be ready for her signature today.

He grabbed his leather bag and left the office without a word to anyone. The closer the hackney drew to Hasterton House, the harder his dread churned. Not because of the duchess, but because of Celia. He resettled himself in the seat, tensed to spring from the hackney as soon as it slowed. Why should he dread a visit? He probably wouldn't even see her, because she surely hated him by now. She probably thought he had arranged the ride to Hyde Park to interrogate her when her guard was down.

When he arrived, he paid the fare and bade the driver to wait. A pair of servants could witness the signing of the copies of the will. Completing the documentation would not take long at all. He vaulted up the front steps and banged the brass ring in the lion's mouth against the plate.

After a surprisingly long few moments, Gransdon opened the door. "Welcome, my lord. Her Grace requests you see her in the privacy of her rooms. Please follow me."

A strange request, since the dowager had said she would attend Lady Bournebridge's ball this evening. Surely, the lady didn't mean to have him bring the papers to her while she dressed. Bracing himself for whatever awaited, Elias dutifully followed, all the while hoping to glimpse his precious Celia, even though he knew she hated him.

Gransdon lightly knocked on a door at the head of the stairs, opened it, and announced, "Lord Raines is here, Your Grace."

"Thank you, Gransdon," came the weak reply.

Only then did the butler step aside and allow Elias to enter.

Duchess Thea reclined on a lounge placed beside a wall of windows. While her color seemed much improved, she appeared weaker and somehow a great deal smaller in her plush nest of pillows and throws.

"Your Grace." Elias offered a respectful bow.

She fluttered her fingers at a nearby chair. "Pull it closer and have a seat, Lord Raines, so we might review the document together. I have no time for niceties or the rules of etiquette today." She pulled in a slow, deep breath, and behaved as though the effort exhausted her. "Forgive me. This afternoon has been particularly trying."

"Think nothing of it, Your Grace." Elias moved the chair as close as he could and had a seat. It pained him to see the lady becoming even more fragile. He pulled the document from his bag and held it so she could read it without expending the effort to hold it.

"Next page," she said repeatedly until they reached the last sheet, then she frowned and squinted at the text. "I do not recall requesting what is noted in item twenty-one, section c."

"Do you wish me to strike it from the copies?" He prayed she wouldn't but refused to dishonor her by arguing his point.

She closed her eyes. "No. I am grateful you thought to include it. It will better protect her."

"There are three copies to sign in front of witnesses, Your Grace."

She winced without opening her eyes.

"Gransdon and your lady's maid can serve as witnesses, then I shall attach the seal, and leave a copy here with you." He glanced up at the butler and the maid. They both nodded.

"And the other two copies?" she said, barely opening an eye and pinning him with a hawkish glare.

"One will be sent to your solicitor in Germany, and the other will be filed at my office in case of any issues in the future." He would not mention her children contesting the will. Upsetting the lady now would be reprehensible.

She smiled and slowly opened both eyes. "Celia can handle them. She is fierce."

It was his turn to smile. "She is indeed, Your Grace."

The duchess turned her head and studied him closer, her expression unnerving. "I charge you with protecting my Celia, Lord Raines."

"I beg your pardon?" The back of his neck tingled, and the hairs stood on end.

She arched a sleek brow and gave him a chiding glare. "I

spoke quite clearly, but I shall repeat it, since I want no misunderstandings between us." She paused and glanced at Gransdon and her maid. She waited for their nods that they would witness her words before returning her attention to him. "I charge you with protecting Celia Bening, Lord Elias Raines. Do you swear to honor this dying woman's last request?"

Elias's heart pounded so hard it made his chest ache. "I will protect Celia any way I can, Your Grace. I swear it."

"Even from herself?" the duchess continued.

"You ask a great deal." He wondered at the woman, and what she truly meant by his protecting Celia once she was gone.

"I am allowed to ask a great deal," she said, "because I am dying." She managed a more congenial smile. "Celia is her own worst enemy, Lord Raines. But if you endeavor to love her and win her love in return, you will discover yourself blessed beyond your wildest imaginings. I promise you that."

"You asked me to protect her," he gently reminded her. "Not love her."

"Love is the greatest protection of all, Lord Raines. If she is loved and knows herself to be loved, she can survive anything." She pointed at him. "And the same goes for you. You should thank me for such words of wisdom."

"And have you told her of this last request of yours?" He could picture Celia's reaction. Vividly.

The duchess managed a weak, lilting chuckle. "At present, she is confused about her feelings for you. But you can change that." She lifted her hand. "Gransdon—ink and quill before my strength fully leaves me for the day."

"Yes, Your Grace." Gransdon hurried over to the table in the corner and fetched them along with a small rosewood lap desk.

"Berta, raise me up." The duchess weakly waved her maid closer.

Berta hurried to prop the dowager higher among her pillows and steadied the desk on her lap while Gransdon held the inkwell for her.

Elias showed the duchess where to sign and initial. Once she completed the task, he handed the copies to Gransdon. "You and Berta sign beside Her Grace's signature on the last page of each copy. Along with today's date, please."

"Yes, my lord." Gransdon tipped a nod for Berta to follow him.

The maid removed the lap desk and carried it over to the table, where Gransdon laid out the three copies of the will.

"Help an old woman settle more comfortably, my lord." The duchess shifted and plucked at her coverings, wincing as though in a great deal of pain.

"Gladly, Your Grace." Elias helped her slide deeper into the pillows and recline even more. "Pardon my forwardness, but did your physician not suggest laudanum for your pain?"

"I refuse to take laudanum," she said. "The dreadful stuff makes me see things I would prefer not to revisit." She patted her chest and pulled in a deep breath. "And it makes it harder for me to draw in a satisfying breath as well."

He knelt beside her and whispered, "My auntie hated laudanum too. But a generous glass of good whisky took its place very nicely."

The duchess smiled and whispered back, "I wonder if we have any?"

"If you do not, I shall send for some immediately." Elias rose to his feet as Gransdon returned the signed and witnessed copies of the will to him. "Gransdon, scour the place for whisky—a good whisky, mind you. If none is found, send for it. It will help Her Grace immensely."

The butler turned to the duchess and waited.

"Please do, Gransdon." She seemed almost relieved.

"At once, Your Grace." He bowed and hurried out the door.

"I shall leave you now, Your Grace." Elias wished he could do more for the lady than recommend whisky to numb her pain. He held up the papers. "Shall I place a copy in the library on my way out?"

The duchess gave another weary chuckle. "If you can make it past the she-dragon hiding in her treasury of books, then yes, by all means, do so." She nestled deeper into her pillows and smiled. "In fact, please do go to the library, Lord Raines. See if you can't find a way to make amends with her and get started on that promise you made to me."

Elias couldn't help but smile. "You are a formidable woman, Your Grace."

She barely shook her head. "Perhaps, once. But no longer." She closed her eyes. "Leave me now. I am tired."

"Rest well, Your Grace." Elias eased from the room, pausing once he stepped into the hall to offer up a silent prayer to ease the woman's suffering. As he lifted his head, a flash of color in the hallway downstairs caught his eye.

The elusive, lovely, and yet most frustrating Miss Bening. No. Not Miss Bening. His Celia. He smiled at the memory of the dowager's charge to win Celia's love and love her in return. He had already completed half the quest. His love for her was the simple part. His beguiling lioness had captured his heart the first time she roared at him.

Papers in hand, he descended the steps with his focus on the library door. Knowing Celia, she had probably locked it. But then again, perhaps she hadn't. Perhaps she believed he hadn't seen her. He paused with his hand on the door handle and listened for movement on the other side. Nothing but the lonely echo of a clock ticking away the minutes came to him. He pushed down on the handle and smiled when it clicked and the door swung open.

"Celia, I know you are in here." He stepped inside, closed the door behind him, and waited for his eyes to adjust to the absence of light. With the heavy curtains drawn and no candles lit, the small fire in the hearth at the other end of the room did little to beat back the darkness. "I brought in Her Grace's copy of the will. Signed and witnessed as is proper and according to her list of wishes." The paragraph he had added for Celia's own good would remain unannounced for now. "I shall place it here in the center of the desk so you may file it wherever you wish."

Elias eased deeper into the room, every sense alert to pick up on the slightest sound or hint of movement. A floorboard on the second floor squeaked and made him smile. "I want you to know that I did not suggest the carriage ride to Hyde Park as a means of getting information from you." He meandered around the desk, eying the upper level as he walked. "I suggested it because I thought it might lift Her Grace's spirits." He listened for the floor to reveal Celia's movements again. "And also because I knew you would come along too—what with your being her companion. I wanted to be with you, Celia. Spend time with *you*. I need you to believe that. You have completely ensorcelled me, dear lady. I can think of no one but you."

Only the ticking clock continued to break the silence. Elias pulled the chair out from behind the desk, scooted it to the foot of the stair, then lowered himself into it. Once fully seated, he angled it so he might comfortably prop his feet on the steps while he waited for his delightful she-dragon to emerge from her lair. "I am not leaving until you come out and talk to me. You will find I can be very single-minded when I decide I want something, and I want you." He couldn't resist a smile. "Come, Celia. As I said, I will not leave until you talk to me."

"You may now leave, Lord Raines. I have talked to you." Her voice came from the second level, but she remained out of sight.

"I never figured you as one to be childish," he dared her. "Or cowardly."

"I am also not one to fall for such a ridiculous attempt to make me appear. Go away."

"Indeed." He stretched out more comfortably and crossed his legs at the ankles. "This chair is quite comfortable. I believe I could nap in it. Are you just as comfortable up there? I hope not, or we could very well be stuck in here for quite some time."

"You are sorely tempting me to throw books down on your head, Lord Raines. All that currently stays my hand is my love for the literature on these shelves." The floor above squeaked again, this time much closer than before. She had to be close to the top of the spiral staircase that led to the second level. "Go away. You have completed the will. Your services are no longer required here."

"On the contrary—Duchess Thea charged me with another task. One I have yet to complete." He laced his fingers together and propped his hands across his middle. He grinned to himself. "And this task could take me a lifetime to complete."

"A lifetime?" she repeated, sounding more frustrated by the moment. "What sort of task would Her Grace give you that could possibly take a lifetime?"

"Protecting you."

"I am quite capable of protecting myself, thank you." But the tremor in her voice claimed otherwise. "Just go away. Please."

The unmistakable sound of tears in her request moved him to rise and silently steal up the stairs. "I am not going away. I made a promise to the duchess and refuse to go back on my word." As he reached the top, light from the round, ornate window in the arch above the bookcases revealed Celia huddling on the floor in front of the shelves, hugging her legs with her chin tucked to her chest and her forehead propped on her knees.

He sat down beside her, stretched out his legs, and pulled her into his lap, holding her close as he had ached to do for so very long.

She twisted and buried her face in his chest, curling tighter into his embrace like a child terrified of the dark. Every breath she drew in became a hitching shudder that she exhaled with a keening sigh. His heart broke for her as she lost the battle with her tears.

"I hate crying!" She thumped his chest with her fist and sobbed even harder.

He stroked her hair and held her, both thankful for the opportunity to do so and amazed at the dowager's knowing that Celia needed him to survive this moment. He pressed a kiss into her silky, jasmine-scented hair and closed his eyes. "There is no shame in tears," he said softly. "Let them flow, dear one, and ease your heart."

"You…do not…understand," she hiccupped, then released another long, high-pitched cry.

"Then make me understand. I am not leaving, remember?"

She didn't answer, just remained silent except for her weeping. But she stayed in his arms, curled on his lap, and for that, he was glad. He hoped neither Lady Sophie nor Lady Ardsmere came searching for her. Calming Celia was his honor alone, and he would guard that honor fiercely.

After a while, she resettled herself until her head rested on his shoulder. He enjoyed sitting like this and hoped it lasted quite some time. Eventually, she hitched in several quick sniffs, then slowly pushed herself upright, but kept her gaze downcast as if ashamed to look him in the eyes. She swiped at his chest as though trying to brush away nonexistent crumbs. "I fear I have completely dampened your shirt. Please forgive me."

He reached up and touched her face, running his thumb across her cheek to wipe away the trails of her tears. "Will you forgive me for our misunderstanding in the park?"

A corner of her mouth quivered upward as though she wanted to smile but wasn't quite ready. "Yes, my lord. I forgive you."

"Elias," he reminded her softly, while gently pulling her closer.

"Elias," she repeated, as though entranced. Her lips parted as her gaze lowered to his mouth, and she pulled in a shaking breath. "Are you going to kiss me?"

"If you will allow it."

"I will," she whispered, then leaned in and hesitantly touched her lips to his. She halted and drew back the slightest bit. "But be warned—I have only read about kissing. Never have I put it into practice."

"Then let us test your comprehension of the literature you studied." He slid his fingers up into her thick, loosely bound hair and cradled her head as he tilted her back. Starting slowly, so as not to frighten her, he nibbled gently across the soft suppleness of her mouth and tasted her with teasing flicks of his tongue. She surprised him by sliding her arms around his neck and opening to him, pulling him in as if starving, to commit fully to the union.

He tightened his embrace and poured every ounce of his yearning into it. She tasted of wonderment, need, and passion, waiting to be unleashed. The soft weight of her on his lap combined with her mouth against his made him groan, then stop himself before doing something rash. This was not the proper time for anything more than a heated kiss. To take advantage of the lovely Celia now, when she was at her most vulnerable, would be an unforgivable disgrace and make him appear to be a rakehell of the worst sort. His Celia deserved better.

"Why did you stop, my lord?" Her breathy whisper almost made him groan again. "Did I botch the kiss?"

"Absolutely not." He cupped her cheek and tenderly stroked his thumb across the plump swell of her bottom lip. "Your kissing is beyond compare." He gently but firmly eased her upright and sat her on the floor beside him. "But I fear, my precious lioness, that if we continue enjoying such forbidden pleasure, we might lose all reason and do something we might later regret."

She gave him a look that hovered somewhere between frustrated, perplexed, and pleased. *"Precious lioness?"*

A soft, huffing laugh escaped him. "Forgive me, but from our first meeting, I have always thought of you as a fiercely beautiful, green-eyed lioness."

"Indeed?" She cocked a brow to a stern slant but then smiled. "And what would you say if I told you that you reminded me of a great, golden-eyed panther I once saw at a menagerie in Hamburg?"

"I would say that we are two well-matched members of the *Panthera* genus." He reached over and took her hand, lacing his fingers with hers. The need to touch her, to remain connected even in the slightest way, raged through him like an unquenchable blaze. "Will you let me protect you, Celia?" he asked softly.

"Draw closer and share every secret so you might finally let down your guard and enjoy all that life offers?"

She shifted with a heavy sigh and drew her hand away, but at least she remained sitting on the floor beside him. "You have no idea what you ask." She drew her knees up again and hugged them, returning to the unhappy position in which he had found her. "You have no idea," she repeated so softly that he almost didn't hear.

"I could have an idea," he gently chided, knowing he risked pushing her farther away rather than closer. "All you need do is trust me. Tell me what troubles you, dear lady. Let me chase your demons away."

Celia pushed herself up from the floor and shook the wrinkles from her dress. "Please excuse me, Lord Raines. It is high time I cease my sulking and return to Her Grace." She paused and took a deep breath, her bottom lip quivering. "She is not well today. Not well at all."

"Lord Raines?" His heart sank even though her tone suggested she did not like using that form of address any more than he enjoyed hearing it. He stood and moved closer, determined to make her see.

She stared up into his eyes, then sadly touched his face and cradled his cheek in her palm. "I am sorry, Elias," she whispered. "It must be *Lord Raines* from now on. For your sake as well as mine." She let her hand drop and moved past him to go to the stairs.

Elias turned and caught her, then gently but firmly pulled her back. "Why, Celia? Tell me why, I beg you."

She pushed away and shook her head. "Goodbye, Lord Raines." Then she skimmed down the steps and out the library door before he could stop her.

CHAPTER SEVEN

"YOU ARE QUITE sure you wish to continue? I do not want you to overdo." Celia took the package of ribbons and combs from her mother as they stepped out of the shop. She handed it to Friedrich, who had waited outside, standing at attention like a personal guard. He accepted the small bundle and placed it with the others he held in the crook of his muscular arm. Celia felt them well protected by the dedicated giant who greatly resembled the Viking etchings in the book of Norse sagas back in her library. She was glad the footman had accompanied them from Germany.

When her mother didn't answer, Celia cleared her throat to get her attention. "Your Grace? Did you hear me?"

"My hearing is exemplary." Duchess Thea turned from perusing items in another shop window and fixed Celia with a warning look. "My tolerance for over-coddling is not." She saucily patted the back of her hat as if ensuring it was tipped to the most fashionable angle. "I am enjoying an exhilarating day of wellness and vigor. Do not spoil it."

"Yes, Your Grace." Celia forced a smile and pretended all was lovely, when in fact, all she wanted to do was curl up and cry. She was miserably lonely and destined to become even more so once Mama died. Especially since she had sent Elias on his way.

But her mother's beaming happiness made her shake herself. Now was not the time to sulk about like a spoiled child. A day of improved health for Mama was a rare gift and deserved better.

She pointed at the next shop in the multitude of businesses lining both sides of the busy street. "I believe Sophie and Frannie are in this bookshop. Would you like to pop in there too?"

Mama wrinkled her nose as though fighting back a sneeze. "While enjoying such energy, I would love to visit the Bond Street bazaar, and then, if time permits, move on to the Pantheon for more browsing. I know you adore poring over the oldest and mustiest of books in the shops, but would you mind very much passing on it this time?" Her smile seemed almost apologetic. "I need the hustle and bustle of people and light right now, Celia. I have been starved of it for so very long."

"I can sort through musty old books anytime," Celia said. "Just give me a moment to see if Sophie and Frannie are ready to come along with us to the bazaars." She turned to Friedrich and gave him a silent *watch over Mama* look.

The footman nodded and moved a step closer to the duchess, all the while stealing glances up and down the street. The devoted man trusted no one, and Celia was glad of it.

She hurried into the small, cluttered shop and collided with Elias just inside the door. Her heart shot into her throat and nearly choked her as she teetered off balance. "Oh my! I do beg your pardon, Lord Raines. Please forgive me."

He steadied her by catching hold of her shoulders, then jerked his hands away as if touching her burned him. Taking a step back, he curtly nodded. "There is nothing to forgive, Miss Bening." Then something both dangerous and exhilarating flickered in his eyes. His rumbling voice deepened to something akin to a warning growl. "Actually, there is much that requires both an apology and forgiveness, but I daresay such matters would be better addressed elsewhere."

She stiffened. How dare he say such a thing where it might be overheard by any number of people? Rather than argue and risk making him say anything more, she gave a deep curtsy, then hurried around him, hoping to escape. She spotted her friends at the counter chatting with the shop owner as they paid for their purchases. She hurried over and took refuge between them as they turned to go. "Duchess Thea wishes to go to the Bond Street bazaar and perhaps the Pantheon. Does that not sound lovely?"

"Indeed." Sophie eyed her as if wondering what was wrong, then looked past her and assumed a polite smile to go along with a belated curtsy. "Good day to you, Lord Raines. How nice to see you again."

"Lady Sophie." Elias bowed to her, then to Frannie. "Lady Ardsmere." He fixed a narrow-eyed scowl on Celia. His jaw flexed as if he was gritting his teeth while contemplating how best to endure her existence.

"Lord Raines." Frannie curtsied, then reached across Celia and caught hold of Sophie's arm. "Come, Sophie. I forgot to show you the book of maps that you simply must purchase for your brother's collection."

"But we already made our purchases," Sophie said while scrambling after her.

"We can make more." Frannie tugged her out of sight around the end of a tall bookcase.

An irritating sense of being abandoned filled Celia as she watched her sisters by choice disappear. No matter. She could handle this alone.

She stoked her courage and faced Elias. Leaning close, she lowered her voice. "You have no reason to be so disagreeable."

"I beg to differ." He widened his stance, as though expecting her to bolt for the door. "I intend to keep my word to the duchess, and you are making my task most difficult. I do not appreciate it when my tasks are made difficult."

She bit the inside of her cheek to keep from blurting out something highly improper in a public place. "I am sorry you feel that way, my lord. Trust me when I tell you that I only do what is best for all concerned."

Her fickle body did not agree. It flashed hot with the memory of his kiss and the delightful warmth of his embrace. She swallowed hard, her cheeks burning while her heart pounded to the point of making her breathless.

His striking appearance didn't help. His navy cutaway coat emphasized his broad shoulders, and his buff-colored pantaloons and polished black boots perfectly displayed his long, muscular legs that had made such a very nice lap on which to sit. Her entire body tingled at the recollection. Thankfully, the smugness of his expression made the breathtaking tingles give way to the indignant anger that helped her regain control.

Celia lifted her chin, ready to fight. "Perhaps you should speak with Her Grace. She is most understanding, and I feel certain would happily release you from your oath." She dismissed herself with a curtsy then went to step around him, and he blocked her way again.

"No, thank you, Miss Bening. I do not make oaths lightly. Nor do I ever go back on them." His entirely-too-perceptive smile widened, irritating her even more.

"Let me pass," she said through clenched teeth. "Her Grace is just outside and should not be kept waiting."

His dark brows ratcheted higher. "Her Grace is outside?"

She refused to repeat herself to this infuriating man. Instead, she moved to step around him again.

And again, he blocked her, but this time he offered his arm. "Allow me to escort you, Miss Bening," he said entirely too loud.

"This is not appropriate." She struggled to keep her tone civil when she would much rather scream and rant at him. "Remember your station, my lord," she said for his ears alone. "I am beneath it."

He moved closer, still holding his arm for her to take. "I do not think so. I suggest you accept the offer of my arm because people are staring. Or is that what you wish?"

A quick glance revealed several patrons were indeed becoming quite interested in their conversation. Probably because Lord Raines not only blocked the door to prevent her exit but kept everyone else from leaving as well. An irritated huff escaped her as she took his arm. "Happy?"

"Quite." He enraged her even more by adding a victorious wink. "Lady Sophie, Lady Ardsmere, would you care to join us?" he called out as he opened the door while bending his arm tight enough to keep Celia's hand imprisoned in the crook of it. To escape, she would have to make a scene by yanking free, and he knew it.

Celia stood at his side and aimed an angry glare at Sophie and Frannie as they emerged from around the bookcase. "Traitors," she accused under her breath as they passed in front of her. At least they both had the decency to duck their heads in a failed attempt at hiding their pride at the success of their treachery.

When she and Elias joined the others outside, the dowager met them, her happiness outshining them all. "What a fortuitous meeting, Lord Raines. Do join our outing, won't you?"

Before Elias could reply, Celia spoke for him. "I am sure Lord Raines is busy with far more important matters than shopping." She tried to release his arm, but before she could escape, he covered her gloved hand with his and held it firmly in place.

"I would be delighted to join you, Your Grace," he said. "Shall we take my carriage?"

"But we are entirely too many," Celia argued, frantic for an escape from this most uncomfortable development. "Even with Friedrich in the driver's box, we are still five."

"Nonsense," her mother said. "Friedrich will bring our carriage with Lady Sophie and Lady Ardsmere. You and I will join Lord Raines for the lovely ride in his barouche that I had to forgo the other day. We shall all meet at Bond Street." She turned to Sophie and Frannie. "Would that suit, my dears? Please say it does. After all, with two carriages, we shall have even more room for whatever treasures we find."

"I think it a splendid idea, Your Grace." Frannie curtsied while avoiding Celia's fuming glare. "What a shame our mothers were trapped into attending Lady Bournebridge's Venetian breakfast. They will be most jealous when they hear of our adventures that they missed."

"Our outing is sure to be more enjoyable than any time spent with Lady Bournebridge." Elias patted Celia's hand again, then gave it an intimate squeeze.

"Release me," she growled under her breath. She wished she could give his arm a painful pinch but knew it would fail through his coat sleeve.

"I will never release you, Miss Bening," he said with an intense look that made it clear he was referring to something else entirely. "Let us be on our way, shall we?"

Sophie and Frannie deserted her once again, but did cast an apologetic glance her way as they hurried along with Friedrich back to the carriage.

A moment after he summoned his vehicle with a tip of his head, Lord Raines's fine barouche pulled up beside them and came to a halt. His driver, Jamison, hopped down, gave a respectful bow, then opened the carriage door.

"Your Grace." Elias helped the duchess into the carriage and watched to make sure she was safely seated. Then he turned and smiled at Celia. He held out his hand. "Miss Bening?"

"You are a true churl, my lord," she said as she took his hand.

He smiled even broader, then leaned in close and whispered, "Such a sharp tongue, my fine lioness. I much prefer the way you used it in the library."

Her cheeks burned so hotly, she knew she must look as if she had used an entire pot of rouge on each of them. She climbed into the carriage, but when she went to sit beside her mother, she discovered the seat blocked by the duchess's cane and reticule. She scowled at the articles on the seat, then shifted her glare to her mother. "Your Grace?"

The duchess assumed a smug demeanor, then unleashed a grin that would rival any Cheshire cat. "Sit in the other seat, Celia. I do not wish to be crowded."

Celia glared at her mother, willing her to move her things. The duchess's eyes danced with a slyness befitting a most impudent child.

"Do be seated, Miss Bening," Elias said. He motioned to the empty seat that faced her impossible mother.

Celia threw herself into it with a very unladylike huff, but she didn't care. How could all of them—Mama, Sophie, and Frannie—turn against her? They knew she could not allow a closeness between herself and Lord Raines. The preservation of *all* their carefully constructed lives forbade it. The idea of seducing the man to manipulate him had been a faulty one indeed. He was utterly intractable. And the devil of it was that she found herself even more drawn to him—almost painfully so.

He settled down beside her and intimately nudged his shoulder against hers. "Oh, I do beg your pardon, Miss Bening." His demeanor shouted that he did not beg her pardon at all and would probably rub against her again if given half the chance.

"I am so glad we came upon you, Lord Raines," the duchess said as they rolled along. "The more the merrier. Do you not agree?"

"Absolutely, Your Grace, and if you will forgive me for making a very personal observation, it lifts my heart to see you enjoying such good health today. Much improved over the last time I saw you."

"It is indeed a glorious day, and I intend to enjoy it." The dowager tapped the toe of Celia's shoe with her cane. "Although there appears to be a little storm cloud among us."

Celia allowed herself an exasperated huff before admitting that Mama was right. She needed to do better and not allow her frustrations to overshadow the gift of this day with her mother in such fine spirits. She offered an apologetic nod. "Forgive me, Your Grace. You are quite correct, and I shall remedy it immediately." She waved her hand in front of her face, then snapped her fingers. "Your winds of happiness have chased the little storm cloud away, leaving nothing but sunshine in its place."

"Well done," Elias said. His deep voice echoed with genuine admiration and approval.

Celia caught herself smiling at him, so she hurried to turn away.

Elias leaned close enough to whisper, "Too late, my lioness. I saw that smile." His warm breath tickled her ear in a most disturbing way.

"A proper gentleman would not comment on such, Lord Raines."

"I neither wish to be proper nor a gentleman in your company." He slid his hand under hers and brought it to his mouth for a kiss. "For the sake of your reputation, however, I shall endeavor to do both."

She swallowed hard and pulled her hand away. Even through her glove, the warmth of his mouth made her yearn for another private moment with him in the library. "Polite Society demands that a gentleman not kiss a woman's hand unless he knows her very well."

"I am working on that part." His lazy smile sent a renewed surge of heat through her.

"On what part?"

His deep, rumbling laugh vibrated through her. "Knowing you *very* well."

"My hearing is impeccable, Lord Raines," the duchess warned with a dark look.

Elias straightened and sat taller. "Forgive me, Your Grace, but please know I only possess the best of intentions when it comes to the charming Miss Bening. I would do nothing to cause her distress or ruin."

"That is good to know, my lord." The duchess's scrutiny of him hardened as she spoke. "I shall haunt you if you cause her heartache or unhappiness. Is that quite clear?"

"As the purest water." He slightly bowed his head, then pressed a hand to his chest. "I gave you my oath earlier, Your Grace. I intend to see it through."

"It is very rude to speak around a person as if they are not present." Celia edged as far from Elias as the padded seat of the carriage allowed. She popped open her parasol and held it out to her mother. "You are facing the sun, Your Grace."

Her mother laughed and waved it away. "I like the sun on my face and no longer have the need to worry about receiving a freckle or two. Shade yourself, dear girl." She wiggled in the seat like a child excited about the outing. "Your carriage gives a most pleasant ride, Lord Raines. Good fortune smiled upon us by crossing our paths today."

"And what do you think, Miss Bening?" He quirked a brow at Celia, devilment in his smile.

"I think I am glad we have arrived." Celia waved at the carriage pulling up behind them as they slowed to a stop. "And Frannie and Sophie have too." She couldn't resist sending a teasing glance Elias's way. "Are you quite sure you are ready to accompany four ladies shopping?"

"I wouldn't miss this for the world." He rubbed his hands together, then jumped out of the carriage and helped the dowager duchess step down.

Celia's traitorous heart beat faster as he turned back and helped her. "Thank you, Lord Raines," she said, then reluctantly removed her hand from his.

He tipped his head her way, then offered his arm to the dowager. "Your Grace?"

"It has been an age since I have walked on the arm of such a handsome young rake," Duchess Thea teased.

A crashing wave of relief, disappointment, and perhaps a bit of envy threatened to drown Celia as she fell in step behind them. Frannie and Sophie caught up with her and took their places on either side, both assuming appropriately crestfallen expressions for their earlier abandonment of her.

"You needed to spend time with him," Sophie whispered.

"In whose opinion?" Celia struggled to hold the fake smile that made her cheeks ache.

"Our mothers." Frannie cut a quick nod at the duchess. "And Her Grace."

"This is utterly ridiculous." Celia slowed her steps so they could fall back and carry on a normal conversation. "A match with Lord Raines is impossible—for the safety of all of us. Our mothers should understand that."

"According to Maman, they all believe that once you inherit the trust, you can allow the sixth Duke of Hasterton to fade from existence and enjoy a *real* life of your own for a change." Sophie's dubious shrug conveyed her opinion that such a plan would fail.

Celia agreed. It would never work. "Since we are clients of the persistent Lord Raines, I doubt my *brother* will be allowed to so easily return to the land of imagination from whence he came." She shook her head. "Ever since he took over for Master Hodgely, Lord Raines has attempted to contact my fictitious twin at least a dozen times. The man is relentless."

"And dashing," Frannie said in a wistful tone. "You can't deny that you are attracted to him."

"And he appears *very much* attracted to you," Sophie said.

Celia paused at a vendor selling small, delicately carved rosewood boxes perfect for holding tiny treasures on a dressing table or nightstand. She traced a finger across one of the creations decorated with hearts entwined with roses. "My heart must remain as empty as this box." She firmly closed the lid. "Permanently."

"You plan to never marry?" Frannie stared at her in open-mouthed wonder.

"You have to marry." Sophie looped her arm through Celia's and gave it a comforting pat. "Frannie and I have no intention of living without love. Neither should you."

"And how do the two of you intend to accomplish such a feat and escape being charged with fraud and hanged for it?" Celia didn't want to sound cruel or waspish, but the Sisterhood created by their mothers was a double-edged sword. While it secured their lands, finances, and places in Society, it also effectively trapped them. Celia couldn't imagine attempting to hide their truths from a husband—nor revealing them. "Well? Tell me how you plan to juggle a family and the lie our lives truly are?"

"I have not thought that far as yet," Frannie said. "But we will sort it. Will we not, Sophie?"

"Yes." Sophie tugged Celia away from the stall of trinket boxes. "And you will too. Come. They are looking back to see what has become of us."

"Did you find a treasure?" the duchess asked when they joined them.

"A little rosewood box," Celia said. "You know how I love trinket boxes." She glanced across the line of stalls her mother had passed. "Have you not found any items too precious to leave behind?"

"We have been admiring the artwork," Elias said before the dowager could answer. He pinned Celia with an intense look. "And talking."

"Talking?" Celia eyed her mother. Instinct warned her that any sort of talk with Elias could only mean trouble.

The duchess smiled but didn't elaborate. Instead, she turned and led them onward with the demeanor of a queen followed by her retinue.

What should have been an enjoyable outing became a subtle form of torture to be endured. And endure it she would. With the utmost grace and style. Following her mother and Elias, Celia chatted with Sophie and Frannie while feigning interest in the expensive finery and wares of the stalls catering to Society's most affluent. As they reached the midpoint of the Bond Street bazaar, she spotted temporary salvation—seats and small tables arranged in front of a merchant selling lemonade. Surely, Mama would agree to sit for a while and enjoy a refreshing drink. While her color and spirits still seemed good, she had to be growing tired.

Celia hurried to the front of their group and drew their attention to the place. "Shall we enjoy a refreshing lemonade before we continue?"

Her mother opened her mouth to speak, but Elias cut her off. "I think it wise indeed. After all, we still have much to see." He eased the dowager into the idea with a convincing tip of his head. "Even the heartiest of athletes know it best to pace oneself in order to finish the race."

The duchess rewarded him with a thoughtful smile. "Of course, my lord. Lemonade sounds like a welcome respite before we continue."

Elias's firm but gentle maneuvering of her mother touched Celia's heart far more than it should have. He was neither a graceless rake nor a jealously avaricious second son, but a kind, caring gentleman.

A wistful sigh escaped her as she watched him help her mother be seated at one of the tables. As soon as the longing breath left her, he lifted his head, and their gazes locked. Somehow, he knew she longed for him. She saw it clearly in his eyes. And perhaps a yearning for her as well.

"Miss Bening?" He held out his hand and waited, knowing she would not be able to resist taking it.

"My lord." She went to him and slid her hand into his.

The faintness of his smile, the way it quirked the fullness of his lips and teased his irresistible dimple into appearing, made her catch her breath. Lord Elias Raines was a danger to all she had ever known—including her heart—and he knew it. How much he knew about her circumstances, she couldn't hazard a guess, but she suspected that it was entirely too much for the comfort of her mind and soul.

He seated her in the chair beside her mother, helped Sophie and Frannie into seats at the next table, then returned and sat next to Celia. With a flick of his wrist, he caught the merchant's eye. "Lemonades all around, my good man. Her Grace must be restored for more shopping."

The stall owner's eyes lit up. "Right away, Your Grace, right away."

"Careful, my lord," Celia couldn't resist warning him. "I am told that posing as a duke can be quite dangerous."

Elias laughed. "My defense will be that the man was speaking to Her Grace and not myself." He winked. "You simply need to know how to phrase such circumstances, Miss Bening."

"Indeed." Celia sorted through the contents of her reticule, more to compose herself than check what she had brought along. The constant wondering about what her mother had confided in Elias had her sitting on thorns.

"I cannot believe we found nothing to purchase other than lemonade," the duchess said with a sad shake of her head. "Perhaps we should return to Oxford Street."

"Whatever you wish, Your Grace." Celia held tightly to the hope that they would indeed go back to Oxford Street and its many shops. From there, if luck smiled upon her, Mama would soon proclaim their outing at an end and be ready to return home. Then Celia could take refuge in either the library or the garden—either would be a haven where Elias most certainly would not be. She hazarded an indulgent glance his way. "I am sure Lord Raines is ready to be on his way."

"Oh no, dear Celia." Her mother paused while lifting her lemonade for a sip. "Lord Raines has agreed to delight us with his company for dinner, even though it will be a simple affair. Isn't that splendid?"

"Splendid," Celia repeated, wondering how Elias had elicited that invitation with such ease. "In that case, should we forgo the shops and return home to inform Mrs. Harcourt?"

Elias waved away her suggestion. "We must not cut the day short. Not when Her Grace is in such fine health. I agreed to dinner because I wish to prolong my presence in your company—not because I seek a meal. A simple plate of cold meats would be a most satisfying banquet in the presence of so many lovely ladies."

Mama, Sophie, and Frannie all responded with silly smiles, appearing to fall victim to the blatant flattery. Celia rolled her eyes.

"Why, Miss Bening." He quirked a brow and leaned toward her with feigned incredulity. "Do you doubt my sincerity?"

"Of course not, Lord Raines." She wouldn't add that it was his intentions she found questionable. She pushed her lemonade away, suddenly finding it too bitter to endure. "I merely felt a bit of dust in my eye."

"Perhaps I should check it for you," he offered. "Come and let me see."

Celia scooted away from the table and hopped to her feet. "Thank you, no. I am quite recovered now. It appears to have resolved itself as quickly as it came." Doing her best to remain a picture of composure, she motioned back in the direction in which they came. "While Her Grace finishes her lemonade, I believe I shall return to the trinket box stall. I have decided I cannot bear to leave the hearts and roses creation behind after all." She curtsied to her mother. "That is, with your permission, Your Grace."

"Do whatever you need to do to get your wants sorted," her mother said. The true meaning of the subtle warning was not lost on Celia. The duchess added a barely perceptible nod. "Indecision is the ruin of many, Celia. Never do anything in a halfhearted manner."

"Yes, Your Grace." Celia only wished it were that easy.

CHAPTER EIGHT

ELIAS SAVORED THE last bite of the delectable syllabub topped with fresh berries. The day had gone even better than he had hoped it would. He would have to remember to add an appreciative amount to Jack's voucher when the Bow Street Runner came to his office for payment. If not for the man's quick action, Elias would never have known where or when to cross paths with the lovely Celia.

From his seat of honor to the right of the dowager duchess, he had studied the ladies at dinner with a more critical eye. The nuances of their glances at each other and their mannerisms provided more information than they realized. The three young women behaved more like sisters than close friends, and the duchess could easily be mistaken for a favorite aunt.

Lady Sophie's mother and Lady Ardsmere's mother-in-law were not present, denying him the possibility of observing them as well. Poor ladies. Probably still trapped at Lady Bournebridge's affair. He couldn't help but grin. His brother, the Duke of Almsbury, was trapped there also, and no amount of blunt could tempt Elias to trade places with Monty. After all, Monty possessed the title. Such engagements were his due.

Elias suddenly realized he had allowed the conversation to lag while thinking back over the day. He forced himself to set his inner musings aside. "A fine repast, Your Grace. Most satisfying." He waved away the footman stepping forward with a salver of sweetmeats and nuts. "No, thank you. I am quite finished, my good man."

The duchess pushed herself to her feet and moved away from the table with the aid of her cane. "What a shame we have no gentleman with whom you could enjoy a glass of port or a bit of snuff."

Elias hurried to stand and bow. "I assure you, Your Grace, I do not miss their company in the least." And he meant it. The mysterious ladies of this household enthralled him—especially his precious Celia. And from what he had observed, they all guarded secrets and possessed no desire whatsoever to immerse themselves in the vicious and highly competitive Marriage Mart of the *ton*.

Of course, fragile health curtailed the dowager's engagements, and Lady Ardsmere was already a wife. But something about that lady whispered that her marital status might be a lie. At one point during their robust dinner conversation, he had mentioned her husband, and she had almost acted as if she didn't know to whom he referred. At that same moment, Celia had nearly choked on her wine and begged to recover in the garden, claiming an urgent need for fresh air. Lady Sophie had then excused herself with the announcement of a sudden headache, and the duchess sent Lady Ardsmere to help her to her room. This household had become a puzzle he itched to solve.

The duchess slowly crossed the room and nodded at the large blond footman who had accompanied them shopping. "Friedrich, please fetch Berta. I am ready to retire." With an apologetic look at Elias, she pulled in a deep breath, then slowly released it. "Forgive me, Lord Raines. I do not mean to be rude, but I find today's adventures catching up with me."

"You could never be rude, Your Grace." Elias genuinely liked the woman and wished fate had granted her a kinder destiny. He fully intended to honor her wishes for him to protect and cherish Celia—and would have done so even without her request. "With your permission, might I step into the garden and ensure Miss

Bening has recovered from her sudden need for fresh air?"

The dowager stared at him, her expression stony and unreadable. "Celia is as fragile and vulnerable as a frightened child at the moment. I understand I bade you protect her. Win her love and love her in return." She moved toward him, thumping her cane harder with every step. "But I pray I have not misplaced my trust in you." She stamped her cane hard one last time and glared at him. "Do not hurt her, or I promise you, there will be hell to pay."

This woman spoke like a loving mother, not an ailing peeress who held a particular fondness for her companion. Elias tried not to take insult over her concerns. "I would never hurt her, Your Grace, but I need her to confide in me so I can help her with whatever puts that frightened look in her eyes." He resettled his stance, trying to find the words to reassure the lady that he only meant the best for Celia. "I know she dreads your death with the whole of her being, but I daresay that is not the entirety of her worries."

The dowager nodded and leaned heavily on her cane. "You may go to her in the garden, Lord Raines." She turned away and slowly headed toward the exit. "Stay as long as required, but do me the courtesy of being discreet when you choose to leave. I will not have Celia ruined." When she reached the double doors that opened to the hallway, she halted and looked back at him. "I shall have Friedrich stand guard at this entrance where he may hear her should she call out for help." Her eyes narrowed again, and this time her expression was quite readable. "Friedrich will do whatever is necessary to protect my Celia. Am I understood clearly?"

"Quite clearly, Your Grace."

"Good." She tipped a curt nod and left him.

Elias turned and eyed the set of glass doors to the sprawling garden. They were opened wide to invite the cool evening air into the dining room. For a London townhouse, such a generous layout was a rarity, and usually only found in country manors. He ambled through the doors and pulled in a deep breath of the refreshing air delicately scented with the earthy new greenness of spring. It beckoned him to come and lose himself in the private oasis.

Torches flickered throughout the intimate layout of the peaceful area. Their golden glow followed the path of stepping stones winding through the maze of shrubbery and raised beds of freshly turned earth that would soon burst with colorful flowers. The gentle sound of trickling water came to him, but he didn't see its source. He also didn't see Celia. Had the lovely lioness somehow escaped him?

"Celia?" He followed the path, easing deeper into the personal Eden that was larger than it had appeared at first glance. "Celia?"

"I wish they hadn't lit the torches," she said from somewhere off to the left. "It makes the stars less bright."

He stepped off the path of stones, rounded a bed of rosebushes yet to bloom, and found her sitting on a bench beside a small, cascading fountain. The water feature fed into a pool bordered by stones that matched those creating the layered levels of the gurgling fountain.

"It is peaceful here beside the water," he said quietly, feeling almost ashamed to speak and break the fragile spell filling the place. "May I join you?"

Without taking her gaze from the rippling pool, she patted the empty spot on the bench but remained silent.

He eased down beside her and leaned forward, propping his elbows on his knees while gazing at the torchlight dancing across the water's undulating surface.

"Quite remarkable," he said with genuine reverence.

"Friedrich built it when the gardener complained of this area always remaining too wet to grow anything." She folded her hands in her lap and seemed to curl into herself, as if withdrawing into the safety of her shell. "Everyone thinks he is *just* a footman, but he has an eye for seeing things before they exist. Somehow, he knows how they should work, and so he creates them. He repaired many things at the manor in Germany." Her soft, musing tone turned bitter. "Such a brilliant man, yet hobbled by being born into the wrong class of society."

Elias watched her, sensing that she wasn't only speaking about Friedrich's lowborn plight. "The world is not a fair place." He straightened and turned toward her. "But I think you already know that better than most."

She shook away his observation with a twitch of her shoulder, then hiked her chin to a defensive angle. Once again, she became the fierce lioness keeping everyone at bay. "It is useless to complain. All one can do is try to change one's circumstances for the better." She attempted a smile but failed. Her bottom lip quivered, and her eyes gleamed with the tears she refused to shed. "I have heard it said happiness is a choice, but I find that concept difficult to put into practice when circumstances have become so disagreeable."

Even though he feared she would pull away, he reached over and gently took her hand. "Happiness is easier when two attempt to create it together."

She bowed her head and closed her eyes, but didn't pull away. For that, he was grateful.

He shifted closer until no space existed between them. "The burden you carry wearies you, my brave lioness. Allow me to shoulder it for you."

"You cannot."

He gently eased his arm around her and encouraged her to rest her head on his shoulder. "I can do many things if given half the chance."

A heavy sigh escaped her, but she remained there, leaning against him and clinging to his hand. "I like the way the torchlight dances across the water." She spoke as if caught in a trance, and either unable or unwilling to break free. "I find the way it lights the ripples calming. Do you?"

"I find this moment both calming and hopeful." He refused to lie. Sitting here with her made everything else fade away. Nothing mattered but keeping her at his side.

"Hopeful?" The leeriness had returned to her tone, but she made no move to pull away.

"Hopeful that you and I could be…" For the first time in a very long while, he struggled to find the perfect word—the word that would please her and put her at ease.

"What?" she prompted. She lifted her head and eyed him as if trying to decide if he was genuine or playing her for a fool.

"I care for you, Celia, care for you with a ferocity that almost frightens me." He huffed a bitter, frustrated laugh. "It frightens me because you wish to have nothing to do with me and refuse to tell me why."

She looked away and once more fixed her sad stare on the glistening pool. "Have you ever been to Germany?"

He stroked the softness of her bare hand that, surprisingly, she still allowed him to hold. "I have not had the pleasure of visiting that country."

"It is quite lovely." She stared straight ahead, and a soft smile slowly curved the bow of her tempting mouth. "I could not have spent my childhood in a better place." She shuddered at the memory like shooing away a bothersome bug. When she returned her gaze to him, her smile was gone. "I must go back to Germany with Her Grace." She swallowed hard and worked her mouth as if fighting back a sob. "When she passes, she wishes to be buried beside her husband." Hard, fast blinking betrayed her battle against tears, and even though she valiantly fought them, a few still escaped. "She intends to die here in London." She angrily swiped her fingers across her cheeks, batting the tears away.

He caught both her hands in his. "I will be here, Celia. You will not go through it alone. I swear it." He didn't bring up that the Duke of Hasterton and his sister would also assist in the laying to rest of their mother. The way Celia spoke as if she were the only one to care for the duchess confused him to no end. "I will help you. You have my word."

She shook her head and looked away. "Go home, Elias," she whispered. "Save yourself from this cruel game."

Cruel game? It occurred to him that neither Celia nor the duchess had ever spoken kindly about the duke. Perhaps the man was a monster in need of a lesson he would not soon forget. "How did he hurt you?"

Celia turned back to him, confusion drawing her dark brows together. "Who?"

"The dowager's son. The duke."

The way her mouth flattened into a hard line told Elias everything he needed to know. "I will make him pay, even if I have to search every country in existence to find him. He will pay for whatever he did to you."

She dropped her gaze to their clasped hands and squeezed his even tighter. "Go home, Elias," she repeated.

"You are my home, Celia." He lifted her hands and gently kissed both of them. "Wherever you are, that is where I wish to be."

"I so wish I could love you," she said so softly he barely heard it.

He framed her face with his hands. "You can. I will protect you from everything you fear." He drew closer and brushed the lightest of kisses across the sweetness of her mouth. "Love me, Celia, and let me love you in return."

She responded with a kiss so urgent, so full of desperation and need, that he gathered her closer, and silently swore to never let her go. She fisted his coat in her hands and held on to him with such a fierceness that his senses roared with a dangerous thundering.

Unable to resist, he smoothed a hand down her back and cupped her bottom, risking what would be a very well-earned slap. But rather than give him a reprimand, she pressed closer, almost crawling into his lap. He helped her shift until she straddled him. The move nearly undid him, awakening him to the severity of the situation. He broke the kiss, held her back, and forced her to look him in the eyes. "Celia—I do not wish to cause you ruin. We must stop."

"I was ruined at birth." She slid her hands up his chest and touched his face with such tenderness that he bit back a groan. "I am so very weary of being alone," she whispered, her sultry voice echoing with despair and aching hopelessness. "Show me, Elias. Show me what it is like to *not* be so lonely. At least for a moment so I can cherish it and remember the feeling."

"Celia." He wanted her with a fury that raged but feared how she would feel afterward. "You do not realize what you ask." It took every ounce of control he possessed to keep from lowering her to the thick carpet of soft grass and indulging in their passions. "I want you, dear one. More than words can describe."

He squeezed her shoulders, aching to join with her, but she had to understand, once he claimed her for his own, she would be his forever. There would be no going back. She was not a woman meant for a casual dalliance, and he was not a man who would use her and toss her aside. They would marry. He would have her as his wife.

"I long for you," he repeated more softly, "but I do not want you unhappy."

"Give me happiness, Elias." She rested a hand on his chest, then slowly tightened her fingers and clutched the front of his shirt. "I ache, but I do not know what I ache for. I yearn but have no idea what I need." She sadly shook her head. "I am so alone in this world, and sick of this dark, desperate feeling. Bring me into the light, Elias. Make the darkness go away—at least for a little while."

He lifted her chin and leveled her gaze with his. "If I do this thing you ask of me, there is no going back. I will possess you completely and never leave." He leaned so close that the tip of his nose nearly touched hers. "You will be mine, Celia. Forever. Do you understand? I will always be in your life. At your side. And you will take my name. Be my wife and I will be your husband."

She locked eyes with him, staring deeply into his soul. So sad.

So lovely. "Are you capable of unconditional love?" she finally whispered.

"With you, my precious one, I am capable of anything."

She tilted her head and barely trailed the tip of her finger across his bottom lip. "Then I give myself to you, Elias Raines. Forever. May God have mercy on your soul."

THE SHADOWY GARDEN made Elias's eyes dark and unreadable, but Celia stared into them anyway. Her complicated world was closing in on her, and he was the only one who could save her.

What they were about to do was immoral, scandalous, and every other judgmental adjective that described the act she had only read about in forbidden books. But she so badly needed to be held, to fully connect with another soul, another heart. She longed to know something besides loneliness, hopelessness, and despair. She would worry about Elias finding out the truth about her at another time. Perhaps what they were about to do would restore her, invigorate her, and reveal the miraculous answer to the stark prospect of spending the rest of her life alone.

Feeling as though in a trance, she watched him remove his coat and spread it across the ground, belatedly realizing he did so to protect her muslin dress from grass stains. She wet her lips and swallowed hard. Soon, she would lie atop that coat—beneath him.

His neckcloth fluttered to the ground. His waistcoat landed on the bench beside her. With the throat of his shirt open enough to reveal a tempting expanse of muscle that made her palms itch to touch him, he held out his hand. She took it and allowed him to guide her to the coat and gently lower her upon it.

He smiled down at her as she lay beneath him. "You are certain?" he asked softly.

"I am."

He bent his head and nibbled slow kisses along her jaw line. An excited shiver stole through her as he continued the tantalizing trail down to her collarbone and across her shoulder that he had somehow bared so easily.

The bodice of her dress suddenly loosened, and she realized he had artfully undone her buttons and slid his hand inside the back to undo the laces of her stays. A gasping breathlessness plagued her as he kissed a wonderfully tingling trail down her front while fondling her breasts in a most pleasing way. "Elias?"

He lifted his head and smiled down at her. "Yes, my lioness?"

She wet her lips, struggling to speak through the pounding of her heart. "This is very nice so far."

"It is indeed." He waited, watching her as if offering yet another chance to stop things before they went any farther.

"I want this," she whispered. "I want you."

"I am glad, Celia. More glad than you will ever know." His whisper was deep and rasping, sweeping across her as tantalizing as a caress. With a tenderness that made her hitch in another quick breath, he brushed her curls back from her face. "I have wanted you from the first day we met when you scolded me for being impertinent."

"Kiss me," she whispered, fearing if he didn't, she might say more than she should. His warm weight gently pressed her deeper into the cushion of grass, making her arch against him, needing him to do more. She wasn't quite sure what that *more* was. Most of the forbidden books had been slightly confusing about that part, and her mother had refused to speak of it.

She closed her eyes and breathed in his scent, an enticing blend of citrus, bergamot, and amber. The solid hardness of his muscular shoulders rippled under her hands, making her greedy to touch him even more. She couldn't get enough of him as he kissed her long and deep, filling her with an unbearable aching that kept growing stronger.

As his hand roamed lower and slipped under her dress, she hugged his head to her chest, reveling in the way his mouth made her tingle and tense with the tightness of an overwound clock. She struggled to breathe as his fingers trailed up her thighs, then found the place no man had ever touched before.

"Oh my." She wrapped a leg around him and arched into his hand. A squeaking sound escaped her as he slid his fingers inside and treated her to the most delicious sensations she had ever experienced.

He lifted his head from her breast and kissed her tenderly as his fingers worked their incredible magic. She ran her hands into his hair and held on tight as the lovely sensations intensified, finding herself unable to stop moaning into his mouth while bucking and writhing into his touch. Then a shocking wave of ecstasy spilled through her with the force of a relentless storm. His arm tightened around her as she jerked and cried out. As the bliss ebbed, a burning rip from deep within made her stiffen.

Elias broke the kiss and stared down at her. "All right, my lioness?"

With the sting already gone, she nodded. "I am better than all right." His gentle preparation of her made her heart soar. Such a caring man. Yes. This had been the right thing to do. She caressed his cheek and whispered, "Now I want *you*."

"As I want you, my Celia. Forever and always." He sealed the words with a kiss as he unbuttoned his falls, then gently slid her skirts up out of the way and settled between her legs. He paused and stared down at her. "I love you, Celia. You understand that— yes?"

Once more, she slid her hands up into his fashionably cropped hair and tangled her fingers in the thick silkiness. "I fear I love you too, Elias." A sadness almost overpowered her, pushing her close to tears. "I am so very sorry."

"Never be sorry, my precious one." He nuzzled a tender kiss across her mouth. "Never," he whispered, then gently rocked his hips forward and eased into her with such a wonderful fullness that she gasped.

She drew her legs up around him and hugged him tight,

arching to meet him.

His teasing thrusts started slow, then gained in speed until reaching the perfect pounding that summoned the crashing wave of ecstasy back—even stronger than before. Giving herself fully to the blissful explosion, she bit her lip to keep from shouting. Elias buried his face in the curve of her neck and muffled his roar. They shuddered together, clinging to each other as the delight washed across them and left them gasping.

He nibbled kisses along her shoulder, neck, and mouth before rising and staring down at her with a solemn expression. "I will never leave you," he said with a gruff softness. The hint of a smile tugged at the corner of his mouth. "Not ever."

Still buoyed by the warm glow, Celia managed a lazy smile. "Never say never, my lord. The future has yet to be written, and the authors of fate are sometimes cruel to lovers."

He rolled and pulled her with him, tucking her into the crook of his arm and settling her head in the dip of his shoulder. "I shall begin writing our future tomorrow by applying for a special license so we can marry within days."

The enormity of what he suggested lodged midway in her chest like a poorly swallowed bite of tough beef. If she married him without revealing the truth, how deeply would he hate her when he found out their marriage was void because she had lied?

"You know I have to return to Germany with Her Grace," she reminded him. "I promised her."

"We can keep your promise to her together." He pressed a tender kiss to her forehead. "That way I can be the one to deal with any issues that might arise with the duke and Lady Cecilia should they choose to treat you ill."

She cuddled closer and remained selfishly silent, knowing the right thing to do would be to tell him now. Tell him everything. Of course, not to put too fine a point on it, she should have told him *before* they did what they just did. But after a lifetime of subterfuge and lies, she loathed the idea of losing this precious moment of closeness with Elias to the ugly truth. In fact, she could not bear it. But a successful way to keep the wool over his eyes currently escaped her.

"Are you all right, Celia?" His arm tightened around her. "You are not regretting what just happened?"

She rose and smiled down at him. "I promise you, I will never regret what just happened."

But instead of smiling back at her, he drew his dark brows together in a worried scowl. "Some will say I married you because of your inheritance." Before she could tell him that the long-tongued fools didn't matter, he continued, "But I added a clause to the will, and Her Grace initialed it. The trust you inherit will always be yours. Set aside for you and our children, should something ever happen to me. I cannot touch a farthing of it, nor even sell so much as a mote of dust from any of your future properties."

She stared at him, taken aback at what he had just confessed. "You did that because you feared the gossips?"

"I did it because I feared losing you." He caressed her cheek. "I never want you to believe that my interest in you is because of your wealth."

Now, she felt even worse about keeping her true identity from him. She pushed herself up and turned her back to him, unable to look him in the eyes. "Could you help me repair myself? With everyone else gone to their beds, I should go too. You know how the servants will talk. Nothing escapes them."

"Quite right." He sat up and worked on her laces, then gifted her with a tender kiss to her nape before doing up her buttons. "I will come around tomorrow and speak with Her Grace." He hugged her back against his chest. "Have you any family I should meet with for their approval?"

She swallowed hard and struggled to control her tone, thankful that he couldn't see her face, for she knew it would give her away. "I have no one other than Her Grace. You might say she is my only family."

He rose and helped her to her feet, then pulled her into his arms and held her. After a long, heavy silence, he whispered into her hair, "What is it, Celia? Tell me what is troubling you." He eased back a step and held her by the shoulders, gazing into her eyes as if trying to delve into her soul. "I am to be your husband soon. Let me vanquish the demons who are tormenting you."

With her hands resting on his chest, she stretched up on tiptoes and kissed him. "You vanquished them by loving me, but you must give me the opportunity to grow accustomed to their absence and realize I can breathe freely once more." The lie soured in the back of her throat and burned her conscience. She kissed him again. "I love you, Elias. You should leave first, so I might hurry up the stairs with as little notice as possible. Agreed?"

"Agreed." He sorted his clothes, then kissed her long and slow before leaving the garden.

As she watched him go, her tears slipped free, cutting hot streams down her face. She had everything she wanted and yet she didn't. All could be lost in the blink of an eye, and the stakes had just risen exponentially.

She hurried to the dining room doors and cocked her head, listening to the hallway to ensure that Elias was gone and Friedrich had gone downstairs.

With all quiet, she scurried up the steps and slipped into her mother's rooms. Knowing Berta slept in the small bedroom adjoining Mama's, Celia crept across the sitting room, using only the light of the night candle on the mantel to guide her. She eased open her mother's bedroom door, slipped in, then quietly clicked it shut behind her.

"Celia?"

"Yes, Mama. I came to check on you. Are you all right?" Celia hurried to the bed and climbed up beside her mother just like she had done as a child when troubled by bad dreams.

Mama took her hand and gently squeezed it. "The question is—are you all right?"

"I am not sure." Celia refused to lie to her observant mother, knowing it was futile. Mama always ferreted out the truth. "He means to apply for a special license and intends to visit tomorrow to speak to you about our marrying." She pulled in a deep breath, then released it with a despairing hiss. "I did not tell him the truth about who I am."

"And do you plan to do so before you marry him?" Mama gently squeezed her hand tighter.

"I thought—probably not."

"The archbishop will not grant a special license if he is unable to verify your eligibility to wed—no matter how well connected Lord Raines is or how much he pays the man." Her mother's heavy sigh echoed through the room.

"Since everything about us is based in Germany, I am certain Elias can manage it." Celia leaned forward, trying to convince herself as well as her mother. "He is a solicitor. Talking his way around things comes naturally."

"Even if he is able to procure the license, you do realize your marriage will be invalid if you do not use your full legal name?" Mama plucked at the bedcovers and shook her head, growing noticeably more agitated. "I do not wish my grandchildren saddled with the titles of bastards."

"I will think of something." Celia hugged herself and felt more frustrated than she had before entering the room. She hadn't thought of those things even though she knew them as well as Mama. What was wrong with her? How could she hope to hide the truth from Elias when she couldn't even effectively navigate this first twist in the plot?

"You must tell him, Celia."

"If I tell him, I will lose him." Celia covered her face as more tears burned down her face. "I cannot bear the thought of losing him, Mama. I love him."

Her mother released another heavy sigh. "I am so sorry, my child."

Sniffing, Celia searched in vain for the handkerchief she always kept tucked into her stays. "Why are you sorry?"

"I am sorry because I thought I was protecting you, but instead, I imprisoned you." Mama reached into her nightstand, withdrew a fresh handkerchief, and handed it to Celia. "I am sorry, my precious child. I swear to you I never meant you any harm." She laced her fingers together and rested her hands on top of her blankets. "Tell him, daughter. Tell him everything. Lord Raines appears to be the sort who might know of a way to undo this harm I have brought down upon you."

The pain and sorrow in her mother's voice cut through Celia's heart. She had to be strong, for Mama's sake—figure this mess out and resolve it so it didn't make her mother's journey to the grave any faster. "I love you, Mama, and I'm proud to be your daughter. You came up with a way to protect me, and now it's my turn to protect you."

She leaned over and kissed her mother's cheek. "Sleep well. We have conquered everything in our path thus far. I see no need to fail now."

Her mother gave her a weak smile and closed her eyes. "Rest well, my courageous one. Tomorrow is another battle."

CHAPTER NINE

"Y ou cannot avoid him forever." Frannie sat cross-legged on Celia's bed.

"And your mother refuses to lie any more to Lord Raines about your feeling unwell." Sophie perched in front of the headboard, slightly rocking as she hugged her knees. "Maman said the poor man is beside himself with worry. This is not fair to him, Celia."

"If I see him, he is sure to want more information to secure the special license." Celia also sat cross-legged on the bed, indulging in the very unladylike position since it was just the three of them in their nightdresses. They had gathered before dawn to ensure the utmost privacy. "Mama said he plied her with questions and is very frustrated that he could not get His Grace the Archbishop of Canterbury to cooperate until more information—and more coin, I am sure—is provided."

"A special license would eliminate the waiting for all the banns to be read and the fuss of a church wedding. Very thoughtful of him, I say, considering your mother's health. With that license, you could marry here at the house in a manner of days." Frannie glanced over at the closed bedroom door, then leaned forward and lowered her voice. "And in my opinion, sooner would be better, since you and he…" She rolled her eyes. "What if you are…" Her concerned gaze dropped to Celia's middle. "Sooner is better because that could not be ignored in the hopes of it going away."

Even though Celia agreed with Frannie's uncomfortably valid points, she didn't need to be bashed over the head with the reminder. "Lecturing me will not enhance my ability to decide what to do."

"I fear Frannie's argument holds merit," Sophie said. "And you have always been the most pragmatic of us, Celia. Now is not the time to lose your power of reason and cower in your rooms."

Celia dropped her head into her hands, wishing she could snap her fingers and make all these complications go away. She loved Elias. Just thinking about him made her breathless, and it wasn't merely a matter of lustful longing. He had snuck into her heart and taken control of it even before their lovely night in the garden.

A heavy sigh escaped. "I cannot imagine what he will do when I tell him the truth. He is a solicitor. If it were discovered that he knowingly supported such a fraud, it would end his career, and a man's career is his identity—his everything." She covered her eyes and rocked in place, ready to scream if not for the fact that it would rouse the entire household. She let her hands drop and slowly shook her head. "For his sake, I should release him and send him on his way." Her heart threatened to break as she decided what she needed to do. "Since I truly love him, I should let him go. And then all our secrets would be safe."

"But what if a child is on the way?" Frannie reminded her in a hissing whisper.

Celia almost bared her teeth in anger. "Then I will finally have someone in my life whom I cannot harm by loving them."

"No." Sophie reached over and gently squeezed Celia's shoulder. "You have to tell him the truth and give him a chance. He has the right to choose." She gently shook her. "Love is not so easily found and should never be cast away so lightly. Remember your mother and Master Hodgely? The loneliness they bore all their lives? Tell him, Celia. It is the only way. If you sign that marriage register as Celia Bening, the union will be void because that is not your legal name. I would think discovering such a thing after the wedding would upset him more than hearing the truth before."

"And you know he won't leave if you simply send him away with no explanation," Frannie said. "He is intractable. Remember?"

Celia held up her hands to quiet them. "If he comes to call today, I will not avoid him—but I am not saying that I won't attempt to stall him until I can think of a way to offer up my explanations in the proper light."

"Proper light?" Frannie repeated, her tone dubious. "Exactly what sort of light softens a lie?"

Celia cut her a hard glare. "Tell me, Frannie, when you decide to choose a husband, as you said you eventually would, how will you tell him that the Marquess of Ardsmere was never real?"

"Mine will be easy. I shall simply kill him off and become his widow."

"You are a virgin," Celia snapped. "Or do you plan on dispensing with that so as not to have to explain it?"

"Sisters!" Sophie interrupted them with a sharp clap. "Turning on each other solves nothing." She glared at them both. "Whatever we decide, we will band together and support one another. Agreed?"

Filled with immediate regret, Celia took hold of Frannie's hands. "Forgive me, I beg you. I am as feral as a cornered animal."

Frannie smiled and twitched a sheepish shrug. "Forgive *me*, dear one. I should not have spoken so harshly about this troubling mess."

Celia scooted off the bed, went to the wardrobe, and opened its double doors. "I suppose we should all dress and prepare ourselves for the day."

"How do you manage without your maid?" Sophie hopped off the bed and shook the wrinkles out of her nightdress.

"Berta comes by after she finishes with Mama." Celia selected her favorite morning dress, the white muslin with the tiny blue flowers and blue trim. "After all, it would seem quite unusual for the duchess's companion to have her own lady's maid."

"Too true," Frannie agreed. "We can help with your stays and buttons." She cast a glance at the window. The new day was making itself known with a soft, pinkish light that gently eased into the room. "After all, it is quite early."

"Early is best for privacy," Celia said. "And if you wouldn't mind helping, that would be lovely. I fear Berta gets little rest because she hovers over Mama so." She bowed her head and hugged her clothes. "I don't know what will happen to poor Berta after…" She couldn't finish because the inevitable was so unbearable. A deep breath and a hard swallow helped her get back on track. She turned to them and managed a smile. "Your help would be much appreciated."

It took no time at all to dress with Sophie and Frannie's help, and Celia was grateful for their company. Her dear friends kept her from wallowing in self-pity.

With her hair pinned up in the simple braided bun she preferred, she descended to the garden while the others finished dressing and tended to their morning correspondence and selection of engagements for the day. It was much too early for breakfast, but a cup of the rich coffee she loved along with the rising sun filling the garden might help her sort her thoughts and forge an acceptable plan.

She prudently avoided the bench beside the water feature. Too many memories there. She would not only become overly warm, but the ability to entertain a logical thought would leave her. Instead, she seated herself at the small table on the opposite side of the garden, tucked away in a circle of hedges. As she sipped her drink, she tried to calm herself, concentrating on the vibrant song of a little wren flitting among the leafy branches in search of a place to nest or perhaps find its morning meal.

The sound of footsteps made her turn and discover Gransdon appearing extremely apologetic and out of sorts.

"Forgive me, Miss Bening, but Lord Raines is here." The butler's huffing snort clearly relayed his opinion regarding early-morning visitors. "I reminded his lordship of the hour and how irregular you might find his calling at this time, but he insists and refuses to leave the premises. What would you have me do?"

The calm instilled by the busy little wren immediately left her. Celia pulled in a deep breath and forced a smile she didn't feel. "It is all right, Gransdon. He is welcome to join me here in the garden. You might ask if he would like a morning coffee or chocolate, since breakfast won't be for a while yet."

Gransdon nodded, then disappeared back inside.

Moments later, Elias strode into the garden and knelt at her side. "Celia." He gently touched her cheek as if fearing she would disappear. "Is your health fully restored? I have been so worried."

"I am quite improved." Although the fluttering of her heart made it difficult to speak. She had longed to see him so much, even though their separation was no one's fault but her own. "I have missed you," she whispered.

Before she could think of anything else to say, he leaned up and treated her to a kiss filled with the same yearning she felt coursing through her veins.

"And I have missed you, my precious lioness." He kissed her again with even more passionate wistfulness.

If he kept this up, she wouldn't be able to think of anything but being in his arms. For the sake of her sanity, and the ability to convince him that she and her mother weren't the worst sort of people, she gently pushed away while tugging upward on his arms.

"You will soil your clothes on the damp ground. Please—sit with me." She lowered her voice and treated herself to a loving caress of his clean-shaven face. "There are far too many bustling about for us to end up in the grass again."

He dragged a chair closer while still firmly holding her hand. "I suppose you are right." He glanced back at the open doors of the dining room. "They did let you know I called twice before?"

"Of course." She eased her hand free of him as a footman appeared with tea. "You do not enjoy coffee or chocolate?"

"Never developed a taste for either. I prefer tea to start my day."

"So, you are aware of the hour," she teased.

Mischief, mirth, and pride flashed in his eyes. "I see I have put Gransdon out of sorts again. Did he call me a doddering rake?"

"Gransdon would never stoop to name calling, and I am quite sure he will recover." She treated herself to another sip of coffee, wishing it was closer to ten o'clock, so they might enjoy the distraction of breakfast with the rest of the household. As it was, it was barely a quarter to seven, and no one would be down for the morning meal before nine thirty. The maids and footmen bustled everywhere to prepare for the day, but Mama and everyone else spent the time before breakfast in their sitting rooms, attending to correspondence and other matters. "And what would you have done if no one had been down from their rooms yet and willing to receive you?"

"Sat on the front steps until Gransdon became so mortified that he allowed me to enter and wait in the library until someone came down."

Celia couldn't help but smile at the thought of Elias perched on the front steps like a beggar. But as he pulled a folded paper out from the inner pocket of his coat, her smile became more difficult to maintain. "What have you there?" She suspected it to be the special license, which would be a disaster, because it wouldn't bear her legal name.

Elias frowned. "Sadly, not what I wish it was. The Archbishop of Canterbury was a friend of my father and, therefore, not a friend of mine or my brother." He unfolded the paper and smoothed it out on the table. "But once I list all the particulars necessary, he will be hard-pressed to refuse me, since I am quite well thought of at the Doctors' Commons."

"Particulars?" She hid behind her cup, pretending to sip again even though nothing remained but bitter dregs.

He glanced at the entrance to the dining room, then turned back to her with a brow arched to a perturbed angle. "I need your full name, Celia. Oddly enough, the duchess was not inclined to share it." He snorted a huff of amusement. "Her Grace gave me the distinct impression that she approved of our match. So, for the life of me, I cannot understand why she refused to share your legal name."

Celia knew very well why. Mama was determined *not* to be the one to explain everything to the inquisitive Lord Raines. Adopting a secretive air, she looked all around, acting as though she were afraid to be overheard. "My name troubles Her Grace," she said quietly, "because it is the same as her daughter's."

"The same as her daughter's?" Elias repeated. His perturbed scowl shifted to a sharper look. "Your name is *Cecelia* rather than *Celia?*"

"My mother always called me *Celia*." That was a truth, albeit a slightly obscured one. "So, it only seemed natural for Her Grace to use that name, since she and her daughter do not currently agree on several matters. Their relationship is quite unsteady at the moment." That was somewhat true. If it had been up to Celia, they never would have left Germany. But, of course, then she and Elias never would have met. Thank the stars Mama had persevered. Or maybe not—depending on the success or failure of the current conversation.

"I see." He eyed her, his expression uncomfortably readable. He didn't believe a word of her version of the truth, and she didn't blame him. It was quite possibly the poorest tale she had ever told.

"My full name is Cecelia Elizabeth Madeline Rose Bening." She left off the surname of Tuttcliffe and tried to recall if all her names were listed anywhere other than her christening records at the church in Germany. As far as she knew, they were not.

"Cecelia Elizabeth Madeline Rose Bening," Elias repeated, his narrow-eyed thoughtfulness more than a little disturbing.

"Yes." She folded her hands in her lap and tried to smile. "But

I really do prefer *Celia*."

"Might we go to the library so you can write it down to ensure I use the correct spelling when I file for the license?" His tone made her tense. It wasn't exactly cold, but it was most definitely suspicious.

"Of course." She rose and led the way, her mind awhirl, searching for any possible way that this could be a misstep. After unlocking the library door with the key hanging from the chatelaine pinned to the wide blue ribbon belted at her waist, Celia hurried to the window and drew back the draperies to improve the light before she lit the candle on the desk.

"I would have thought the maids would have already been in here." Elias meandered deeper into the room, eying the banked hearth and the remainder of draperies waiting to be drawn.

"Mrs. Harcourt misplaced their key," she lied. "And they have yet to get another. Mine is currently the only one."

"Why not leave it unlocked?"

"Her Grace prefers it locked, since this is where she keeps important papers she brought from Germany." Somewhat of a truth, but more like a lie. Celia swallowed hard to keep from groaning. Lying to Elias had become almost painful. She lit a second candle and held out her hand. "Do you wish me to write on your paper or use a fresh piece of parchment?"

He placed it in her hand. "Please do write on this paper. There is space enough for your name and birth date directly below mine."

She took a seat, signed, then filled out the date, February 7, 1794. While wafting the paper to dry the ink rather than using sand, she stared at her handwriting, knowing if the special license listed that name, the marriage would be void. Rather than hand it to Elias, she placed it back on the desk and stared down at it.

"Celia?"

She refused to look up at him. The way he said her name roared that he knew she was a liar, and this paper was just the trap he needed to prove it. "Yes, Elias?"

"Is there something else you wish to tell me?"

Her hands slowly closed into fists on either side of the paper as she lifted her head and leveled her gaze with his. "Nothing that I am sure you have not already surmised." She drew in a deep breath and released it with a heavy sigh. "Perhaps it would be better if you told me."

"Why do you not wish anyone to know that you are Lady Cecilia?" He restlessly paced back and forth in front of the desk, reminding her yet again of the great panther confined in the cage at Hamburg.

She decided to answer with a question of her own. "How long have you known?"

"I suspected it the first day we met." He leaned across the desk, splaying his large hands on its top as if he was about to vault over it. "You and the duchess share a remarkable resemblance." He slowly shook his head. "Your subterfuge makes no sense."

"I did not wish to be plagued with any concerns other than my mother and her health," she said, knowing that to be only a small part of the truth. "I refuse to be bothered with being presented at court, visiting the modiste for gowns, or enduring ridiculous visits from those only interested in my exorbitant dowry and my ability to birth them an heir." She lifted her chin. "Celia, the companion to Her Grace, has a great deal more freedom than Lady Cecilia, daughter of the fifth Duke of Hasterton."

"Not every young woman attending the Season is required to come out," he argued with frustrating accuracy. "You would not have been forced to participate in any of those things you mentioned."

"You are quite incorrect, my lord, and you know it. A duke's daughter of eligible age? Visiting from Germany? Her first time in London, and yet she does not wish to present herself to the *ton*? The gossips would have pounced on such oddness and feasted upon it for weeks. Whispers and looks would have plagued us everywhere we went and ruined Mama's visit."

"Fine. Then when did you plan on telling me?" The eerie quietness of his tone frightened her. It was dangerous and filled with anger. "You didn't think that the man you gave yourself to and promised to marry had a right to know your true identity? What else do I need to know about you, my lady?"

She drew her fists down into her lap and glared up at him, refusing to look away. Now was the time to sever the tie and save him from ruin because of her. "All else you need to know, my lord, is that I release you from your promise." Blast her eyes. They burned with the tears that her heart screamed for her to shed. But she could not. "Now, please take your leave and do not be bothered with this household any longer. Mama and I have decided that all further legalities shall be handled by our solicitor in Germany." She blinked harder and faster, refusing to release the tears. "After all, Mama will be laid to rest in Germany, and that is more my home than London could ever hope to be."

"Is that what you truly wish, *my lady*?" He towered over her with nothing but the too-narrow mahogany desk between them.

She forced a cruel smile. "Your tone betrays you, my lord. Is that not what you wish?"

He reached out and cupped her chin in his hand. "No, Celia. You answer first. And I want the truth this time."

"We are a mistake that would be better resolved by separating rather than made worse by matrimony." Her eyes burned, and her throat ached with the need to sob. Her heart dropped like a stone into the pit of her stomach. "I release you, Elias, and I apologize for wasting your time."

When his hand dropped away from her, she should have escaped out the door, but she didn't. The struggle to hold the act together took everything she possessed. She sat there staring up at him, hoping that since she was powerless to move, he would leave in her place.

He didn't. Elias rounded the desk, grabbed her up by the shoulders, and pulled her to him. "You apologize for wasting my time?" He yanked her closer and locked his arms around her.

"You consider what we shared a waste?"

She had no words and tried to look away, but he wouldn't allow it. He buried his fingers into her thick braid and held her head tilted back, forcing her to look up at him to witness the wildness and hurt in his eyes.

"I release you," she repeated softly, helpless to say anything more.

"I do not release you," he said in a low growl. "You not only gave me your word but sealed the promise with your body. I do not take such things lightly."

"It is for your own good," she said, thankful for a sudden burst of indignation restoring her ability to speak. He might own her heart, but she would not be his prisoner. "Save yourself, my lord. Trust me when I say this is for the best."

"Tell me the truth!" he roared. "Tell me why!"

The library door burst open. Friedrich charged in and pulled Elias away.

Elias rounded on the man and punched him in the face. Blood streamed from Friedrich's nose.

"Stop this at once!" Celia shoved between them, one hand on Elias's chest, the other held out to keep Friedrich at bay. "Friedrich, it is all right. Lord Raines and I were merely having a very heated discussion."

"Shall I see him out, my lady?" The hulking blond footman took a threatening step toward Elias. "To the door with him— yes?"

"I am sure Lord Raines can find his way out all by himself," she said, shocked but thankful for the calm numbness that had settled across her. "Go tend to your nose, Friedrich, and thank you for responding when you thought me in distress."

"Are you certain, my lady?" The footman's thick German accent made her long for home and simpler times.

"Positive, thank you. See to yourself now. That nose looks quite bad." She kept her hand on Elias's chest until Friedrich left the room and closed the door behind him. Then she turned and faced Elias, determined to make him leave and never come back. "We cannot marry. It would mean the end of all you have worked so hard to attain. I will not be responsible for your ruin. Nor will I watch you come to hate me. Now, go."

"I love you," he said with his teeth bared like a cornered animal. "And I know you love me."

She huffed a bitter laugh. "Love is a wicked demon sent to curse the weak into believing it will save everything and last forever. But then it fails. Burns out like a spent candle. Does nothing but create torment and pain." She shook her head and pointed at the door. "Save yourself, Elias, and be thankful I freed you from this slow death."

He caught her close and tried to kiss her, but she turned away. He dropped his arms from around her, stepped back, and glared at her with such pain that she had to hold her breath to keep from sobbing. After what felt like forever, he shook his head and backed toward the door. "This is not over, Celia. I do not go quietly, and I always return. Remember that, my love."

Celia held herself locked in place. Chin up. No expression. Hands tightened into fists. She would not react and betray the utter desolation tearing her to pieces.

Elias stormed out of the library and slammed the door behind him.

Only then did she drop to the floor right where she stood. On her knees, she hugged herself and rocked back and forth with tears streaming down her face. She made no sound, just wept in silence and swore to herself—never again. Allowing oneself to *feel* had proven to be the greatest of errors. Such a fool she was. Such a lonely, misbegotten fool that would have been better off never being born.

CHAPTER TEN

"I WANT TO know everywhere they go before they even think about going there." Elias fixed a stern glare on Jack Portney, willing the Bow Street Runner to understand the severity of the request.

Mr. Portney accepted the task with a curt dip of his chin. "It will be done, my lord. Several reliable contacts now exist within the household. I shall keep you informed on a regular basis—hourly, if necessary."

"Good man." Elias dismissed him with a nod and returned his attention to the paper Celia had signed with everything but her title and surname. He had suspected her identity from the beginning but wanted so badly to trust her, to believe she would never deceive him, that he had shoved his suspicions aside. Never again would he make the mistake of going against his instincts.

And now he would solve the rest of his precious lioness's mystery. If she had released him with the excuse that she had tired of toying with a second son, a solicitor, he *might* have accepted her reason at face value. He jerked his head with a hard shake and threw himself back in the chair. No. He would not have accepted that reason either. Heartache had filled her eyes along with that same strange leeriness he had noticed the first time they met. She loved him as much as he loved her. Celia was his, and he would win her back after obliterating whatever foolishness she had spouted about refusing to ruin him. Ruin him how? He could not be ruined.

"But she very well could be," he muttered. What if she carried his child? Yet another reason to solve this riddle and convince her to marry him. Never would he abandon his own or be a cruel, heartless bastard like his father. He picked up the slip of paper and slowly rubbed his thumb back and forth across her flowery signature. "What is your secret, Lady Cecilia? What is this web of lies you have woven?"

His brother, Aurelias Montseton Raines, fourth Duke of Almsbury, affectionately and sometimes not so affectionately known as Monty, strolled into the office without the courtesy of knocking. "Your summons sounded both urgent and slightly rude, little brother." He softened the accusation with an affectionate smile as he dropped into the chair facing Elias's desk. "What sorry business has you so crusty?"

Elias ignored Monty's usual flippancy. "You are widely traveled. Have you ever crossed paths with the Duke of Hasterton?"

"Hasterton, you say?" Monty scowled as he pondered the question, then shook his head. "I don't believe anyone has, old man. Why?"

"He is my client, yet never responds to correspondence unless he initiates it. His dying mother had me draw up her last will and testament to leave all her worldly goods to her devoted companion, Miss Celia Bening. According to the dowager duchess, her son was much too busy to escort her to London for a final visit, and her daughter's frail health prevented her from coming also." Elias leaned forward and thumped the desk. "Her Grace also extracted an oath from me to protect and *love* Miss Bening, who I have since discovered is, in fact, her daughter, the Lady Cecilia."

Monty squinted as if sorting through all Elias had just said caused him physical pain. He straightened in the chair, then leaned forward. "Her Grace's companion is actually her daughter?"

Elias nodded.

"Why would her daughter pose as a companion?" Monty grimaced. "Is she too unpleasant for Polite Society?"

"Unpleasant?" Elias snorted. "Only in attitude. Her beauty is beyond compare, yet she is the most stubborn, infuriating, unreasonable woman I have ever met."

"And you love her," Monty observed with a shrewdness only a beloved brother could possess.

"Yes, damn you." Elias raked his hands through his hair. "And she said she loved me. I even applied for a special license so we could marry before death claims her mother." Another disgusted snort escaped him. "But, of course, that was when *Miss Bening* revealed her true identity and decided to send me packing with the claim that she refused to be responsible for my ruin."

"Your ruin?"

"Yes, and she would not elaborate on how exactly that might occur." Elias threw himself back in the chair again and scrubbed a hand across his mouth. "How the devil could the woman possibly ruin me?" He gritted his teeth, then made up his mind to confess all to his trusted brother. "It is her that could be ruined if our evening in her garden results in more than a single night of pleasure."

Monty cringed and slowly shook his head. "You never do things halfway, do you, little brother?"

"Apparently not." Elias yanked open his bottom desk drawer, pulled out a bottle and a pair of glasses, and poured them both a drink. "I love her, Monty, and I mean to solve this infuriating puzzle and make her my wife."

"What do you need from me?"

"Do you know of anyone who has met Hasterton? Has the man ever warmed his seat in the House of Lords? I have been unable to find anyone who personally knows the man, but your connections cast a much wider net than mine."

Monty shook his head again. "The man is an enigma. Never seen but known to be the shrewdest businessman and investor London has ever seen in our time. Do you know I even heard he devised a system of shops all across the Continent? And every single one of them is a roaring success. All have the same business model, and all are run by women. Some sort of combination tea and biscuit book shops or some such nonsense. I cannot recall the details about that particular venture, but according to the prime minister, anything Hasterton touches turns to gold." He sampled the whisky, gave an appreciative nod, then took a deeper sip. "As his solicitor, you know the extent of his successes. You know the man's wealth, and his ability to ferret out yet another success." Monty turned thoughtful. "Do you mean to get the man to force his sister to marry you? Is he her guardian?"

"She is of legal age." Elias tapped on the date beside Celia's name. "His twin, in fact. Both are three and twenty."

Monty leaned forward, his mouth sagging open. "You are telling me that cunning fellow who is probably richer than Croesus by now is a mere three and twenty?"

"Yes." Elias wouldn't go into detail about Hasterton's wealth, but the dowager duchess and the young duke had done quite well with the estate, increasing it several times over.

"What about your man, Mr. Portney? Has he been able to discover anything?" Monty slid his glass onto the desk but shook his head when Elias offered to freshen it. "He's the best of the Bow Street Runners. Even better than old Elkins."

"I have had him on the case for a while. So far, nothing." Elias swirled the whisky in the glass. The way the golden liquid caught the light helped him think. "It is almost as if the duke does not exist."

"I know quite a few individuals down at the Exchange who would beg to differ. The man's every move is watched and mimicked in the hopes of reaping at least a portion of his successes."

"Yet the only servants or employees willing to offer us information about him are those most recently hired for his London townhouse. And even they have never seen him." Elias slowly shook his head, then lifted his gaze from his glass and settled it on his brother. "I love Celia, and she will be mine."

Monty returned a sympathetic look. "We will work this out, brother. I swear it." His expression of sympathy furrowed into a studious frown. "Lady Bournebridge mentioned spotting you in the park the other day." His frown slowly shifted to an amused smirk. "Quite beside herself, she was, because neither she nor her cackling hens-in-waiting could identify the two lovelies you treated to a ride in that fine barouche I gave you."

Elias smiled at the memory. "The raven-haired goddess was my Celia. The fetching redhead was Lady Sophie, sister to the fourth Earl of Rydleshire. I believe the Rydleshires spend most of their time in France, just as the dowager duchess and Celia have spent the lion's share of their lives in Germany." He cocked his head and arched a meaningful brow. "And Lady Sophie is unattached."

"Our task at hand is to get you married, dear brother. Not me." Monty tapped on the desktop again. "Lady Whitfield's dinner party is this evening. An intimate gathering of sixteen to twenty persons, as I understand. Did you receive a card for it? I know her husband thinks quite highly of you after your handling of that rather delicate affair for him last year."

Elias glanced at the basket on the corner of his desk. It over-flowed with messages and cards in dire need of attention. "I have yet to sort through the correspondence from the past few days." He dismissed the issue with a shrug. "I fail to see how Lady Whitfield's soiree is relevant to my dilemma with Celia."

"According to Fords, the aforementioned Lady Sophie and the dowager Countess of Rydleshire, Lady Ardsmere, and her mother-in-law, *and* the dowager Duchess of Hasterton and your Lady Cecilia will be in attendance." Monty preened like a peacock and added a wink for good measure.

"How the deuce did your valet come by such information?" Elias wondered if he should hire Fords to discover more about Celia rather than Mr. Portney.

"Fords knows I prefer to read the table before I take part in the game." Monty fiddled with his gloves. "It's open season on eligible bachelors, and the marriage-minded mothers are cunning and relentless. One must carefully prepare before treading such dangerous grounds." He twitched a knowing shrug. "Servants know everything. One must simply listen." He nodded at the overflowing basket of envelopes. "Dig for the card, dear brother. What better place to observe and haunt your elusive Lady Cecilia than when she is trapped at a dinner party?"

Elias shuffled through the papers, tearing open seals and scanning the sheets for the gist of the contents and the sender. He paused long enough to toss a handful of the unopened ones into Monty's lap. "Make yourself useful."

Monty joined in but moved at a slower pace. One of the notes grabbed his interest. He leaned forward and stroked his chin, enraptured by the multi-page missive. "I had no idea he had that many illegitimate children."

"Monty!" Elias snatched it out of his hands and set it aside. "Find the Whitfield invite—not fodder for gossip at the club."

"We do not gossip."

"You lie. I have witnessed it." Elias looked closer at the words scrawled across the note in his hand. "Here. Found it." Now that he had confirmed he was officially invited, he could more effectively plan his attack. He glanced up from the invitation. "You do plan to attend, yes?"

"I wouldn't miss it for the world now," Monty said. "You have piqued my interest regarding my future sister-in-law. Shall I come by and fetch you, since heavy rains appear to be the way of it today?"

"Yes, I fear the barouche offers little protection against the weather." Elias refolded the card and tucked it safely into the inner pocket of his coat. "I shall be ready at a quarter past eight. That should enable us to arrive at an opportune time that is also acceptable to our hostess. I shall send my response to the Whitfields immediately."

"We shall arrive early enough to watch for the arrival of

those from the Hasterton household." Monty rose, donned his hat and gloves, then winked again. "You shall be married before the month is out, dear brother. Never fear." As he sauntered toward the door, he glanced back and proudly patted his chest. "And I shall be an exemplary uncle who spoils his beloved nephews and nieces with the finest of gifts."

"Let us not get ahead of ourselves." Elias gathered his hat, gloves, and satchel, and followed his brother out of the office and the building.

"Care for a ride?" Monty paused with his foot on his carriage's step.

Elias glanced up at the overcast sky. The heavy bank of grayness looked ready to split open and pour. "I would, actually. Thank you very much."

When they came to a stop in front of his modest home, he turned to his brother. "Thank you."

For once, Monty became quite serious. "You can always depend on me. I hope you know that."

"I do, and it is much appreciated." Elias alit from the carriage, closed the door, then thumped on it before vaulting up his front steps and hurrying inside.

Mrs. Camp met him in the entry hall with a look of surprise. "Home early, my lord? Not feeling poorly, I hope?"

"I am quite well, Mrs. Camp, but I forgot to tell you I shall be going out this evening. Please have Henry ready the bath, and I shall require my evening dress seen to, of course." An amused huff escaped him as he added, "It may be in need of a good dusting." Elias rarely made it a point to attend such parties unless it would improve a relationship with a client. Tonight, however, he needed to impress upon Celia that he would not go quietly, and wherever she went, he would be there as well.

Mrs. Camp sprang into action, gathering his hat, gloves, and satchel from him. She waddled down the hallway at an impressive speed, considering her generous girth. "Right away, my lord," she called back without slowing. "I shall have Henry shine your good leather shoes once he finishes carrying the water. I know you'll not wish to wear your Hessians with your evening dress."

If Wellington had troops as efficient and lively as Mrs. Camp, the war would have ended ages ago. Elias didn't bother responding, since the housekeeper had already disappeared downstairs to rally the troops—or *troop* as it were, since her son Henry was the only servant other than a maid to help her with the housekeeping. Jamison, the driver of his coach, lived above the stable at the back of the house.

As Elias climbed the stairs, it struck him that he kept quite a modest home. But as a bachelor and a worker of long hours, he didn't need anything more. He halted on the landing, turned, and stared back downstairs at the sparse hall devoid of paintings, small tables, vases of fresh flowers, and any other unnecessary items that merely created clutter and required dusting. He failed to see the need for such things.

As the daughter of a very affluent family, Celia came from opulence and excess—the best of everything. While he did quite well at the firm, he could never provide her with such a lifestyle. Was that the true reason she had spurned him? Had she said she was protecting him from ruin to save his ego?

He pulled in a deep breath and slowly whistled it out through clenched teeth. Now was not the time to second-guess himself. A deep knowing, a raw feeling that gnawed at him, insisted there was more to Celia's release of him than she had revealed. And while riches dripped from her name, she had never behaved like a spoiled darling of the *ton* intent on showing everyone that only the very best satisfied her. After all, as *Celia the companion*, she had always dressed with a modest intent of not outshining the dowager duchess. There was a worrisome mystery to be solved here, and he would not rest until he untangled it.

The door to the servants' stair at the other end of the hall thumped open with a loud bang. Henry ambled out of it, toting steaming buckets of water. "Sorry for the noise, my lord." The young man gave Elias an apologetic look. "I was paying more attention to not spilling than catching the door."

"Give me the buckets, lad, and you can run down and get more." Elias went to take them, but Henry backed up with a horrified look.

"If Mother found out I let you carry the water..." The boy gave a hard shake of his head. "I'll not risk that sort of wrath, my lord. If you could open the dressing room door, though, that would be grand."

Elias crossed the bedroom, opened the door, and stepped aside, noticing that his black evening coat had already been brushed and placed on the clothes horse. His newest white shirt—one *without* ruffles, just as he preferred—and his waistcoat waited there as well. His black trousers rested across the foot of the bed. He often wondered if Mrs. Camp was a ghost, because the woman had perfected the ability to move about the house with amazing speed and complete every task without being heard or seen. A freshly starched cravat was laid out on top of his dresser, as well as short drawers, stockings with their garters, and braces for his trousers.

As Henry hurried out for more water, Elias started shedding his clothes and pondering what Celia's reaction would be when she saw him. *If* the dowager duchess's health permitted them to attend, as Monty's valet had reported. If the poor lady's day had not gone well, then all his preparations would be for naught.

"Think positive," he said aloud while approaching the one luxury he indulged in—a metal tub large enough to stretch out his long legs in and hopefully, someday, use for an amorous bath with Celia.

Either Henry or his mother had already lined the vessel with linen. A hint of steam rose from the small amount of water barely covering the bottom of the tub. A pair of kettles hanging over the fire in the dressing room's small hearth were at the ready for rinsing or making the bathwater hotter.

Henry reappeared, red-faced and huffing for air as he emptied two more buckets into the tub.

"Henry." Elias halted the lad as he grabbed up both buckets and started to dash back out. "Running is not necessary."

"Not according to Mother." With a knowing dip of his chin, the boy turned and ran for more.

Shaking his head, Elias settled down into the shallow water and started washing with a fresh bar of Pears soap. The clean scent of rosemary, thyme, and a slightly floral note filled the small room but failed to alleviate his tension as it usually did. Too much was at stake for him to relax. Once he reached the Whitfields' and discovered whether Celia and her mother attended, his tense state would be easier managed. At least, he hoped so.

Henry continued toting water until it reached slightly above Elias's waist. Taking pity on the winded lad, Elias told him, "That'll do, Henry. If I need extra for rinsing, the kettles on the hearth will be just fine."

"Thank you, my lord." The young man bowed and quietly closed the door on his way out to keep the warmth in the room.

Elias finished bathing, scrubbed himself dry, then rubbed in his favorite blended oils of citrus, bergamot, and amber. Scents branded themselves upon one's memories, and he wanted Celia to think of him any time she came across these. She had placed the same curse upon him. To his dying day, whenever he happened upon the fragrance of jasmine, he would think of her.

After dressing, he sat on the bench at the foot of the bed and secured the ties of his freshly polished black shoes. He preferred boots, but that simply would not do for a dinner party. He stood and eyed himself in the mirror, then laughed. Father had often insulted him by saying he looked like the Prince of Darkness himself whenever he wore black. The somber shade accentuated his black hair and the golden eyes he had inherited from his mother. His looks had made his father hate him even more.

"To the devil with you, Father." He tipped a nod at his image and marched out, more determined than ever to make this evening a success. Monty had mentioned marriage before the month was out. If Elias had his way about it, the union would take place within a matter of days. With the knowledge of Celia's true identity, there would be no questions impeding the issue of the special license.

Mrs. Camp met him at the bottom of the stair. "I've brushed your topper, and with the weather what it is, I thought your greatcoat would be in order." Her ever-amiable expression hardened into a slightly scolding, motherly look. "You should have worn it this morning. Even with it being spring, a soaking rain could be the death of you."

"Yes, Mrs. Camp." He'd learned long ago not to argue with the housekeeper. She only had the best of intentions, and he found comfort in her caring nature.

"Shall I send Henry out to hire a coach?" She turned and frowned at the window as the rain sluiced down even harder across the panes. "The barouche won't be protection enough on a night like this."

Elias inwardly smiled. Mrs. Camp fretted about him drowning in the deluge but had no trouble tossing her son out into the storm for the sake of her employer. "That won't be necessary. My brother should arrive soon in his coach."

Mrs. Camp beamed the round-cheeked smile of a young girl hoping to be noticed by a lad. "His Grace is too kind."

Elias tried not to roll his eyes. Monty had that effect on women, no matter their age, marital status, or social standing. "He is indeed."

"I'll have Henry watch for him. He knows His Grace's coach."

Before Elias could stop her, she'd hurried down the hallway bellowing her son's name. He checked his timepiece, then donned his hat, greatcoat, and gloves before opening the door and squinting out into the weather. Monty always arrived early, and there came his coach around the corner. The battle was nigh.

CHAPTER ELEVEN

ELIAS SUBTLY MANEUVERED around until he stood with his back to the wall, behind a section of chairs arranged for the pleasure of the guests. From this prime spot, he could easily carry on a polite conversation while watching for Celia to arrive. Movement in the corner of his eye drew his attention to Lady Whitfield flitting around the large room like a nervous butterfly, checking every detail before more guests appeared.

He and Monty *had* arrived unfashionably early. While it was regrettable, Elias was glad they were the first of what looked to be a sizable gathering. Monty's valet had guessed sixteen to twenty. From the lines of chairs arranged around the perimeter of the room and in sizable clusters in the center, a great deal more was expected.

The muffled rumbling of distant thunder concerned him. With the dowager duchess's frailness, he wondered if she and Celia would venture out on such a night. While he wished the woman no ill will, he hoped they would still risk it.

"I believe we arrived a touch too early," Monty remarked in a low tone. He subtly edged closer and nudged Elias. "You do realize you will need to move about the room and carry on at least a smattering of conversation with those in attendance?"

"I am aware." Elias kept his gaze locked on the archway leading to the hall.

"Then stop watching the entrance like a leopard waiting to

pounce." Monty caught hold of his coat sleeve and tugged him into motion. "Elias," he said loudly, then snorted with an obviously fake laugh. "You must be joking."

Elias spared his brother a curious glare. "What the deuce is wrong with you?"

Monty cut his eyes to the side, subtly directing Elias's attention to their host, who was blatantly staring at them with an irritated glower. The man was obviously not pleased about their early arrival.

Realizing they had noticed him, Lord Whitfield sprang into action and motioned for a servant just entering the room with a tray of drinks to serve Elias and Monty. "Your Grace, Lord Raines, I do apologize. You should have been offered drinks ages ago."

"It is we who must apologize, Whitfield. I fear my penchant for timeliness made us arrive quite early." Monty accepted a glass and turned to Elias. "I have always suffered from over-punctuality. Have I not, brother?"

"Indeed. Were my brother a condemned man, he would arrive early for his own hanging." Elias accepted a glass, then almost snapped its stem as the Duchess of Hasterton and Celia entered the room. He attempted to recover and make idle chatter even though he kept his gaze locked on Celia. "Have you been quite well, Whitfield? It has been a while since last we spoke."

Lord Whitfield turned to follow the line of his stare, then turned back to him with a smile. "Even illness has not diminished the dowager duchess's beauty." He cast another nonchalant glance their way as the rest of the Hasterton household joined them. "My Daphne says that the lovely young thing at Her Grace's side is her companion, but the resemblance of the two is uncanny. Do you not agree? Surely, they must be relations."

"Both are quite breathtaking," Monty said. His overly appreciative tone made Elias consider elbowing him in the ribs. Hard.

Elias turned and set his drink on the wall's narrow ledge running waist-high around the room. "Her Grace is my client. I believe I shall go over and greet her."

Celia turned and spotted him before he reached her. His precious lioness looked poised to flee. A bright rosiness flared across her cheeks and panic flashed in her pale green eyes. It didn't escape his notice that her mother latched on to her arm to prevent her from stepping away.

"Your Grace," he said to the dowager with a heartfelt smile and a bow. "You braved the weather. I do hope that means the *good* days are outnumbering the bad."

Her resulting smile seemed genuine, filling him with relief. "I love the rain," she said, "and it is quite good to see you again, Lord Raines."

The weariness in her tone concerned him. He feared the lady pushed herself too hard. "Thank you, Your Grace." He cut a sharp look at Celia, then gentled it back at the duchess. "I worried you might never wish to see me again."

The dowager's smile turned sad. "As I said, it is quite good to see you."

Celia jutted her chin higher, and although she remained silent, the delicate fronds of the plumage arranged in her hair quivered with her trembling.

Elias offered her a bow. "And it is lovely to see you again, *Miss Bening*."

She returned a curtsy. "Lord Raines."

As Monty joined them, Elias stepped to one side and inclined his head toward his brother. "Allow me to present my brother, His Grace, the fourth Duke of Almsbury. Monty, this is Her Grace, the dowager Duchess of Hasterton, and her companion, Miss Celia Bening."

Celia curtsied deeply. The duchess held tightly to her cane and gave a nod. "Forgive me, Your Grace. I fear my days of managing a curtsy are long behind me."

Monty gracefully accepted the apology by bowing to them both. "It is an honor to meet you, Your Grace. And you as well, Miss Bening." With a sly smile directed at Celia, he added, "Elias has told me a great deal about you."

The feather in Celia's hair quivered more noticeably. She turned to the duchess. "Shall we get you seated, Your Grace? Standing so long can be quite wearying for you."

"Allow me," Elias said before Duchess Thea could answer. He stepped in and offered his arm. As she took it, he leaned down and whispered, "I am trying to keep my oath to you, Your Grace. Any assistance you could offer would be most appreciated."

She gave him a sad smile. "I fear that must be Celia's choice." With the slightest shake of her head, she added, "I wish it was mine to make for her."

As he led her to a chair, he allowed himself a heavy sigh. "I am quite stubborn, Your Grace. This is not over until I decide it is."

The duchess folded her hands in her lap and avoided looking him in the eyes. "Good luck to you, Lord Raines. I pray that I live to see you prosper in this endeavor." Then she stared straight ahead, as though dismissing him.

Lady Sophie stepped in to block his way as he turned to go to Celia. "She still says *no*," she whispered, with a sympathetic wrinkling of her nose. "Go away."

"I do not wish to be rude," he said with a smile to throw off anyone observing them. "But you would be well advised to step aside, Lady Sophie. Celia will be mine."

The lady made a face, then moved around him as though she wished to greet another guest who had just arrived.

As Lady Ardsmere blocked his way and opened her mouth to speak, he gave her a warning glare and slightly shook his head.

She closed her mouth, stuck her nose high in the air, and joined her mother-in-law at the dowager duchess's side.

Celia edged a step back, glancing all around as if trying to decide the best direction in which to flee.

"Might I have a word, Miss Bening?" he said in the politest tone he could manage.

"I should see to Her Grace, my lord. Perhaps after dinner?"

She sidled to the left, smiling and nodding as more guests poured into the room.

"Her Grace is quite comfortable." He effectively herded Celia to the right until they reached a slightly secluded area beside the windows. It was suitable for a quiet conversation, yet still open enough to the other guests to be considered appropriate. "Did you inform Her Grace that you refused to marry the man who adores you—the man you shared yourself with, I might add?"

She pressed her mouth into a hard line and glared at him.

"Shall I take that as a *yes*?"

"Take it however you wish," she said coldly. "As I told you before, it is for the best." She glanced away and pressed her gloved fist to her mouth. After a quick sniff and a visible swallow, she gave him a look that melted him. "I do this because I love you," she said softly. "Please trust me."

"A strange request from the woman who refuses to trust me."

"I have trusted you with more than you realize." She gave him a cryptic look that made him grit his teeth. "Have a good evening, Lord Raines. This conversation is over." She hurried away, sweeping across the room with the grace of a swan gliding across a waterway.

More guests filed into the room, closing her off from his sight.

Elias rolled his shoulders and stretched his neck, wishing he hadn't tied his cravat so tightly. His tensed muscles ached, and he couldn't breathe due to the need to chase after Celia, ranting and raging until she came to her senses. He sucked in a deep breath and hissed it out through clenched teeth, struggling to regain a sense of calm. With the heavy rains, a walk outside to cool down was impossible.

"Any luck?" Monty appeared at his side and handed him another drink.

"None whatsoever," Elias answered sourly. He tasted the liquid that smelled like port, then caught himself before revealing a grimace that would be perceived as quite rude. "What is this ghastly stuff?"

"Not sure." Monty lifted his glass and frowned at it while smacking his lips. "I believe it was port before they watered it down. They invited so many bloody people to this incorrectly described *intimate* dinner party that they probably feared running short. If Prinny shows, as I heard that he might, for their sakes, I do hope they offer him something better."

"Might I suggest you run, dear brother?" Elias didn't look at Monty. Just kept his gaze focused straight ahead.

"Why?"

"The odious Lady Bournebridge and her rather pinched-face daughter are headed this way, and I know they are *not* coming for me."

When Monty failed to answer, Elias turned his way and discovered him gone. He laughed and forced down another swallow of the disgusting port. When they were children, Monty had often slipped past Nanny and the governesses to bring Elias the treats their father had always denied his second son. It was good to know that his brother hadn't lost his gift of being neither seen nor heard.

As predicted, Lady Bournebridge puckered a fiercer scowl and halted midway with her daughter in tow. She gave Elias an unpleasant smirk that he assumed she meant as a smile, then grabbed her daughter's hand and changed course, parting the guests much as Almighty God had parted the Red Sea.

Elias took the opportunity to forge his way through the mingling masses to rejoin the dowager duchess and Celia. The duchess still sat where he had placed her. Celia sat beside her, and the rest of the Hasterton entourage hovered nearby as though on guard. Placing himself in front of the duchess and Celia to keep the crowd from pressing in on them, he said with forced brightness, "Lovely gathering. Is it not?"

The duchess arched a cynical brow and resettled her fingers on the handle of her cane. "It is quite the gathering." She turned to Celia, then tipped her head in Elias's direction. "Do be a dear and fetch me some refreshment. With this many in attendance, I fear that the light repast we were promised will either fail to be served or completely run out before it reaches us. I am sure Lord Raines would be happy to go along to ensure you are not trampled."

"I would, indeed." Elias squared his shoulders and smiled, daring Celia to refuse.

Her eyes narrowed the slightest bit before she forced a polite smile. "Thank you, Lord Raines. Your assistance is most appreciated."

The dowager waved Lady Sophie's mother out from behind the chairs and patted Celia's seat. "Hurry and sit, Nia, before we lose the chair."

Elias laughed as he edged into the throng and cleared a path for Celia. When she reached his side, he casually extended his arm behind her for protection but took care not to touch her in what anyone might perceive as an embrace. He cleared their way with his other arm, edging sideways until they reached a long banquet table that had very little remaining in the way of food or drink.

"This is ridiculous," he said for Celia's ears alone. "Intimate dinner party, my eye. Hurry and snatch something for yourself and your mother."

Panic flared across Celia's face, but she recovered quickly. "I shall get something for *Her Grace*," she said louder than necessary, then shoved forward, snatched up a napkin, and started filling it with whatever she could grab.

Elias felt like kicking himself. If anyone had overheard his mistake in referring to the duchess as Miss Bening's mother, word would spread faster than red wine spilled on fresh linen. "I shall fetch Her Grace something to drink, Miss Bening," he called out loudly. "And one for yourself as well."

She cast a nervous smile back at him, then forged onward, trying to gather up the meager pickings.

If the prince regent did show up, Lord and Lady Whitfield would be ruined even more than they already were by putting on such a disastrous affair. Elias elbowed his way farther down the table and claimed the last two glasses of punch. He held them high to protect them from sloshing and made his way back to Celia.

"The last two," he said to her.

"Well done, you," she said with such sincerity that his heart swelled. She held up the bulging napkin. "A bit of cheese and bread was all that was left, but hopefully, it will be enough to keep Her Grace steady until we get home."

By the time they worked their way back to the duchess, the poor lady was fanning herself. Elias hurried to hand her the punch. "I am sorry it took so long, Your Grace." The woman's pallor concerned him. He bent closer and whispered, "Shall I get you to a less crowded room?"

Celia knelt beside Duchess Thea and looked up into her face. "I shall order the carriages brought to the door immediately. You do not appear well at all."

"Do not fuss and draw attention," the dowager told them both. She sipped at the drink, then hugged the delicate cup to her chest and bowed her head.

Elias decided to take matters into his own hands. "We are done here, Your Grace." He flagged down Monty and gave him the signal they had worked out long ago that meant *time to leave*. Then he caught the attention of a footman and waved the man over. "Her Grace's carriages. To the front door. Immediately."

The man bobbed his head and took off as fast as the crowded room allowed.

"I did not tell you I was ready to leave, my lord," the duchess said.

"I did not ask, Your Grace." Elias held out his hand to help her rise, determined to get her out of the place before it did her ill.

The dowager took his hand, started to stand, then sagged like a windless sail.

Elias caught her as she fell forward and swept her up into his arms. "Clear a path," he bellowed. "Now!" He paused only long enough for Celia to reach his side. The fear on her face made his heart ache. He prayed this wasn't the end. Not now. Not with so many watching. "I said clear the way! Her Grace is not well."

As he stepped into the far less crowded entry hall, Lady Whitfield hurried forward and opened a side door. "Here! In here. You may lay Her Grace in here."

The duchess's eyes fluttered as though she fought to keep them open. "Do not let me die here," she rasped.

Celia gave him a teary-eyed nod and tugged him toward the front door. "Her Grace wishes to leave," she called to Lady Whitfield.

"My carriage already awaits," Monty said as he yanked open the front door. "Take it."

"Your things, Lord Raines!" Lady Whitfield shrilled, revealing her panic.

"Give them to my brother," Elias shouted without looking back. He bent as he stepped out into the rain, trying to shield the duchess as much as he could. He clambered up into the carriage and eased down into the seat with her, keeping her propped upright as much as possible.

The coachman helped Celia enter. She slid in next to Elias and draped her mother's legs across her lap. "Mama," she whispered with a soft cry. "Not yet. Please."

His heart aching, Elias wished with all his soul that he could carry this burden for Celia. He wrapped an arm around her and hugged her so she might get closer to her mother.

"We shall have you home soon, Your Grace," he reassured the dowager. "Stay with us."

The duchess barely opened her eyes. She caught Celia's hand and placed it on Elias's chest. "I want you married to him, Celia. He is a good man, and good men are in such short supply."

"Rest now, Mama. We can worry about that later." Celia hiccupped a soft cry while trying to hold her mother's hand, but the duchess placed it back on Elias's chest.

"Swear to me you will marry him," the dowager said. "I will not rest without knowing such a man cares for you."

Elias held his breath, unsure whether or not he wanted Celia to take the oath. He wanted her to love him—not marry him out of guilt.

"Mama—"

"He will understand, Celia. Tell him everything. Give him the chance I never gave to my dearest Raymond. Do not marry your work and live out your days in loneliness and regret. Land and riches mean little in the end." The duchess wheezed in a deep breath and weakly coughed it out. "Swear it, my dearest daughter. You are my precious treasure, and I cannot rest if you are not protected and happy."

"I will marry him, Mama. I swear it."

Elias closed his eyes and slowly exhaled, feeling both elated and sorrowful. This was not the way he wished for Celia to choose to be his wife, but he would deal with that later. For now, all he could do was support her in what was about to be a very difficult time. He tried to make the dowager more comfortable in his arms. "Rest, Your Grace. We will sort this all out once you regain your strength."

The duchess closed her eyes and whispered, "I admire your optimism, dear boy."

Celia gently shuddered against him with silent weeping. He tightened his arm around her and rested his cheek on her head, wishing he could take this terrible pain away.

The coach rolled to a stop in front of Hasterton House.

"We are here, Your Grace," Elias said quietly as he carefully lifted her and climbed down from the coach.

"Good," the duchess whispered.

Celia hurried ahead, ran up the steps, and pounded on the door. She stepped to one side and looked back at Elias, waving for him to hurry.

When Gransdon opened the door, open-mouthed shock registered on his face. "Berta!" he shouted in a very uncharacteristic bellow. "Friedrich! Fetch the physician! Now!"

Elias strode into the house and hurried up to the second floor. The frail duchess weighed nothing, and her limp silence concerned him. He feared she had already passed.

Berta rushed into the dowager's room and turned down the covers of the bed.

Elias eased her down among the pillows, then stepped back so Celia and Berta could tend to her. He bowed his head and prayed that the noble lady had not yet left them. He knew it was selfish to wish her more days of weariness and pain, but he had grown quite fond of her and loathed the idea of never seeing her again.

A light knock at the door made him hurry across the room in the hopes that Friedrich had already returned with the doctor. His hopes were answered.

"Dr. MacMaddenly to see Her Grace," said the spindly man with a heavy Scottish burr. Dressed all in black, for some uncomfortable reason, he gave Elias the impression of an undertaker rather than a physician. The gentleman squinted at him over the thick lenses of his wire-rimmed spectacles. "I understand there is some urgency." His tone left no doubt he was telling Elias to step aside.

Elias swung the door open wide and waved the man inside. "That you for coming so quickly, doctor. It is quite urgent."

Dr. MacMaddenly snorted and hurried to the bedside, unceremoniously shooing the women out of the way. After setting his large black bag on the bedside table, he leaned over the duchess. "Kindly open your eyes, Your Grace," he gently coaxed her. When she failed to respond, he straightened and pointed at the door. "Her Grace needs privacy during my examination. Out with the lot of ye. I shall send for ye when I am ready, ye ken?"

"I would rather stay with my mother," Celia said.

The doctor eyed her with a stern puckering of his mouth. "I need to have a look at your mother, m'lady. So I can help her. It will not be long, and 'tis better that ye wait outside." He pointed at the door again. "Now, go. For her sake. Aye?"

Elias gently but firmly pulled Celia away. "Come, dear one. We need to get you some tea. Let Dr. MacMaddenly do what he can. Let us go downstairs to the parlor."

"I don't want her to die without me here." Celia kept her gaze locked on her mother but allowed Elias to ease her into his arms.

The physician looked up from where he held the duchess's wrist between his finger and thumb. "Pulse is rapid and weak but steadier than I expected. If that changes, I shall get ye up here immediately. Now go and allow me to do what needs doing."

"Celia, come." Elias curled his arm around her and nudged her out through the sitting room, into the hall, and to the top of the stair.

She stiffened in his arms, stuck in place, then twisted around to stare at her mother's door. "I am not going any farther. What if she needs me?" Terror filled her eyes. The tremor in her voice begged him to understand.

He took her hand and kissed it. "Then we shall sit right here on the step." To show he meant it, he plopped down, looked up at her, then held out his hand. "Join me, my lady?"

Despair and hopelessness slumping her shoulders, Celia dropped beside him and covered her face with her hands.

Wrapping an arm around her, Elias leaned her against him and held her while she wept. Knowing she had tossed her reticule somewhere between here and the front door, he offered her the use of his handkerchief. "I have heard of Dr. MacMaddenly," he said quietly, hoping to offer her some sort of comfort. "Schooled in Edinburgh and highly sought after by those members of the *ton* needing care."

"There is no hope." The handkerchief she clutched to her mouth muffled her voice. "I brought in doctors from all over. None have helped her."

"There is always hope." Elias tipped her face up to his. "We will not give up until she tells us farewell."

Her face crumpled, and she unleashed a pitiful wail while thumping his chest with her fist. "I do not want her to leave. She is all I have."

He hugged her close again, rocking and shushing her, realizing his fierce lioness was inconsolable. It would do no good to remind her of her brother. Or of himself. She would not be alone in this world, but now was not the time for logic. Now was the time to be there for her.

After what seemed like hours, the door behind them creaked open. Elias turned, and Celia lifted her head.

"I would speak to you both." The doctor motioned for them to join him.

Celia jumped up and rushed into the sitting room. Elias followed close behind.

Standing in the center of the room, Dr. MacMaddenly shrugged on his greatcoat as he spoke. "How long has Her Grace suffered with this condition?"

"For the past year," Celia said. Bitterness sharpened her tone. "And no physician in the civilized world has helped her. All of them clucked their tongues and told me to order her grave prepared."

The doctor appeared unimpressed as he donned his hat and peered down his nose at her. "Obviously, none of those physicians were Scots trained in Edinburgh." He picked up his bag, then shot a glance back at the bedroom door. "Her Grace suffers from a weakness of her heart. I administered a dose of digitalis tincture and watched her closely. She appears to be tolerating it well enough, but dinna hesitate to fetch me if the need arises. I shall return tomorrow to check for improvement. I will need to see her daily to settle on the exact amount required each day in order for her to enjoy life a bit more than she enjoys it at present. 'Tis a grand drug for cases such as hers, but also exceedingly dangerous." He dismissed them both with a curt nod. "Good evenin' to ye. I shall call again tomorrow." Without waiting for their response or questions, he left.

Celia stared after him for a moment, then whirled about and rushed into the bedroom.

Elias debated for a moment whether to join her, then decided to wait. Celia needed private time with her mother. Filled with an edginess that forbade standing still, he idly paced around the small room. It occurred to him he hadn't sent Monty's coach back to the Whitfields', but surely the driver had taken it upon himself to do so.

A quiet click made him stop and turn toward the bedroom door. A surge of relief crashed through him as Celia gave him a tremulous smile.

"She is resting peacefully," she said, "and enjoying deeper breaths than she has in quite a while."

He closed the distance between them and took her hands in his. "That is the best of news."

Celia agreed with a weak nod, then lowered her gaze to their hands. "I promised her I would speak with you before you went home this evening."

The hesitancy in her voice caused him concern. Was this where she would go back on her word and send him packing again? "Speak to me?" he repeated, carefully controlling his tone.

"In the library." She eased her hands out of his and took a step back, placing an arm's length of space between them. "I need a drink. Something stronger than tea. Would you like one too?"

"I would, indeed." His infallible instincts told him he would need it.

CHAPTER TWELVE

CELIA TRIED TO pour the brandy without spilling, but with her trembling, she was less than successful. She had promised Mama to tell Elias the whole of it and give him the chance to either accept or refuse their life of lies. Mama still regretted never giving Master Hodgely that choice.

"I have brandy this time rather than Madeira," she called back over her shoulder.

"Anything is fine after this evening's events."

She bit her lip, knowing the events weren't over. Before turning from the shelf of decanters, she sent up a silent prayer that what was about to happen would go well. After a deep breath, she forced a smile and joined Elias in the seating area in front of the small hearth. A cheery fire crackled within, its flames dancing behind the grating. It beat back the chill of the damp evening but did little to warm her hopes that Elias would understand. She handed him the glass with the genteel nod of a perfect hostess. "Here you are, my lord."

"Elias," he gently corrected her. In the firelight, his golden eyes shimmered with a richer warmth than usual. "You frighten me, Celia."

"Frighten you?" She seated herself beside him on the small sofa in front of the fire and set her glass on the oval table beside it. She couldn't drink. Not just yet. "How on earth have I frightened you?"

"Do you mean to send me away again?"

His bluntness almost caused her to choke. She swallowed hard and wet her lips. "I will not send you away again," she said with a carefulness she hoped was convincing. "Not ever."

Then she stiffened her spine and folded her hands in her lap. Might as well be on with it. Delaying it would not make it any easier. The problem was, she wasn't sure where to start. Perhaps a bit of layering was in order. "As a solicitor, I am sure you are well aware of the laws regarding the ownership of entailed property?"

He blinked as though unsure he had heard her correctly. "Yes. I am well aware of the laws. Why?"

"Then you know it cannot be sold because the entailment commonly ties it to several generations of heirs. *Male* heirs. Farther down the line of succession."

"I am quite familiar with the laws of primogeniture." He sipped his drink, his unflinching gaze locked on her.

What could she say? How could she make him understand? "My father died before I was born, turning my mother into a young widow, expecting her first child—the child who would decide her future."

He said nothing, watching her like a cat watches a cornered mouse about to make its last fatal attempt at fleeing.

"I was told my mother sobbed when I was born. Both from joy and fear. Joy about my good health and yet fear for what would become of us—financially, socially, where we would live." She waited for him to comment. When he didn't, she continued, "You see, by the time I was born, my mother had not only lost my father but all her family as well. Influenza, you understand. She was completely alone except for a few loyal servants."

"But you and your brother are twins." The puzzlement revealed in the slight furrow of his brow didn't match the dawning realization smoldering in his eyes. "I am sure your mother was relieved when he was born a few moments later. The duke's heir."

"She would have been—had he ever been born." Celia waited, bracing herself. "I am not a twin. Never have been. Not even while in my mother's womb."

He frowned and slowly tilted his head to one side. "You do not mean to suggest…"

Celia rose, went to her desk, and signed a sheet of paper with the same signature she used for all business dealings. As she returned to Elias, she gently blew on the ink to dry it. Without a word, she handed it to him, then settled back in her seat and waited.

"This is not possible." He barely shook his head while staring down at the official signature of Charles Tuttcliffe, the sixth Duke of Hasterton. "Surely, you cannot mean to say…"

"That we created Charles to protect our entailed properties, our money, our place in Society? The title? That over the years, with the help of some well-paid and extraordinarily loyal individuals, we took the somewhat strained Hasterton holdings and formed the comfortably powerful estate we enjoy today? That my mother, a woman of brilliance, successfully carried off this subterfuge until I took over the reins seven years ago at the gentle age of ten and six?"

"Subterfuge?" He tossed back his drink, then pointed the empty glass at her. "This is not subterfuge. It is fraud. A fraud of the scale that would see you both hanged. Impersonating a peer?" He shook his head. "No. Not impersonating a peer. Pulling one from your imagination."

"And now you know why I tried to protect you from ruin." Her throat ached with the need to break down and sob, but she refused to give way to tears. At least, not yet. "An intimate association with me would make you just as guilty—whether you knew about our scheme or not."

"I still could be deemed guilty." Elias lurched to his feet and stormed back and forth in front of the hearth. "The entire firm could be charged after overseeing the Hasterton accounts all these years." He halted and stared at her. "At the time of your birth, your mother had the Bening accounts protected by her marriage contract. Those were rightfully hers to use as needed. Why did she not rely on them instead of creating this farce?"

"At that time, the Bening accounts would not have provided enough for a dormouse's survival, and the crumbs left from my father's will were laughable. His many debts had to be settled." Celia stood, unable to sit any longer. "Like many young women of the peerage, Mama was pressured into marrying my father for all the usual reasons. Her parents as much as forced her to give up the man she truly loved. Yet when she gave birth to a daughter sired by a man she never wanted, she was expected to become a pauper until she found another man to pay her way." Celia thumped her chest, anger at the injustice of it all setting her on fire. "Just because I was born female, legally, I was denied the properties, money, and status that would have rightly been mine had I been blessed with a cock and a pair of bollocks." She tapped her temple. "Neither my nor my mother's brains, nor our ability to reason and make sound business decisions, mattered. Without my mother's ingenuity, the title would have gone extinct. The entailed properties would have gone fallow until the Crown decided which of its favorite fawners deserved them. Any money left in the Hasterton accounts would have gone to the Crown's coffers too. All while my mother was forced to make do with very little until she found a man of the peerage willing to buy her body and feed her infant daughter. Merely because I was born a girl and not a boy. Is that fair, I ask you?"

"What the two of you did—still do—is not legal," Elias said loudly enough to make her rage burn even hotter.

She jabbed the air, pointing at him. "And *that* is exactly why I delayed telling you, and also why Master Hodgely was never told. Men do not care about the women they profess to love or supposedly wish to protect. All they care about is themselves and their precious little world, where a woman's place is only in their beds or padding their accounts with a fine, fat dowry."

"That is not true."

"Is it not?" Celia closed the distance between them and poked him in the chest. "Then why do you stand there looking ready to vault over anything in your way to be free of this place and never look back?"

He raked a hand through his cropped hair, making the black curls stand on end. "Your mother could have sold off the Bening lands."

"There were no Bening lands until we purchased them with Hasterton profits three years ago. All other lands are entailed to the Hasterton title and could not be sold. You know that." She was furious with herself for giving this unfeeling man both her heart and her virginity. Devil take her. She had been such a fool. "And besides, what purpose does *your mother should have done so* advice do now other than belittle a dying woman who valiantly took care of her daughter without having to become anyone's whore?"

His crestfallen look gave her a hollow victory. He shook his head. "That is not fair, Celia."

"Life is not fair, *Lord Raines*. It is high time you realized what I was forced to learn at birth." She hiked her chin higher. "Now you know all of my truths. I have entrusted you with everything. All I ask is that you refrain from turning us over to the authorities because of Mama's health. Once she dies, if you still feel the need to see me hang, then, by all means, do what you will. But until then, I beg upon your sense of honor and your Christian decency to let a frail, lonely old woman die in peace."

She hated the revulsion in his eyes. But she had been the one to put it there, so by rights, she guessed she deserved it. "Well? May I have your word that you will take no action until after Mama dies? She has suffered enough—or has she, according to *your* standards?"

His eyes turned flinty, and his expression settled into an unreadable mask. "What do you intend to tell Her Grace about this conversation?"

"That is none of your affair." But he was right. Mama would

ask. What would she say?

"On the contrary, *Lady Cecelia*." Elias swaggered toward her, backing her up a step. "You know as well as I that Her Grace will ask if you told me and will also wish to know my reaction. What do you intend to say? After all, she is a dying woman whose last wish was to see you loved and protected by me." He hit his chest with his fist. "*Married* to me. If you tell her I did not take it well—"

"Which you haven't—"

"May I please finish?" He glared at her, obviously incensed by the interruption.

She rolled her eyes and flicked a hand. "Go on."

"As I was saying before I was so rudely interrupted..." He scowled at her, daring her to do so again. "If you tell her I did not take it well and that we two shall no longer become one, do you not fear how that will affect her health?"

"It will not affect her nearly as bad as prison or a trip to the gallows!"

"Perhaps not. But it will still affect her. Are you willing to risk it? Risk sending her on her way faster with a heady dose of regret for bringing you to London?"

"I hate you." She fisted her hands so tightly that the seams of her gloves pinched her fingers.

"I hate you more," he growled, then shook his head. "But I do not wish to be a part of sending your mother to her grave any faster than she is already going."

Celia eyed him, barely controlling the urge to throw something at him. "What do you suggest, Lord Raines? Being a *male*, I feel sure you have a far superior plan than I, a mere female, could ever hope to dream up."

"We will reveal your identity to the world and marry as she wishes. Your *brother* will continue his travels on the Continent." He towered over her and shook his finger. "And we will be perceived as the epitome of a happy, loving couple—until Her Grace leaves this world and is laid to rest beside her husband in Germany."

"And then you will turn me over to the authorities and claim you never discovered the scheme until Mama died, and I confessed that Charles did not exist." Celia glared at him, clenching her teeth until her jaw ached. Elias was a hellhound of the worst sort to offer such a hardhearted plan, but it would protect Mama. "Fine. I will do so to protect the happiness of my mother's last days."

"Fine," he said, looking ready to spit. He suddenly shifted and appeared to be listening in the hallway's direction. "It sounds as though the rest of your household has arrived. Might I suggest keeping our agreement between ourselves? The fewer who know, the better."

Celia would not betray Sophie or Frannie's trust, and she would take their secrets to the gallows with her to protect them from the same fate. She would never lie to them. From this moment forward, however, she would lie to Elias every chance she got. "The terms of our agreement will be between us alone."

While he granted her a nod, he did not seem fully convinced. Fine. She would seal the bargain with a meaningful declaration usually reserved for lovers rather than the enemy Elias had become.

She stormed over to her desk and rummaged through the drawers until she came up with a short length of ribbon and the scissors she kept for the emergency trimming of loose threads. After tying the ribbon around a small lock of her hair, she snipped it off, marched back to him, and placed the sacrificed curl in his hand. "To bind our agreement and the secrecy thereof."

He politely bowed. "So be it, my lady." He tucked it into the inner pocket of his coat and offered his arm. "Shall we greet them with the doctor's report and our decision for an immediate marriage?"

Celia glared at him as she took his arm, determined to show him she could not be outdone. "A fine idea, my lord. Let the final scheme begin."

Concentrating on relaxing her clenched jaw, she walked with

him out of the library and called to the ladies heading down the hallway, "I know this evening has been too worrisome to bear, but if you could join us in the parlor, Elias and I have some pleasant news to counter the horridness of the day."

The four women she had known all her life stood there staring at her. Celia read their leeriness as if it was her own. They knew something was terribly amiss. After releasing Elias's arm with a subtle yank, she hurried forward and opened the parlor doors. "Please. If just for a moment. I promise to share only good news."

"Of course." Sophie linked arms with her mother and Frannie and tugged them forward.

"Yes, we could use some good news after enduring the Whitfields' *faux pas* and then dear Thea's collapse," Frannie's fake mother-in-law but true mother said. "Please assure us she is resting well."

"She is indeed," Celia said, forcing a false smile. Once the ladies had seated themselves, she continued with the only actual good news there was to share. "Dr. MacMaddenly has determined that Mama has a weak heart. The esteemed doctor has a medication that will hopefully help her cope with the condition. In fact, he administered the first dose this evening, and Mama is resting much better than before."

At her reference to *Mama* rather than Her Grace, all four women cut sharp looks over at Elias where he stood by the door.

"Do not worry." Celia held out a hand, beckoning him over. "He knows I am Lady Cecilia and plans to write to Charles about our intentions."

With a charming smile that made her heart even heavier, Elias strode forward, took her hand in his, and pressed it lovingly to his cheek. "We are to be married immediately," he announced. "And while we would like the blessing of the duke before we marry, His Grace often takes quite some time to reply, and we are not willing to wait."

"Yes," Celia said, struggling to keep her voice from cracking.

"Mama has given us her blessing, and that is enough."

Sophie was the first to break the awkward silence that followed. She hurried to hug Celia. "Congratulations, sister! I am so happy for you."

Frannie, her mother, and Sophie's mother followed suit.

"And when will this glorious event take place?" Frannie asked with a forced brightness that made Celia cringe.

"As soon as I obtain the special license," Elias said. "With any luck, before the week is out."

"Splendid," Sophie said, then turned to Celia. "Do forgive us, sister, but we really must retire now. The evening has been quite draining, but I am so pleased it ended on such a happy note." With a startled look, she turned to Elias. "My lord, do forgive me, but your brother waits for you in his carriage. He refused to come inside because he feared that the news about the duchess would not be good. I nearly forgot to tell you."

"Think nothing of it." Elias took Celia's gloved hand once again and bowed over it. "Until tomorrow, my dearest. Rest well."

She forced herself to beam up at him with a loving smile while managing a curtsy. "I shall dream of you," she lied, damning him with all her heart. She held her breath until her odious judge and executioner exited the house, and she heard the front door close behind him. As soon as it thudded shut, she sagged down into the nearest chair and held her head in her hands.

"Sister!" Sophie and Frannie cried out in unison as they rushed to her side.

"Tell us this instant," Frannie ordered her. "What was the meaning of the charade we just witnessed?"

Celia lifted her head and gave Frannie and Sophie's mothers a stern look. "You must not tell Mama any of what I am about to tell you. Swear it."

Lady Rydleshire and Lady Ardsmere both held up their hands and shook their heads.

"No. Whatever it is, do not speak of it until we leave the room," Lady Rydleshire said.

Lady Ardsmere nodded as she hurried toward the door with Sophie's mother. "Thea, Lavinia, and I made a pact long ago that we would never keep secrets from each other. If there is anything that must be kept from our sister, even if for her own good, then we would be more comfortable not knowing about it, so we do not break our word to her."

Celia nodded and waited until they left the room, then closed the parlor doors behind them.

Sophie patted the seat between her and Frannie. "Now sit and tell us what happened."

With a despondent huff, Celia flopped down between them, leaned back against the cushions, and covered her eyes with her hands. "On the way home from the Whitfields', Mama *extracted* a promise from me." She let her hands drop and stared up at the ceiling. "She wanted me to marry Elias so he could protect me."

"And?" Frannie prompted.

"And she also made me swear to tell him the truth." Celia kept her gaze locked on the cream-colored plaster roses decorating the pale blue ceiling. "So, I did."

"You didn't," Sophie whispered.

"I did."

"All of it?" Frannie asked.

"All of it," Celia repeated. She folded her hands and sat straighter, then gave them both reassuring looks. "The only thing I withheld was information about the Sisterhood. As far as he knows, my deception is the only case of fraudulent behavior. I will take your stories with me to the gallows."

"To the gallows?" Sophie shrieked so loudly that both Frannie and Celia lunged to cover her mouth. She batted them away and lowered her voice to a whisper. "Who is sending you to the gallows?"

"Elias." Celia pulled in a deep breath, determined to harden herself and accept the deal she had made with the devil. "To give

Mama peace until her time comes, he said we should marry and give her the perception that we are a loving couple. Since she is already well on her way to the grave, he said his conscience couldn't bear it if he were the one to make her last days unbearable by sending us to prison and then on to be hanged. But once she is gone and laid to rest in Germany, he will turn me over to the authorities. After all, as a solicitor, he cannot be privy to any activities as reprehensible as impersonating a peer and committing innumerable fraudulent activities."

"He actually plans to turn you in after your mother dies?" Frannie asked in a horrified whisper.

"To protect himself, his career, and his illustrious firm." Celia pushed herself up from the sofa, crossed the room, and yanked on the golden bellpull embroidered with rich green leaves of ivy. When Gransdon entered, she no longer had the energy to manage a smile. "I know it is quite late, Gransdon, but please bring us any cold meats and cheeses Cook might be willing to prepare. And wine, Gransdon. Copious amounts of wine."

"Right away, Miss Bening."

"And Gransdon," she called out before he lumbered down the hall. "Miss Bening the companion no longer exists. Please spread the word that everyone may relax and call me Lady Cecilia."

Gransdon behaved as though the request was as normal as any other. "Yes, my lady." After a proper nod, he turned and left.

"Raines cannot mean to do this to you." Sophie rose and worried her way back and forth across the room. "The man told you he loved you. You said you loved him."

"Men will say anything." Much to her shame, Celia's voice cracked, and tears escaped. "I am a damned fool for believing him and shall pay for it with my life!"

"Oh, Celia!" Sophie rushed to her side, and Frannie joined her.

"And another thing." Celia sniffed and forced herself to hold it together. "He said not to tell either of you the truth of our arrangement. The fewer who knew the better, he said." She huffed a bitter laugh. "I told him I wouldn't tell you." More tears escaped, and this time, she didn't fight them. "I will lie to him, but I will never lie to you, my sisters."

All three of them wept together, then hurried to turn away and hide their sorrow when Gransdon and Friedrich entered with their late repast.

"Will that be all, my lady?" the butler asked, a hint of concern shading his tone.

"Yes. Thank you, Gransdon." Celia offered a nod, then quickly turned aside again.

"Lady Cecilia?" Friedrich said. "Can we help you?"

"I fear I am beyond helping, Friedrich, but I very much appreciate the offer." She managed a smile and waved them away. "Go to your beds, gentlemen. I know you are weary. When the ladies and I finish, it can be cleared away tomorrow."

Gransdon and Friedrich each gave her a somber bow, then departed and closed the doors behind them.

Frannie hurried to the table and poured them each a glass of wine. Her eyes narrowed as she handed one to Celia. "Perhaps you might become a widow soon after your mother's death. *Before* your beloved husband has a chance to turn you in."

"I am a fraud, Frannie. Not a murderer." Celia took a very large, unladylike gulp.

"You don't have to be the one to kill him," Sophie said while picking through a platter of sweetmeats.

"Both of you stop." While thoughts of slapping Elias might currently bring her no small amount of pleasure, Celia couldn't imagine actually killing him. After all, the crime was hers to pay for. And damn and blast it all! She still loved him.

"So, you truly mean to marry him?" Sophie asked as she held out a platter of cold meats.

"That was the agreement." Celia waved away the food, opting for more wine instead. "The price of his silence until Mama passes." She stared down at the ruby liquid swirling in the glass. "It is the least I can do after Mama chose me over the man she loved. She deserves peace."

"Surely, the marriage will be in name only?" Frannie snapped off a bite of apple while arching a brow.

"I would imagine so, judging by the revulsion on his face when I told him that Charles did not exist." Celia lowered herself back onto the sofa, crossed her legs at the ankles, and rudely propped her feet on the low table in front of her. The memory of the disgust in his eyes made her tears spill over again.

"A shame, really," she said softly. "Because I really did love him." She trembled with a sad little shrug. "Still do."

CHAPTER THIRTEEN

"T ELL ME, DAMN you!" Monty circled him. "You've been at this since I got you home, and it's nearly dawn."

Stripped down to his waist, sweat streaming down his body, Elias pummeled the long black leather bag suspended from a rafter in the ceiling of his cellar. "I am not yet ready to speak of it," he said between hard punches.

"In the carriage, you said the doctor from Edinburgh left you with the impression that he might help the duchess. At least grant her a bit more comfort in her final days." Monty caught the bag and stopped it from swinging, then widened his stance to prepare for a more vicious attack. "Fortuitous news—correct?"

Elias hit the bag with another series of rapid-fire blows, envisioning passages of law regarding entailed properties, primogeniture, and the punishment for fraud. All those damnable things had ripped his beloved Celia from the life he had envisioned for them. He attacked the bag again, knocking Monty back several steps.

Monty pushed away from the bag, yanked off his coat and waistcoat, and rolled up his sleeves. "Either talk to me or fight me." He held up his fists in a vulnerable pose that Elias would never use against him. "Talk or fight, little brother. What will it be?"

With an enraged roar, Elias tore into the heavy leather punching bag with renewed fury. "I signed a contract with Satan, damn you, and have yet to find a loophole."

"What the deuce are you talking about?" Monty let his fists drop.

Elias turned away from the bag and thumped Monty in the chest hard enough to back him up. "What I am about to tell you does not leave this room. Do you give me your word?"

Rubbing the spot Elias just hit, Monty scowled at him. "Of course."

"I mean it, Aurelias Montseton Raines. I will have your word!"

Monty lifted both hands and retreated another step. "You have my word. Just don't use my full name again. You sound like Father."

"Calling me that will not help your cause." Elias strode over to the worktable and started unwinding the strips of cloth he used to protect his knuckles. "I met the Duke of Hasterton."

"Truly?" Monty joined him at the table. "The famed duke no one has ever seen? What's the fellow like?"

Elias locked eyes with Monty. He knew he could trust his brother—but this damn secret was dangerous. "The duke is Celia."

"You mean he looks like her?" Monty shrugged. "Stands to reason, old boy. They are twins."

Elias shook his head. "You misunderstand me. He *is* Celia. Celia *is* Hasterton."

Monty squinted one eye shut as if trying to sight a pistol. "What do you mean *Celia is Hasterton*? That is impossible."

"Why? Because the man can do no wrong when it comes to investments? Because none of his many businesses have ever failed to turn an astounding profit?" Elias propped his hands on the table and bowed his head, still amazed at the duchess and Celia's ability to manage such a grand scheme with such extraordinary finesse and precision. He turned and thumped Monty again. "They made him up, man. Charles was never born. Never existed. Lady Cecilia is the only child of the Duke and

Duchess of Hasterton."

Monty's expression turned incredulous. "What are you saying?"

"The duchess *pretended* to have a son so as not to lose everything and end up a pauper, because the funds guaranteed by her marriage contract and her husband's will were far from adequate. The brilliant woman ran the estate herself until Celia took over seven years ago and increased their wealth and holdings tenfold."

"Gads." Monty scratched his head as he meandered over to a wooden stool and plopped down on it. "How bloody brilliant," he said with a snorting laugh.

"How bloody fraudulent," Elias snapped. "Fraudulent enough to see them both hanged."

"Only if they get caught." Monty thoughtfully pursed his lips and shook his head. "My dear brother, I see your overactive sense of morality rearing its ugly head." He rose to his feet. "Good heavens, man. The duchess is already dying, and the other cunning criminal is the woman you love."

"This farce cannot go on." Elias threw his hands in the air. "Someone will discover it, and then I will hang with them. Such a scandal could bring down the entire firm."

Monty scratched through the morning stubble on his chin. "As I see it, old boy, the scheme has survived quite well for twenty-odd years now. Why should it not continue to thrive?"

"I am a solicitor. A partner with a prestigious law group." Elias snatched up a generous square of linen off the table and scrubbed the sweat from his face and chest. "How can I knowingly condone such a thing?"

"Because if you love the woman, you will do anything to keep her safe." Monty scowled at him, slowly prowling closer like a predator about to attack. The nearer he drew, the more he tilted his head to one side. "What have you done?"

"Behaved like a complete ass," Elias said as he hung his head.

His contempt for his father's questionable dealings and lack of morals had caused him to become a self-righteous devil determined to see that the dishonest got what he felt they deserved. His pompous sense of proper ethics painted everything black or white. There was no middle ground. No shades of gray. No justifications for any choice or action. It was either right or wrong. Legal or not. And those who shunned the law deserved the damnation they received.

He huffed a bitter laugh. "I begged her to trust me. To tell me what was troubling her so I could help her and her mother."

"And when she did?" Monty's hard-jawed look said he already knew the answer.

"When she did, I turned on her. Reacted like her assigned solicitor instead of the man who loves her with an all-consuming fury."

Monty clasped his hands to the small of his back and meandered back and forth in front of him. "You mentioned signing a contract with Satan?"

"Her Grace took a liking to me." Elias snorted another mirthless laugh. "Why she did so, I have no idea. But she did, and on the day we completed her will—which is now invalid, I might add—she extracted an oath from me to win Celia's love. To marry her. To love her and protect her."

"And how is that a deal with the devil?" Monty stopped pacing and pinned him with a confused frown.

"Her Grace also drew a promise from Celia to marry me." Bitterness churned through Elias. "Her Grace is a sly one. No wonder the estate thrived under her care." He rifled through his clothes draped over the back of a chair. His chest burned with his breaking heart as his fingers closed around Celia's precious lock of hair. "After Celia told me everything, she begged me not to turn her and her mother over to the authorities because of her mother's failing health. I told her that her mother expected us to marry, and if we did not, Her Grace would not only be upset in her final days, but had also insinuated she would not enjoy peace when she died."

"And?" Monty prodded while moving closer.

Elias held up the silky black curl and showed it to his brother. "I suggested we marry and assume the appearance of a happy, loving couple to make Her Grace's last days as pleasant as possible. Celia agreed and gave me this to seal the bargain that once her mother is laid to rest in Germany, I can then turn her over to the authorities. She will admit her guilt, state that neither I nor the firm were aware of the scheme, and will go to the gallows without argument."

Monty's mouth went ajar with an incredulous stare. "In all my days, I do not believe I have ever met such a damned fool."

"Nor have I." Elias cradled the lock of hair in his palm, staring down at it, wishing it meant happiness instead of the cruel bargain he had been too stupid and stunned to stop at the time, the bargain that had broken Celia's heart. He had utterly failed her. "When I suggested we marry for the duchess's sake, I did not say I wanted to turn Celia in once her mother died. She was the one who suggested it, and idiot that I was, I did not contradict her." He slowly shook his head. "I wanted her as my wife. At least for a little while. I hoped…"

"You hoped what? What the deuce did you mean to do after the dowager died?" Monty glared at him in disbelief.

"Devil if I know." Elias carefully tucked the treasured curl back inside his coat pocket. "I was still in shock, I suppose. From learning the truth."

Monty moved to stand in front of him, eying him with what appeared to be both sympathy and frustration. "I realize a childhood of mistreatment created your rather extreme perception about what is right and what is wrong." He threw up his hands and turned away. "I wish you had known Mother. She would have saved you from this…*debacle*."

"Well, I didn't know her." Elias hoisted himself up onto the sturdy worktable and sat there, sagging forward with his head in his hands. "And I do not know how to make this right."

The table groaned as Monty joined him. "Do you love her?"

"More than I thought it possible to love anyone."

"Then that is all that matters." Monty shifted back and forth, making the table creak again. "They harmed no one with their scheme. In fact, they very well could have harmed themselves if they had not shown such initiative. You know what has happened to poor widows and daughters without proper provisions. And Celia and her mother have also educated the business world immensely. Been a boon to the economy. The *duke's* every action on the Exchange or any other venture is studied and replicated in an attempt to achieve the same success. Some have done quite well. Others—not so much. But that is no fault of Celia's or her mother."

"She thinks I have the lowest opinion of her now. Because of the way I reacted."

"Fall on your knees and beg the woman's forgiveness, for heaven's sake. Have you never done that before?" Monty thumped him on the shoulder. "Tell her how you feel, man."

Elias straightened and shook his head. "She will never believe me. I saw it in her eyes. I cut her too deeply."

Monty blew out a heavy sigh. "But she means to marry you according to your *deal*, yes?"

"Yes."

"Well, it's rather putting the cart before the horse, but it appears to me that you need to woo your wife to win back her love and trust in you." Monty swung his feet, making the creaking of the table louder.

Elias clamped hold of his knee and stopped him. "Sit still, damn you."

"Sorry." Monty hopped down and brushed off the seat of his trousers. "Win your wife's heart and convince her that no matter what happens, you will not escort her to the gallows."

Blowing out a heavy sigh, Elias scrubbed his gritty eyes. His brother always made everything sound so easy. Too easy. And it never worked out that way. "And I suppose I turn a blind eye while she carries on with the scheme as usual?" That thought made him inwardly cringe. Years of raging against the unlawful curdled in his gut. "It cannot possibly go on forever. At some point, people will suspect something is not right. A duke of three and twenty constantly traveling is one thing, but an older duke who should be married and fathering an heir will draw too much attention." He stared down at the floor, drowning in despondency. "I cannot bear to lose her, Monty. Not now, and not years in the future."

"Have you not heard of recluses who never marry?" Monty shrugged. "Or once the duchess dies, kill the man off in an accident. Drown him at sea or claim him eaten by cannibals or some such nonsense."

"But then Celia would eventually lose the vast estate she and her mother built." He already knew his lioness was proud of all she and her mother had achieved and would not be likely to stand idly by and watch it float away. "And you know how difficult it is to have a missing peer proclaimed legally dead. It could take a decade or more." He pinned a hard glare on his brother. "Do not even suggest it. I am not about to *purchase* a body for a funeral."

Monty shrugged again. "Waiting for him to be declared dead would buy you several years of bliss. But it sounds as if losing the entailed properties and whatever monies had not been transferred to a safe account is not on the table. You are positive there are no other relations, even on the very fringes of the Hasterton line, who could lay claim to the estate were the duke to die?"

"According to Celia and from what I recall of the records, there are not." Elias thought back over his conversations with Master Hodgely. His mentor had mentioned no one who might contest the peerage. "And if there were, I feel sure we would have known by now, considering the wealth involved. The Crown would happily take it all at the first opportunity. You know that."

Monty's ever-mischievous smile turned quite sly. "The patent for the Dukedom of Hasterton could be amended to allow Celia and her sons to inherit the dukedom successively after the death of her brother leaves no heirs. Surely, you are familiar with Parliament's act amending the Dukedom of Marlborough?"

Hope pounded in Elias's chest as thunderously as his heart. He stared at his brother. "Why did I not think of that?"

"Because raw emotion temporarily incapacitated you. I have heard it said that love can be quite toxic." Monty shook a finger at him. "That is why I avoid it at all costs." He clapped a hand on Elias's shoulder. "I could see that the act gets the proper support and attention to pass without issue." He preened like the proudest of birds, smoothing back his longish black curls that badly needed a trim. "I am well thought of in both the House of Lords and the House of Commons, if I do say so myself."

Elias held up a hand. "Not yet. Timing is critical. If we attempt such a thing at the same time my marriage becomes public knowledge, it will appear very suspicious. Especially with the duke so young, and quite alive, so to speak."

Monty agreed with a thoughtful nod. "Yes…and then, if we claimed him dead immediately thereafter, it would look even more suspect. So, how shall we go about this?"

Elias slid off the table, scooped up his clothes, and headed toward the stairs. "Come. I need food and drink to think straight."

"Several hours of sleep might do you wonders as well." Monty followed him.

Mrs. Camp and Sarah the maid turned as the pair entered the kitchen, then whirled back around and gave Elias their backs.

"Good morning, my lord," Mrs. Camp said. She curtsied without facing him. "Up quite early for our exercise, are we?"

Monty thumped him on the back. "Shirt, man. Have you no manners?"

"Good heavens! Forgive me, Mrs. Camp. Sarah." Elias shrugged on the shirt. "It is safe to turn now, ladies. I am properly covered."

Mrs. Camp turned, gave him a relieved smile, then pointed at the door. "A second pitcher of water for his lordship's room, Sarah. He'll be wanting an ample wash before he goes out today."

Sarah dipped a curtsy to Elias and Monty both, then scurried out to follow orders.

"I believe she is saying you are a bit ripe, old man," Monty teased.

"Why no, Your Grace." Mrs. Camp aimed a quick curtsy at Monty. "I would never say such a thing to his lordship." But mirth twinkled in her eyes and her plump cheeks turned even rosier.

"Mrs. Camp, would it be a terrible imposition if my brother and I ate our breakfast here in the kitchen—alone?" Elias seated himself at the worktable in the center of the room and motioned for Monty to do the same.

"*Now*, my lord?" She glanced back at the stove that she and Sarah had just lit. Several sticks of wood lay nearby, waiting to be added to the newly kindled flame. "You never eat before ten a.m."

"The Whitfields' dinner party was a complete disaster," Monty told her in a gossipy whisper. "They completely ran out of food within the first hour and were watering down the port to make it last."

"Oh my, they will be ruined, will they not?" Mrs. Camp greedily took in every word with surprising satisfaction. She wasn't usually a woman who took such great pleasure in the pitfalls of others.

But then Elias remembered that Mrs. Camp and the Whitfields' housekeeper had maintained a long-running feud. He smiled and joined in to get his breakfast cooked faster. "Too many guests. Too little food and drink." He leaned toward her. "And it was said that Prinny was going to show."

Mrs. Camp gasped. "Did he?"

Elias shrugged. "I am unsure. The heat of the crowded room overcame the poor Duchess of Hasterton, and my brother and I had to see her home."

"Oh my, you have had nothing to eat in ages, then." Mrs. Camp whirled about and started chucking wood into the stove. "Let me get this going good, then I'll fetch the cakes from the pantry and hurry with the tea and chocolate. That'll get you started while I cook the eggs, kidneys, chops, and liver. I understand you don't usually eat such a large breakfast, but you must be famished." She turned and shook a finger at him. "Why did you not wake me when you arrived home? I would have set you out a late supper." Without waiting for an answer, she bustled out of the room, disappearing into the pantry.

"Well played," Elias told Monty. "How did you know a juicy *on dit* would get her moving?"

Monty fixed him with a superior look. "I know women."

Stretching to watch the pantry door, Elias leaned across the table toward his brother. "I have been thinking. If I tell Celia of our plan to have the original patent amended to name her as the heir, she might forgive me."

"She might also take that as your saying you cannot love her unless she is legitimate rather than a brilliant fraud." Monty leaned back in his chair and made a face. "I advise you to play this carefully, brother. You said you hurt her deeply after she trusted you."

"Do not remind me." Elias pinched the bridge of his nose and rubbed the inner corners of his burning eyes. The memory of the hurt on Celia's face haunted him. She felt as if he had betrayed her—and he had. "I am as monstrous as our father."

"No, you are not." Monty leaned forward to say something else but stopped as Mrs. Camp whisked back into the room.

"Start on these, Your Grace and my lord." She placed two platters piled high with slices of plum cake, seed cakes, and Elias's favorite saffron cake. "Tea is next. The kettles on the hearth are almost ready." She set the table with cups, plates, and silverware, then rushed over to the hearth, poured steaming water into the teapot, and brought it to the table as well. Examining her work with a critical eye, she threw her hands in the air. "Milk, sugar, and honey. Where is my mind?" She dashed back into the pantry, then returned with those.

"Well done, Mrs. Camp." Monty filled his plate, then sat back out of the way as she poured his tea.

"You cannot have her," Elias said, knowing his brother's tactics.

Mrs. Camp went uncharacteristically silent with the praise, offered a pleased curtsy, then turned to the stove and started preparing the rest of the breakfast banquet she had promised. There would be no more privacy until she finished.

As Elias washed down a bite of cake with tea, he decided Monty was likely right about Celia's reaction if he told her of their plan before they married. In fact, she might even refuse marriage if she became the legitimate Duchess of Hasterton. He would not risk that. Celia would be his wife, and he would win her love again. Somehow.

CHAPTER FOURTEEN

"D R. MACMADDENLY IS such a charming man. Do you not think so?"

Celia looked up from the book she might as well put back on the shelf. All she could think about was Elias and their cruel bargain. "Forgive me, Mama. What did you say?"

Her mother smiled as she gently tugged a vibrant blue thread up through the body of a partially embroidered bluebird. "I think Dr. MacMaddenly is quite charming. Do you not find him so?"

The physician was a pompous, overly proud Scot, but Celia decided not to say that, since Mama appeared much improved under his care. "I find him very knowledgeable."

"Very knowledgeable?"

Celia turned the page she had read at least three times and still couldn't remember a word of. "Yes. Very knowledgeable. Your color is better than it has been for months, and your energy is increasing. We are very fortunate that Friedrich found the good doctor."

"Are you unwell?" Her mother lowered her needlework and studied Celia with a suspicious scowl.

"Unwell?" Celia asked. It was far better to repeat the question than answer it truthfully. Mama had no idea just how unwell she had been since confessing all their sins to Elias.

"You are never diplomatic, and you always repeat the question when you do not wish to answer it honestly." The duchess cast a disapproving look down her nose at Celia. "Why are you so distracted? Is it because Lord Raines has not called upon us for almost a week?"

Lord Raines hadn't called upon them because the man more than likely could not tolerate the sight of them. But Celia could not admit that either. Instead, she forced an indulgent expression. "He sent a note begging our forgiveness, remember?"

Her mother's eyes narrowed.

Celia clenched her teeth, belatedly remembering that Mama was not one to swallow a lie easily. To fool her required Herculean effort. It had been so long since Celia tried to trick her mother about anything that she had forgotten what a chore it was.

Resettling herself in the chair, she lifted her book as though aching to get back to it. "We cannot expect him to postpone a request from Prinny."

The duchess appeared to accept that answer. "As long as you know that in your heart." She leaned forward and lowered her voice. "There is not *something else* troubling you, is there?"

"Something else?"

"Stop repeating my questions!" The duchess smacked the chair arm with a hard spat.

"You are in a temper." Celia smiled. Her mother hadn't had the energy to be so ill-tempered in a very long while. "I honestly do not know what *something else* you are referring to. Forgive me for my ignorance."

"Flowers." The way the duchess drew out the word could only mean one thing. "After all, is it not nearing your *time* to bloom?"

"Rest assured, Mama, someday you will be a grandmother," Celia said. "But *not yet*."

Her mother seemed disappointed with that news and even reacted with a frustrated huff. "Did Lord Raines tell you when he would call again? After all, we must give the modiste a time to finish your gown."

"He did not say. I am sure he will call on us as soon as he can." Celia lifted her book again, determined to hide within its pages.

The loud clacking of the front door's brass knocker made her cringe. Deep down in her soul, she knew it was Elias. No, not Elias. It was her judge and executioner—and soon, her husband, who would bide his time and heaven only knew what else until he could be rid of her.

"Lord Raines," Gransdon announced as Elias joined them in the parlor.

Celia gritted her teeth and struggled to hold a pleased expression as Elias bowed to her mother, then turned and took her hands in his.

"You do forgive me for not calling until now, yes?" The sincerity in his voice almost crumbled her composure.

"Of course," she said over-brightly. Scolding herself for sounding false, she swallowed hard and resolved to do better. "One cannot put off the prince regent."

Elias's hopeful smile faltered and something akin to pain filled his eyes. Pain? How ridiculous. She had to be mistaken. It was more than likely his disgust for her that he was trying to hide.

She eased her hands out of his and motioned to the chair beside her mother. "Do sit. Gransdon already knows to bring tea."

"Yes, do," her mother told him. "Tell us about your doings for the prince regent."

Elias shook a finger at the duchess as he took a seat. "Now, now, Your Grace. Not everything can be shared—as much as I would like to. But I will say it does my heart good to find you enjoying an afternoon here in the parlor."

"Dr. MacMaddenly is a truly gifted physician." The duchess placed her needlework on the side table, rose from her chair, and, with arms aloft, slowly turned in a graceful circle. "I am well enough to dance at the next ball we attend."

Rising, Elias took her hand and bowed over it. "Wonderful

news! You will save me a spot on your dance card?"

Celia watched their byplay, her cheeks aching with her forced smile. When Elias held out his hand for her to join them, she bit the inside of her lip before standing and sliding her hand into his. "With Mama so recovered, I am sure her dance card will fill quite quickly."

He tugged Celia closer and made her knees weak with a smoldering gaze. "Ah yes, but surely she will save a dance for her daughter's future husband?" He turned and aimed the deadliness of his charm at the duchess. "Will you not, Your Grace?"

"But of course, my lord." The duchess patted his hand, then released it. "Do forgive me, but I just remembered some correspondence that I absolutely cannot allow to wait a moment longer."

"But your tea," Celia said, panicking at being left alone with Elias.

"I shall have Gransdon bring mine to my private sitting room." The duchess gave them a saucy wink. "And since the two of you are soon to be married, I will indulge you with an afternoon without a chaperone." She pointed at them both. "But I shall leave word with Gransdon that if anyone calls, I am to be fetched immediately to return before any visitors are let in—for appearance's sake."

"Before you go, Your Grace," Elias said. "I have the special license." He beamed an excited smile first at the duchess and then at Celia. "All we must do is name the day I can bring the clergyman to perform the ceremony."

Celia braced herself, determined not to sag to the floor and sob. Elias was quite a convincing actor. If only all this was real.

She almost snorted. The marriage would be real, or at least legal. But the love she had hoped to nurture and grow was gone.

Celia weakly fluttered a hand. "The modiste is finishing my gown. As soon as she is done, we can marry."

The duchess patted his arm. "Two days, dear boy. I shall tell the modiste we must have the gown in two days' time. Will that do?"

He turned to Celia. "What say you, my precious lioness? In two days' time, will you become my wife and make me the happiest man alive?"

"Yes," she said, frustrated that her voice was determined to quiver. When she made this damnable bargain, she'd had no idea how difficult it would be to carry it out. "Two days will be perfect."

"Celia?" Her mother reached for her hand and gave it a gentle squeeze. "I have never seen you so pale. Should you go up and rest?"

If she took the opportunity to escape, Mama would suspect something for certain. Celia shook her head. She had no choice but to stay. "I simply need a biscuit. All I took the time for at breakfast was a cup of chocolate."

The duchess appeared unconvinced but released her hand and turned back to Elias. She gave him a stern look. "Remember your oath, Lord Raines. See that she eats."

He bowed to the dowager. "I shall, Your Grace."

The duchess kissed Celia's cheek, then cast a knowing smile back at them as she left the parlor doors wide open.

Elias took Celia's hand before she realized what he intended. He gently tugged her over to the sofa. "Sit, Celia. Your mother is right. You are as pale as milk. Are you certain you are well?"

As she lowered herself to the seat, she snatched her hands out of his grasp. "Of course I am not well," she hissed after a glance at the doors. "I am finding our agreed-upon act quite difficult. But worry not, I shall conquer my weakness and play the part accordingly." She looked away, determined not to meet his gaze. She could not bear the revulsion she knew she would see there.

Gransdon entered with the tea and served them. "Will that be all, my lady?" he asked.

"Her Grace wishes to take her tea in her private sitting room, please." Celia sampled hers, wishing it was brandy.

"Yes, my lady. I shall see to it." The butler strode out and closed the doors that the duchess had previously left open.

"Shall I open them?" Elias asked quietly.

Celia lowered her cup to its saucer, clenching her teeth, as her trembling made the porcelain rattle. She set it on the table beside her, clutched her hands in her lap, and kept her gaze lowered. "Whatever you wish."

"I wish for you to be happy," he said softly. "But I fear that with me, you will never be."

She found both his tone and his words not only confusing but horrendously cruel. Was that his intent? To toy with her emotions the entire time they were together? To torment her all the way to the gallows? She pulled in a deep breath and released it, bracing herself for whatever he might say next. She focused on her hands in her lap.

"Can you ever forgive me, Celia?"

"Forgive you?" She eyed him, bracing herself for the lash of taunting words.

"I begged you to trust me, and when you did, I failed you." Elias touched her cheek with such excruciating tenderness that she shied away. "I am more sorry than you will ever know. Please try to find it in your heart to forgive me."

This had to be a terrible game. He was trying to trick her into letting down her guard again, so he could crush her hopes even harder. Like teasing a starving animal with the promise of food.

"Forgiveness was not a part of our bargain, my lord." She cleared her throat, damning herself for allowing her emotions to choke her. "Our terms were marriage, a peaceful goodbye to my mother, and then your freedom with my eventual imprisonment and hanging." She twitched a shrug. "And as I said before, I shall endeavor to become more convincing so everyone will believe we are genuine."

He leaned forward and peered up into her face. "I truly am begging your forgiveness for being such a callous fool. This is not some cruel trick. I would never do that. And I shall never have freedom from you, Celia. Nor do I ever want it. My heart will always be yours."

She finally lifted her gaze to his. "I do not believe you," she said. "And I never will."

"Then I shall spend the rest of my days trying to convince you of my sincerity." His expression was an unreadable mask, and his eyes were dark and swirling with shadows.

She ached to believe him but couldn't. This was a trap. He was the hound. She was the fox. And he was determined to punish her by ripping her heart to even smaller shreds. It was time to change the subject to something safer. Cold, hard details. She handled details much better than feelings. "Where shall we live once we marry?"

He studied her for a moment, then said, "Wherever you and your mother wish to live. I assumed your mother would live with us. Did I assume correctly?"

"Yes." Celia retrieved her cup but left the saucer on the table. Better to avoid the rattle. After a small sip, she set it back down. "If it is amenable to you, it would be easier for Mama to live here. She is doing quite well, but I am unsure how well she would weather another move. Even one as simple as to a different street in London."

"Then we shall live here." He sat there, staring at her so long that it made her skin crawl.

She forced herself to meet his stare with a cold, hard gaze. "What?"

"I would like to bring my staff here. My housekeeper, Mrs. Camp, her son Henry, and the maid, Sarah, have been with me for years. I haven't the heart to let them go."

"I did not realize your lordship had a heart." She probably should not have said that, but there it was.

His chiseled jaw hardened even more, and his nostrils flared. He bowed his head. "I deserved that and accept it fully."

"By all means, bring your staff here." Celia rose and went to the window overlooking the street, but saw nothing but her dismal future. "Mrs. Harcourt, our housekeeper, plans to leave us at the end of the week to care for her sister. Your Mrs. Camp can replace her."

The heat of him embraced her, warning of his presence directly behind her. The man moved as silently as the deadly predator that he was. "I believe you will like Mrs. Camp," he said. "She mothers everyone."

Celia didn't bother answering, just stared through the lacy curtains at the dreary day that perfectly mirrored her feelings.

Taking hold of her by the shoulders, Elias gently turned her, then took her hands in his and went down on one knee. "I beg your forgiveness, my precious one. I was a pompous, judgmental, cold-hearted bastard to you, and I will regret it for the rest of my life. Please, Celia. I do not say this to trick you or give you false hope. I say it because I love you, and I am ashamed of the way I behaved."

Her blasted tears slipped free no matter how hard she blinked to hold them back. "Damn!" She yanked her hands out of his and swiped at them.

Elias remained on his knee, looking up at her with such a convincing expression that she ached to drop onto the floor and dive into his arms. But she didn't. She could not trust him again. Not yet.

She sniffed and cleared her throat. "Forgive my language, my lord."

"I can forgive anything as long as you can find it in your heart to forgive me." Still on one knee, he slipped his hand inside his coat and pulled out the lock of hair she had given him. "I want this to symbolize our eternal union," he said. "Not that heartless bargain I should have shouted down rather than agreed to." He reached into his pocket again and drew out a dark blue velvet box. "For you, my lady. To mark the bargain I should have insisted upon. The uniting of our lives forever and a day."

Celia stared down at it, wanting so badly for everything he said to be real. Rather than take it, she pressed her hand to the base of her throat and willed her heart to stop pounding so hard and fast. "What is it?"

His mouth set in a hard line, Elias eased open the box's lid and held it out to her. "I had it made for you. Another reason I delayed my visit until today."

The necklace resting on the satin pillow inside the box took her breath away. Gold beadwork bordered the heart-shaped locket covered with delicately frosted grape leaves and tiny bunches of golden grapes. Draped across the widest part of the gold heart was a garland of gemstones.

"It is so beautiful," she said in a breathless whisper.

"The gemstones have meaning. The order they are in." Elias rose and pointed them out. "Ruby, emerald, garnet, aquamarine, ruby again, and diamond. Their first letters are an acrostic that spells REGARD. Regard means *to see* and also *love.* This locket means *I saw you and fell in love.*" He lifted it out of the box by its golden chain. "Inside is a lock of my hair and also part of the curl that you gave me." The longing in his eyes beseeched her to believe him.

She hurried to turn away, unready to face what she saw in his eyes. "Put it on me, please?"

"Gladly, my love." He placed it around her neck.

As his fingers brushed her nape, tingles shot through her, making her draw in a quick breath. After the locket fell in place between her breasts and warmed to her flesh, Elias pressed the tenderest of kisses to the back of her neck. "I love you, Celia," he whispered. "Please try to love me again."

"I want to," she said before she could stop herself. "But I am so afraid."

He gently turned her into his embrace. "I will never betray your trust again. Not ever."

She rested her hands on his chest and stared up at him, her darkly handsome panther, the man who could either uplift her or destroy her. "What about your firm? Your integrity as a solicitor?"

"That is not my greatest worry," he said softly.

"And what is your greatest worry?"

"Losing you forever."

"If this is not real—"

He silenced her with a kiss that sent her headlong into an overwhelming conflict of doubts and the aching need to be loved. His arms tightened around her, molding her against his hard, muscular body and making her yearn to sink into his embrace and never emerge again. He tasted of truth and sincerity, but above all, he tasted of danger. He knew all her secrets. Dare she forgive him and allow him access to her battered heart yet again?

"I love you," he rasped across her lips, breathing his emotions into her. "Love me again, Celia. Love me."

She caught his face between her hands and held him there, her mouth mere inches from his. Staring into his eyes, she willed him to understand. "I have never trusted easily. My survival and that of my mother depended on taking the greatest care. When I trusted you with not only our truth but my heart—"

He cupped her face between his hands just as she held his. "I know. All I can do is continue to beg you for forgiveness."

"No," she said, searching his eyes for the slightest hint of betrayal. "Do not beg. My forgiveness will be yours once I learn I can trust you again."

A hint of a smile tugged at the corner of his mouth. "Will you grant me the rest of your life to teach you?"

"For now," she said softly, then sealed the oath with another kiss.

The loud crack of the front door's knocker against the brass plate jolted them apart. Celia patted her hair and smoothed the wrinkles out of her dress. She rushed to the window and peered through the lace at the carriage in front of the house. "I am not familiar with that crest, are you?"

Elias joined her, then groaned. "Brace yourself, my lioness. It appears the esteemed Lady Bournebridge has come to call."

"Oh, good heavens. Mama finds that woman unbearable, and Lady Bournebridge is certain to be even more unpleasant since Mama not only missed her ball but also declined to attend the woman's Venetian breakfast." Celia caught Elias by the arm and tugged him toward the other end of the room. "That narrow door over there is a rather winding route to the kitchens, if you wish to escape."

"I will not leave you and your mother at the mercy of that woman." He ushered her back to her seat, then took his. "We are doing nothing more than having a pleasant visit over tea. Gransdon has surely gone to fetch your mother."

As soon as they settled into their chairs, the duchess rushed in through the narrow door Celia had just pointed out. "I cannot imagine why that woman is coming here." She shot an irritated glance at Gransdon where he waited at the double doors leading into the hallway and gave him a sharp nod. "I wish the ladies had waited to attend the Royal Academy's exhibition," she told Celia. "When meeting Lady Bournebridge, it is important to have ample allies present."

"Lady Bournebridge and her daughter, Lady Temperance," Gransdon announced, then stepped aside and bowed.

The two swept into the parlor, casting a critical eye all around as if the place might not be worthy of them. Elias rose to his feet but remained silent as Celia and her mother stepped forward to greet the unwelcome visitors.

"Lady Bournebridge, Lady Temperance, how good of you to call." The duchess gracefully directed their attention to Elias. "Allow me to introduce you to Lord Raines."

Lady Temperance curtsied, but her mother did not. Lady Bournebridge gave him an up-and-down scowl as if sizing him for a roasting pan. "Lord Raines, yes. He is my husband's solicitor." She granted him a tip of her head when he bowed.

"And this is my daughter, Lady Cecilia," the duchess continued.

"Your daughter?" Lady Bournebridge perked like a cat spotting a juicy mouse. "According to many at the Whitfields' gathering, this lovely young lady was Miss Celia Bening, your companion."

Celia bit the inside of her cheek so hard that she tasted blood. Before her mother could counter Lady Bournebridge's rather ineffective attack with a firm parry, she fluttered away the words as if they were a swarm of flies. "I would not consider the Whitfield party a reliable source for anything. Poor Mama fainted dead away from the overly crowded room and lack of sustenance to ease her." Before Lady Bournebridge could counterattack, Celia directed them to the sofa while the rest of them returned to their seats. "Do join us for tea. Gransdon will soon be in with additional settings."

After settling among the cushions like a fat, nesting hen, Lady Bournebridge turned to Celia's mother. "How dreadful for you at the party. Are you fully recovered now?"

"Oh yes, quite recovered," the duchess answered with a smugness that made Celia proud.

"Well, you know," Lady Bournebridge drawled, "I was quite concerned when you failed to attend my ball after confirming, and then when you declined the invitation to my Venetian breakfast, I was certain some terrible misunderstanding had arisen. I simply had to visit to ensure all was well."

"Quite well," the duchess said. "Traveling from Germany simply proved to be more taxing than I anticipated. Do forgive me for not easing your mind with a note of explanation."

Lady Bournebridge gave a rude, dismissive smirk. "Think nothing of it, Your Grace. You were clearly overtaxed by travel. Very understandable."

Gransdon and Friedrich entered with more tea and additional platters of cakes. They served the ladies with a quiet efficiency that had Lady Bournebridge and her daughter watching them as they left the room.

"Excellent servants are so hard to find of late." Lady Bournebridge sipped her tea as if testing it for poison. With a pained puckering of her mouth that left Celia wondering if the woman was about to choke, she turned back to the duchess. "This is my Temperance's first Season, and we have been very pleased so far." She slid a wicked glance Celia's way. "Everyone at the Whitfields' soiree must have thought your Cecilia a companion since she dressed so modestly, and has neither openly come out for the Season nor been presented at court."

Before her mother could respond, Celia laughed and leaned forward as though about to share the juiciest bit of gossip. "With this being my first visit to London since I was a child, I wanted to survey the hunting grounds before joining the fray." She took a slow sip of her tea and allowed herself a wicked smile. "I prefer to be the hound rather than the fox."

Lady Bournebridge stretched back as though Celia had slapped her. One of her spindly brows arched almost to her hairline. "I see," she said, then eyed Celia as she sipped her tea.

"And my Cecilia has already found love," the duchess said. With an affectionate smile, she held out her hand. "Lord Raines has asked for Cecilia's hand, and we have accepted."

Lady Temperance snorted and tittered a rude laugh, before making a show of modestly turning her face aside.

"Something wrong with your tea?" Celia asked while fighting the urge to lob her cup at the rat-faced little chit.

"My Temperance is quite delicate," Lady Bournebridge hurried to say. She fixed her daughter with a pointed look, then turned back to Celia and the duchess with the smugness of a professional thief. "She sometimes chokes if the temperature of the beverage isn't a suitable match or quite up to the standard which one would normally desire."

If the tea didn't choke the insufferable little ape leader and her mother, Celia would. How dare they sit there and openly insult Elias by implying he wasn't good enough for her to marry?

"Poor dear. Perhaps if she traveled more, her palate would be more able to recognize exemplary quality when it is presented— rather than judging a tea simply by its *title*," the duchess said, her tone dripping with sarcasm.

Touché, Mama. Celia politely hid her smile behind her cup.

Elias sat there openly grinning, obviously enjoying the entertainment.

"Perhaps we should go," Lady Bournebridge said, her expression sourer than usual. "We simply wished to call after that horrid incident at the Whitfields'." She set her tea on the table and gave an impatient flip of her hand at her daughter. "It is good to see you quite recovered and to learn no misunderstandings exist between us." With an imperious sneer that appeared to be meant as a smile, she nodded first at Elias, then at Celia. "And congratulations. Much happiness to you both."

"Thank you, Lady Bournebridge," Elias said with a mocking bow before taking Celia's hand and pressing a kiss to it. "And may Lady Temperance's hunt be as successful as my Celia's."

Lady Bournebridge's eyes flared wide, and Lady Temperance emitted a high-pitched yip as though someone had pinched her. "Good day to all," the lady haughtily said before they both stormed from the room.

"You have to marry now," Celia's mother said with a faint smile. "We shall probably read all about your engagement in tomorrow's gossip sheets."

"Good," Elias said with a proud jutting of his chin. "I want everyone to know."

Celia pressed a hand over the lovely golden locket and prayed he truly meant it—and that somehow, he would find a way to come to terms with her being the true Duke of Hasterton.

CHAPTER FIFTEEN

E LIAS RAN A finger behind the over-starched cravat that was about to strangle him. Mrs. Camp had outdone herself upon learning that today was to be the auspicious day of the wedding. She had cleaned, starched, and brushed his clothes within an inch of their lives, and clapped her approval when Monty presented him with an exquisite waistcoat whose pattern possessed a silvery sheen. Along with the new waistcoat came a fresh shirt of the finest linen adorned with the ruffled front and cuffs that he hated.

"You settled the vicar in the drawing room with the others?" he asked his brother while shrugging on the waistcoat.

"Yes. And he is still sober. So far." Monty stepped back and nodded his approval as Elias presented himself before donning his coat. "But I cannot guarantee for how long. After all, Reverend Neville has been retired for quite some time and enjoys his evening brandies immensely."

"Yes, but you said the man was a favorite of our mother and Father hated him." Elias smiled at his reflection in the mirror. "The perfect clergyman for this day."

"Mrs. Neville has promised to keep him focused and also brought their grandson, the newest vicar of our old parish, and his wife to ensure everything is properly recorded in the register."

Elias stopped tugging at his clothes and faced his brother. "And you are generous enough to house them for the night in your townhouse. Whatever in the world would I do without you, brother?"

"You would founder miserably." Monty frowned at Elias's cravat and adjusted it. "Gads, man. You should have allowed me to loan you Fords. He would have tied that thing properly." He threw up his hands as if there was no hope for it. "By the way, while I hate to impart bad news on this glorious day, you do realize the two of you have caused quite the stir. Polite Society does not appreciate a solicitor, even one as esteemed as yourself, snatching up one of its wealthiest darlings."

"I assumed there would be talk." Elias checked his timepiece, grinning at the memory of Celia and her mother giving no quarter to the odious Lady Bournebridge and her equally unpleasant daughter. Monty's unusually solemn expression gave him pause. "Out with it, man. I prefer to be forewarned."

"One displeased old dowry hunter, Lord Mabryton, approached me at the club to confirm the rumor, and two other drowning-in-debt lords mentioned it during the recess at yesterday's session." Monty's concerned scowl hardened even more. "I fear such discussions may cause issues when we bring the letters patent to Parliament."

"We shall have to bide our time, then. Wait for the *ton* to shift their attention elsewhere." Elias hated the thought of delaying their carefully plotted course. He wanted Celia legally safe and proclaimed the legitimate heir to the empire she and her mother had created.

Monty clapped him on the shoulder. "Forgive me. I should not have brought up such troublesome worries on today of all days." He adjusted the ruffles at Elias's wrist. "And all is well now between yourself and your lady love?"

"Not entirely well, but much improved." Elias offered a rueful look and sadly shook his head. "I have learned a painful lesson, brother. Trust must be earned over time, and once lost, it is even more difficult to reclaim."

He squared his shoulders, pulled his timepiece from his pocket, and checked it again. Almost time. An excited edginess filled him. The wagging tongues of the *ton* were right—Lady Cecilia was most definitely above his station. But no one could ever claim to love her more than he did.

"Mother's ring will bring you luck." Monty patted his pocket while admiring himself in the mirror.

"Are you quite certain you wish me to use it?" While he appreciated his brother's offer of their mother's ring, Elias couldn't help but feel undeserving of the honor. By rights, the ring should go to Monty's future wife—whenever the rogue decided to choose one.

"Absolutely, old boy." Monty smoothed back his hair, then turned toward the door with a curt nod. "I may never marry." He ushered Elias forward. "However, it is now time for you to do so."

Elias led the way, forcing himself to maintain a composed demeanor when he would much rather dash down to the drawing room and sweep Celia up into his arms.

When he and Monty stepped through the double doors of the room, a hint of disappointment filled him. His precious lioness had yet to descend from her suite. A subtle glance revealed everyone else was already seated and beaming with happiness. Lady Rydleshire and the dowager Marchioness of Ardsmere flanked the dowager duchess. Celia's chosen sisters, as she always fondly referred to them, Lady Sophie and Lady Ardsmere, excitedly perched on the edge of their seats closest to the drawing room doors.

The retired Reverend Neville, his wife, grandson, and grandson's wife lined up in front of the windows. They greeted Elias with happy nods, then returned their attention to the entrance flanked by a pair of large vases filled with sprays of ivy and delicate pink rosebuds just beginning to open.

An excited expectancy filled the room, but as each minute ticked away, the waiting took on a life of its own, changing into a worrisome uncertainty. The reverend cleared his throat and barely tipped an inquisitive nod in the duchess's direction.

"Nervous bride." The duchess leaned forward and eyed the doorway as if willing Celia to appear. "I feel sure she will join us soon." She resettled her clasped hands in her lap and looked to Lady Sophie. "Sophie, was she nearly ready when you left her?"

Lady Sophie gave a quick nod. "Yes, Your Grace. Lady Cecilia said she would be right down after she changed her shoes for the third time." She cast a congratulatory smile Elias's way. "She wanted everything to be perfect for her husband-to-be."

Perfection was one thing. This waiting was unnecessary torture. Elias resettled his stance and glanced toward the hallway again. Had she changed her mind? Decided to jilt him for revenge? No. Surely not. Her kisses and the wistfulness in her pale green eyes had confirmed her willingness to forgive and start again.

Monty cleared his throat, disappeared into the hallway briefly, then returned to his place beside Elias with a shake of his head. "No sign of her, brother," he said quietly.

Elias had had enough. "I'm going upstairs to see about her. Something is terribly wrong. I feel it." He exited the drawing room and charged up the stairs, taking the steps two at a time. A glance back told him Monty, Lady Sophie, and Lady Ardsmere followed, but he didn't slow. An increasing dread pounded through him, warning that all was not well.

He rapped on the door to her private sitting room, hitting it so hard it rattled the hinges. "Celia?" When only silence answered, he pushed inside, fears mounting higher at the emptiness he found within. He strode to the bedroom door and pounded on it. "Celia! Are you all right?"

Still no answer. He tried the latch and discovered it locked. "Celia! At least answer so I know you are not unwell."

"She was fine earlier, and quite excited," Lady Sophie called out from behind him.

"Something is wrong." Elias waved them off. "Stand back. I am breaking it down."

Monty shielded the ladies as he shuffled them away.

Fueled by a raging protectiveness he had never known before, Elias kicked the door open, splintering the frame and leaving it hanging by a single hinge. "Celia!" he bellowed as he surged into the room.

It was empty and entirely too disheveled for his liking. He turned to Lady Sophie, and his gut clenched with a certainty he wished he could deny. The young woman's pallor and wide eyes confirmed that the room had not been this way when she left Celia a short time ago.

"I want everyone in this household brought to the drawing room. Now. Every servant. Every guest. Every person who darkened the halls of this townhouse since we last saw Celia. No one is to leave this property under any circumstances."

"I shall see to it," Monty said. He nodded toward the exit. "Ladies, after you."

Elias carefully moved around the bedroom, then checked the dressing room, scrutinizing every detail. The curtains hanging from the frame of the four-poster bed were not neatly tied back, as would be usual for this time of day. At least, only one of them was. The other hung at an odd angle, as though almost yanked down. The windows were shut and would not be a feasible entry or exit from this height. And, as usual for London, it was raining. Neither the curtains nor the floors were the least bit wet. Whatever had become of Celia had originated from within the household, and from the state of the room, it had not happened with her consent. Fury set his blood boiling.

He examined the door latch closer, noting it could be locked from either side, but only with a key. Celia and the housekeeper should be the only persons in possession of one. A forlorn satin slipper of the palest pink lay on its side beside the shattered opening into the sitting room. He crouched beside it, clenching his jaw until it ached. One side of the precious shoe was frayed as though it had been dragged on the floor and treated roughly. A black mark stained the toe. He snatched it up and studied it closer. A pungency identified it. Shoe polish. With a rub of his thumb, the mark smeared across the material. Whoever had taken Celia had just polished their boots or shoes.

With the dainty shoe in hand, he stormed downstairs and strode into the drawing room. All eyes turned to him. He showed the slipper to Lady Sophie. "Was she wearing this when you left her?"

Her eyes filling with tears, Lady Sophie clutched a handkerchief to her mouth and sobbed. Confirmation enough for Elias.

"Who has taken my baby?" Duchess Thea's enraged wail cut through the room. She stamped her gleaming cane hard against the floor as she thundered toward the servants. "Who has come into this house and betrayed me? Who dared hurt my Celia?"

Gransdon turned and glowered down the line of those assigned to keep the household in order. "You will each give Her Grace an account of yourselves throughout this day," he growled. "Every moment up until this very last minute!"

With a furious scowl, Mrs. Camp turned, tugged her Henry out of the way, and glared at the wide-eyed maids, footmen, gardener, and cook. "Where are the grooms and coachman?" she asked.

Elias stepped forward, weighing their expressions, noting their nervous shuffling in place. It hit him that one very familiar face was missing. "Where is Friedrich?"

The duchess whacked her cane against the wall, appearing ready to beat the information out of some unlucky soul. "Where is he?"

Gransdon stepped out of line again and paced back and forth in front of the other servants. He stopped in front of the footman named Reginald and jabbed a finger at him. "You were with Friedrich earlier, setting up extra seating in the dining room and removing the dividing wall between the parlor and anteroom. Where is he?"

The tall, spindly young man stood there, opening and closing his mouth like a fish out of water. "Not certain, Mr. Gransdon. Last I saw of him, he had gone to fetch another table from storage. Told me to finish up here in the drawing room and that he would tidy up the rest." He proffered a nervous bow to the duchess. "I swear, Your Grace. That was last I saw of him, and I been nowhere near Lady Cecilia all day." He shook his head so hard that he stumbled sideways. "I would never hurt her ladyship, Your Grace. Not for no amount of money."

"Money," Elias repeated. That had to be what this was about. "I want the man found, and I want the Bow Street Runners sent for. Ask for Jack Portney."

"And Thomas Elkin," the duchess added. She whacked her cane against the wall again. "Do it now!"

Mrs. Camp shoved Henry toward the door. After the boy bobbed his head at Elias, he took off like a shot.

Elias turned to Monty. "Have your coachman get with the grooms to search the stable and check for missing horses."

"I can show you the shorter way, Your Grace." Reginald stepped forward and waited for permission to do so.

Elias waved him on, and Monty rushed out after the footman, heading toward the back of the house.

"You. Gardener. Your name?" Elias pointed at the older gentleman clutching his hat and work gloves against his middle.

"Abraham, my lord. Abraham Mulderny."

"It is my understanding that Friedrich helped you with certain areas of the garden. Is that true?" Elias moved closer, glaring at the man who seemed either unwilling or unable to look him in the eye. "You would do well to answer honestly. I have no patience whatsoever at the moment."

The man bobbed his head, then nervously scrubbed a gnarled hand across his sparse tufts of white hair. "That Friedrich boy built that there waterfall in the corner where it stayed too wet for anything to grow." He twisted his hat and gloves as if trying to wring them out. "But that was all. That one there—" He shook his head and looked ready to spit. "That one didn't much care for digging in the dirt or planting. Just wanted to build stuff that ain't never been done afore so he could tell you how smart he was.

Awful braggart, he was."

So the man probably not only wanted money but also crowing rights about what he had done. Elias turned to the duchess. "How long has Friedrich been in your employ?"

"Years." The duchess frowned with a faraway look in her narrowing eyes. "At least five or more. He was with us in Germany and—"

Elias held up a hand and stopped her. "We should speak in private, Your Grace."

She nodded and turned to the ladies who seemed to Elias to be a great deal more to the duchess and Celia than mere friends. "You know I trust you, my dearest sisters, but please avail yourselves of the food in the dining room." A shuddering breath left her as she appeared to be struggling to maintain her composure. "We must all keep up our strength for when we find Celia and can proceed with the ceremony."

Reverend Neville and his wife came forward, sympathy filling their faces. "We shall pray for Lady Cecilia's quick and safe return, Your Grace," he said. They turned in unison to Elias. "Have faith, my lord. Your lady will be found."

Damn right she would be, but Elias didn't speak the vow aloud. He gave a perfunctory nod, then offered his arm to the duchess. "The library or the parlor, Your Grace?"

"Library." She took his arm and marked each of their steps with a hard *ping* of her cane against the marble floor of the hallway.

Strangely enough, the maids had lit the candles in the room. While Elias found that somewhat odd, he decided to check into it later. At the moment, finding Celia was all that mattered.

He led the duchess to one of the more comfortable chairs in front of the hearth, helped her settle into the seat, then crossed back to the door and closed it. "I need a drink, Your Grace. Would you like one?"

"Most definitely," she said with a flick of her hand in the direction of the liquor cabinet. "Do help yourself, Lord Raines, and do not give me cause to accuse you of a stingy pour."

As Elias poured a generous brandy for them both, he tossed a concerned look at her back over his shoulder. "Should we send for Dr. MacMaddenly?"

Her eyes flared with alarm as she pressed a trembling hand to the base of her throat. "Do you fear Celia harmed?" Her voice broke, making Elias wish he had phrased the question in a more considerate manner. The woman had a bad heart and was tormented enough as it was.

"I do not fear Celia has been harmed," he said, hoping that was true. "My concern was for you, Your Grace. This situation does not promote a healthy state for anyone—much less someone with a weakness of the heart."

With a tight-jawed nod, the duchess accepted her drink from him and also seemed to accept his explanation. "We can send for Ian once the Bow Street Runners arrive. I do not wish to send anyone else out of the household until we have thoroughly questioned them as to their whereabouts, and what they might know about Friedrich's disappearance as well."

Ian? Elias noted the duchess's intimate use of the physician's first name but chose not to mention it. That was none of his affair, and now was not the time to put his interest where it didn't belong. All that mattered was finding Celia. He settled in the chair beside the dowager, wishing he had poured himself a whisky instead of brandy. "You said Friedrich had been with you for over five years. In Germany?"

"Yes. At least that many. Likely more." She kept her gaze locked on the hearth, as though mesmerized by the glowing coals of the dwindling fire. "Mrs. Thacker, our housekeeper there, recommended him after he lost his entire family to consumption. Celia felt quite bad for him, and so did I. We both believed him to be close to her age, but according to Mrs. Thacker, he was much older—at least ten years or more. As an act of charity, we chose to give him a chance to prove himself." She slowly shook her head without taking her focus from the fire. "It would seem that no good deed goes unpunished, and misplaced trust is quite deadly."

Elias shifted in the seat, wondering how much she knew of his and Celia's trust issues, but now was not the time for that discussion. "How much does he know?" he asked quietly.

The duchess sipped her drink, then released a heavy sigh. "Servants tend to know a great deal more than we wish for them to," she said. "That is why Celia and I always made a point of paying them well for their loyalty." She locked eyes with him. "I fear he knows enough to force us to pay for his silence in exchange for Celia's safe return."

"Before I allow him to compromise Celia's safety or yours—I will kill him."

"Good." The duchess lifted her glass in a toast. "I want my precious Celia back. No matter the cost."

A light knock on the door made Elias turn. "Enter."

Monty strode in with Jack Portney and Thomas Elkin, the two best Bow Street Runners, following in his wake. "The grooms report no horses missing. I've set them and our coachmen into combing the stables, grounds, and attached alleyways." He nodded at the two Runners. "Forgive the interruption, but I felt sure you would wish to speak to these gentlemen immediately."

"Indeed, we do." Elias turned back to the duchess. "I trust Henry. Shall I send him for the doctor now?"

The dowager's troubled scowl turned almost thoughtful and definitely calculating. She shook her head. "No. Now that I have thought more about it, Friedrich was the one who fetched Dr. MacMaddenly the night I collapsed. Until we are certain his finding the physician was a completely innocent happenstance, I do not wish for the man to be brought back into this household and be made aware of anything he doesn't already know. My trust in anyone connected to Friedrich runs quite thin at the moment."

Elias was beginning to understand how this shrewd woman

had successfully pulled off such an intricate charade for so many years. "As you wish, Your Grace." He rose to his feet, too knotted up with damned helplessness to sit any longer. The unknown tormented him. Was Celia alive? Was she injured? What had Friedrich done to her?

"You feel certain the footman took her?" Mr. Elkin asked the duchess.

"He is the only one in the household who did not report to the drawing room when called. Why else would he go missing at the same time that Celia disappeared from her bedroom?" The duchess turned back to the coals in the hearth, staring at them as if hoping to summon Celia into the library. "No one else could have taken her," she said, almost growling out the words. "Because of my health, Celia and I have not exactly taken London by storm, and only our closest friends are here with us today." She huffed a bitter snort. "I doubt very much the retired vicar and his family would even conceive of such a cruel kidnapping."

"Friedrich seemed overprotective for a footman," Elias said, more to her than the Runners. "I bloodied the man's nose once when he burst in on a rather loud conversation between myself and Celia. Has he always been that way?"

The duchess resettled her grip on her cane's ornately decorated handle, making her knuckles whiten with the effort. "Friedrich was always protective of us both." Her mouth flattened into a hard line. "I once considered that a blessing. But now it appears to have turned into a curse."

"Are you aware of any jib doors in the home, Your Grace?" Mr. Portney asked. When the duchess shook her head, then closed her eyes as though in dire need of silence, he turned to Elias. "Your brother said Lady Cecilia was last seen in her private suite. If there is a jib door in one of them, that would explain how the footman got hold of her with no one's notice. Might even give us a clue where he took her, since they're on foot—what with no horses or carriages being gone."

"And on such a stormy evening," Mr. Elkin interjected, "if he took to the streets with her, there would be few people to notice and far too many shadows he could put to good use. I shall send for more men to aid in the search. We must cover this area as quickly as possible. Time is of the essence."

Elias crouched beside the duchess, loath to plague her with more questions but knowing it had to be done. "Forgive me, Your Grace, but do you know if any of the townhouse's construction floor plans or drafts might still be here in the library? Master Hodgely said your husband commissioned this home to be built as a wedding present. Would he have kept the plans?"

She lifted her head and frowned at the memory. "Edmund would have kept them. But I have no idea where they might be." She closed her eyes again, but a tear slipped free and rolled down her cheek. "Celia would know. This room was her haven."

Elias flagged Monty over. "Her Grace needs comfort that I fear we men cannot give her. Would you be good enough to see her into the dining room? Her ladies are there. They will take far better care of her than we can."

With a gentle nod, Monty bent and whispered something in the duchess's ear that somehow drew a teary-eyed smile from her. She allowed him to help her to her feet and tuck her hand into the crook of his arm. Before moving to the door, she looked at Elias. "You will keep me *fully* informed?"

"I swear it, Your Grace."

She drew herself up as if gathering every last shred of courage she possessed. "Very good. I shall be in the dining room."

As soon as the door clicked shut behind them, Elias turned back to the Bow Street Runners. "Lady Cecilia has to be alive. How else could the man get a ransom?"

The men's grim expressions offered him no comfort.

Mr. Portney ambled over to a cabinet that held at least a dozen or more narrow drawers—the sort of drawers that might hold collections of maps or large papers. "It depends on his intentions," he said. "Or if he's gone mad."

"That is why we must work fast." Mr. Elkins took the candle

from the desk over to the unusual cabinet and held it above each drawer as Mr. Portney pulled them open. While thumbing through what turned out to be a collection of useless maps, he paused and scowled at Elias. "Do you have any notion how long the man was with them?"

"Over five years." Elias lit another candle and headed for the door. "Send Henry for the additional men," he told Mr. Portney. "I trust him. And in the meantime, I shall be upstairs, searching Lady Cecilia's rooms again. The bastard has to have hidden her here on the premises. In this part of town, it would be too difficult to take her anywhere else without someone noticing."

Without waiting for a response, he shielded the candle's flame and hurried up the stairs. The storm's gloom and the evening hours had brought a bleakness with them. Long, cold shadows shrouded everything. When he reached Celia's sitting room, he lit every precious beeswax candle he could find. Damn the cost of them. He needed light, and prayed that wherever his Celia was, she had light too and was unharmed.

He walked around the perimeter of the room, running his hand along the walls. What he couldn't see, he would feel. The slightest bump or space would reveal what he sought—the hidden door the devil had used.

Disappointment churned along with his building frustration, as the space held no secrets to share.

Then he remembered the locked bedroom door. Either the bedroom or her dressing room had to possess a way to a concealed passage. It made sense. Many townhouses contained such an arrangement so the servants could move about and tend to their duties with as little bother to their employers as possible, unseen and unheard as they carried out their master or mistress's every whim.

The bedroom walls proved as solid and unyielding as the adjoining sitting room. He lit a fresh candle and headed for the dressing room but halted before passing through the door. Was that a poorly matched seam in the vibrant blue and white willow tree pattern decorating the walls above the solid white wainscoting?

Bringing the light closer, he discovered the seam perfectly met where the wood panels abutted each other. This was the door. He shoved against it. It gave the slightest bit but failed to open into the space on the other side. Friedrich had either blocked it or the thing had jammed. Or perhaps, rather than swing into the space, it somehow opened out into the room and could then be pulled shut again from inside the passage.

With a careful, bouncing shove, the jib door clicked, then opened enough to be pulled out the rest of the way.

He entered the musty space and paused, listening for the slightest hint of a sound. Holding the candle high, he noted it was in fact a passage and not merely extra storage or a priest hole for safe hiding. In white paint that had dripped and run down the wall was a circle with a cross extending out of its bottom rim. Friedrich had marked the door with the gender symbol for the female. Apparently, the footman was more educated than he let anyone know.

Elias crouched and shined the light on the floor. Scuffed marks cut through the dust, creating fresh tracks that revealed the bastard had gone this way. No one had used the passage until recently—until Friedrich.

Elias straightened and stared into the darkness the lone candle fought to illuminate. He needed a weapon before he gave chase. A frustrated huff escaped him. His double-barrel flintlock, a gift from a slightly dubious client, had yet to be moved to the townhouse, since he had not thought to need it anytime soon. He strode back into the bedroom in search of something else to use for defense besides his fists.

The iron poker on the hearth held promise. He snatched it up and rushed back into the passage. His Celia would be back in his arms before this day ended.

CHAPTER SIXTEEN

CELIA BIT HARDER into the cloth knotted between her teeth. Out of breath from kicking, thrashing, and trying to scream through the gag, she glowered at Friedrich. She took great pride in the deep, bloody scratches she had raked down his face, and only wished she had clawed him more. It was her sincerest hope his wounds would be clearly visible from the gallows, so all would know that Lady Cecilia Tuttcliffe relinquished nothing without a fight.

The sorry blackguard had the audacity to wink at her. "Our children will be fierce." He hooked a finger in a jug and drank before stowing it back into the shadows at the foot of the cot he had unceremoniously dumped her on, then lashed her to when she tried to escape.

"As soon as you see reason, I will remove the ropes and gag." He scooted a short barrel closer to the wooden crate beside the bed and sat on it. A sputtering tallow candle gave out very little light in the tight, dingy space that looked as though it had been carved out of the earth with a spade. It had to be a root cellar or some such storage, considering it had a wooden door embedded in the wall between a pair of massive timber braces.

"All your money will be mine, and you will too." He thumped his chest and smiled. "The wife I deserve. I will be the real duke instead of that fairytale man you and your mother made up."

Was he actually that great of a fool? To think he would become the duke by marrying her? Celia looked away. She couldn't stand the sight of the vile scrub any longer. At least he had allowed her to sit with her back against the wall before lashing her wrists to the cot's corners.

And thankfully, he had wound the rope over her legs and under the cot, starting at the ankles and securing it all the way up to her waist before knotting it to the frame. She sent up a silent prayer of thanks that he appeared to have no intention of forcing himself upon her.

She almost gagged at the thought. Bile rose and burned in the back of her throat, which was already raw from trying to make herself heard through the gag. A scuffling sound, like the scratching of tiny claws somewhere in the shadows, made her draw into herself as much as the ropes allowed.

"Rats." Friedrich tore a strip of cloth from the hem of his shirt, wet it with whatever liquid the jug held, and dabbed it against his bleeding face. From the way he cringed, the container contained some form of alcohol.

She hoped it burned like the dickens. "I hate you!" she slowly forced through the gag, exaggerating every syllable so he couldn't fail to understand her.

The fool laughed. He pulled a long-bladed dagger from his boot and threw it at the dirt floor in some sort of ridiculous, repetitious game. "You will learn to love me as I love you." He retrieved the blade then pointed it at her. "I have loved you since I first saw you all those years ago." He threw out his chest. "You should thank me. I protect you now from a man unworthy of you." His expression shifted to one that gave her chills. "You will either share your wealth and learn to love me as your husband, or I will have you hanged for..." He frowned as though unable to remember the word. "Fraud," he said with a victorious dip of his chin. "Yes. That is what he shouted at you that day when I tried to save you, and you sent me away instead of him."

She fixed him with a narrow-eyed glare. She would die in this hole or at the end of a rope before she gave herself to this mad devil.

He returned to throwing his knife to make it stick straight up in the ground. "You will discover I am a patient man," he said. "I can wait as long as it takes for you to realize I am the one for you. My father taught me that women never know what is best until a man shows them." He nodded and threw his knife again. "You will see."

Celia turned her face away from him again. The greasy smoke of the sputtering candle gave her an idea. Friedrich claimed to love her. If he truly did, in his own irrational way, then surely he would remove the gag if she acted as though she were choking. Then if she lied and agreed to marry him, he would bring her up out of this hole, and she could make her escape. Or scream. Or both. Whatever it took to help Elias come to her rescue.

Because Elias would save her. She knew that with every fiber of her being. Her only concern was *how* Friedrich intended to marry her. What if the crazed fool thought committing the carnal act would make them husband and wife? She shuddered at that possibility.

"You are cold?" Friedrich rose. The low ceiling of the dank room forced him to bend slightly. He unrolled a blanket from the foot of the bed and tucked it up around her shoulders. "Better?"

She closed her eyes and turned her face away, frustration making her grind her teeth harder into the cloth.

"You are stubborn." Taking hold of her chin, he forced her to face him. "I am more stubborn. We will stay here as long as it takes."

Celia silently damned him to the hottest level of hell.

Friedrich pried open the small keg he had used as a seat and pulled out a cloth sack. From its depths, he pulled a half-eaten crust of bread that he must have rescued from the scrap bin. He wafted it under her nose. "You do not eat or drink until you are my wife. Understand?"

She glared at him, refusing him the satisfaction of the slightest reaction.

"Understand?" he bellowed mere inches from her face.

She still didn't react, refusing to even blink even though her eyes burned with the need to do so.

"You are mine!" he shouted again. His hot breath reeked, but she refused to give him the satisfaction of turning away.

A thunderous crash and the splintering of wood seemed to shake the room. Elias's enraged roar as he plowed into their midst shook the space harder.

Celia's heart leapt as he brandished an iron rod like the mightiest of swords.

Friedrich recovered entirely too quickly, dodging and lunging while slashing his knife at Elias. The low ceiling and close confines hindered both of the tall, muscular men.

Cringing and ducking as much as her bonds allowed, Celia braced herself. One or both of them could easily land on her. She yanked at her bonds until her wrists burned and felt wet with a warm stickiness that had to be blood. She didn't care. Unladylike or not, she champed at the bit to join the battle and punish the beastly Friedrich for not only ruining her wedding day but also for ruining her new dress and satin slippers.

Elias slammed the iron rod hard across the crazed footman's arm.

Friedrich grunted with the pain and staggered back. With his wounded arm tucked against his chest, he shifted his hold on the long-bladed dagger and stabbed and slashed with abandon.

"You will die for this!" Elias roared with a resounding swing of the iron that caught Friedrich in his side.

The footman flung himself across Celia. He held the knife high as though ready to end her. "She either lives with me or dies with me," he growled.

Elias went still and backed up. "If you hurt her…"

"What?" Friedrich spat at him. "What will you do? You cannot talk yourself out of this one, Englishman. She is either mine or she is dead. I offer no other option."

Deafening gunfire exploded from the doorway. "I prefer my option," Monty said, then fired again. "No one torments my brother or those he loves."

Pinned beneath Friedrich's crushing weight, Celia struggled to breathe as he held the knife raised above her as though determined to live until he carried through his threat. His only movement was the slightest tremor that traveled through her. She felt the disgusting warmth of his blood soaking into her gown.

He slowly shifted his crazed scowl from Elias to her, bared his teeth, then forced out, "I meant what I said," before slashing downward.

The searing burn made her throw back her head and sob a muffled cry through the gag.

"Celia!" Elias dove onto Friedrich and dragged the man off her.

She heard a sickening gurgle and then blessed silence. Silence had to be good. It had to mean Elias had prevailed. She lifted her head and opened her eyes to his terrified gaze.

"My beloved lioness," he breathlessly repeated over and over while tearing away the damnable gag. "Fetch the doctor," he shouted while sawing at her bonds with the very knife that had caused her so much pain. At least, she thought it was the same knife. Perhaps not. From the terrible burning and warm wetness covering her chest, the blade might still be in her.

"I knew you would come," she said, hoping he could hear her. A loud roaring in her ears made it hard to tell how loud she was talking.

"I was going to find you if I had to tear London apart brick by brick."

"Am I going to die?" She closed her eyes. It took so much effort to breathe through the hurting, she had no strength left to keep her eyes open. The thought of dying angered her. She had spent all her life alone, living a sham and allowing no one near her to protect the charade. She didn't want to die that way too. Elias had broken her heart at first. But now… "Promise we will marry before I die."

"You will not die," he said, his deep voice stern but as warm and comforting as his embrace. "I forbid it, Celia. Absolutely forbid it."

"Promise we will marry as soon as you get me out of this hole." If he would promise her that, this horrid pain would be so much easier to bear.

"I swear it, my precious one." He gently slid his arms under her shoulders and legs. "Hold fast, my love. I know moving will cause you more pain, but I must get you to your room."

"And then we will marry," she said through a cry of pain as he lifted her. "Before the doctor does anything. Before I die." His arms tightened around her, and the tender brush of his kiss across her forehead made her cry. "Promise me," she whispered through the burning ache that pounded through her with every beat of her heart.

"I promise, my love. Only a little farther and we will be back in your bedroom."

Celia pressed her face against his throat and concentrated on his reassuring scent of citrus, bergamot, and amber. The clean, sharp, yet sultry notes always took her back to the garden. The feel of his skin against hers. His heat of him as he rose above her, then joined with her, branding her with his delicious scent.

Worse pain shot through her as he kicked the door open and stepped into her bedroom. "I may be sick," she warned. Her head spun and her stomach churned—and all the while her chest burned as though hot coals were piled upon her.

"Here is your bed, my love." Elias gently lowered her onto the pillows, then kissed her forehead again. "Hold fast, my courageous one." He held her hand tightly, then shifted beside her.

Biting her lip against the terrible aching, she cracked open one eye. "Send for everyone so we can marry." She could no longer make out his face. Everything was so dark and blurry. "And light more candles, please. It is so dark—and cold." She let her eyes close again and vaguely sensed something falling across her.

"A blanket, my love," Elias whispered, brushing his lips against her cheek. "Monty is fetching everyone. I do not mean to cause you more pain again, but I need to change the cloth on your wound and check the bleeding."

"Change it?" She puzzled over his wording. To change it meant he had already used a compress on it. Had she blacked out and not realized it?

At a resurgence of pain, as though the wound had a cruel personality of its own and had gotten its second wind, a hitching groan escaped her. "Damn," she said. After the past few hours, she had the right to such profanity, and dared anyone to deny it.

"My Celia!"

"Mama." Celia smiled and breathed easier. "Is the reverend here too?"

"Yes, my darling, but you do not have my permission to die. Do you understand?" her mother said through a soft sob. "We can have the ceremony once you heal. Dr. MacMaddenly is on his way."

"Now," Celia whispered. "I do not want to die alone, and Elias promised."

Muffled whisperings swirled around her, but she dared not risk opening her eyes. She needed to conserve her energy for the vows.

"Elias?"

"I am here, my love."

The warmth of his hand cradling hers as he sat on the bed beside her brought her comfort. "Tell the vicar to get on with it," she said, trying to sound stern but failing miserably.

"Reverend Neville?" Elias gently squeezed her hand, then kissed it. "The briefest ceremony possible, if you please."

"Do you, Cecilia Elizabeth Madeline Rose Bening Tuttcliffe,

take Elias Raines to be your lawfully wedded husband until death shall part you?" asked a man whose voice Celia didn't recognize.

"I do," she said, hoping everyone could hear her. The roaring in her ears seemed to get louder.

"And do you, Elias Raines, take Cecilia Elizabeth Madeline Rose Bening Tuttcliffe to be your lawfully wedded wife until death do you part?" asked the same voice.

"I do. And even beyond death, because she will never have my permission to leave me." Elias's mouth was so close to her cheek that his warm breath tickled across her.

Celia smiled as something slid onto her finger. A ring. Perhaps she would look at it later when she had less pain distracting her. And if she didn't live to see it. Maybe her spirit could tarry long enough to glimpse it.

"I now pronounce you man and wife," the reverend said, suddenly seeming in a greater hurry. "Let no man attempt to part that which God has joined. Kiss your bride, my lord, and then have her mark the register as best she can."

"I love you, Celia. The doctor has arrived. Promise me you will fight to live." Elias barely brushed his mouth across hers, and she vaguely became aware of a quill between her fingers.

"I love you, Elias. Help me mark the register. I don't have the strength to open my eyes." Her hand moved, then the quill went away, and her arm was once again at her side. "Tell Mama I am sorry, and that I love her."

"There is nothing to be sorry for," her mother said, her voice sounding far away.

"Everyone out," Dr. MacMaddenly said. "Now!"

At least, she thought it was the rude Scot barking like an angry dog beside her bed. But it didn't really matter now. She was not alone anymore. She sank into the darkness knowing that she was Mrs. Elias Raines.

ELIAS KEPT HIS gaze locked on the slow, steady rise and fall of Celia's bandaged chest, smiling at the realization that his breathing had matched itself with hers. He closed his eyes and sent up another prayer of thanks that she had survived the terrible ordeal. He had feared her doomed because of all the blood. But Dr. MacMaddenly had approved of the wound bleeding so much. The arrogant Scot had informed him that her bleeding cleansed the wound better than any splash of whisky could. Praise God that the deepest part of the stabbing slash was closer to Celia's shoulder than her heart or lungs.

He opened his eyes and smiled at his precious bride, his fearless lioness. Even though her wound had required quite a bit of stitching, the doctor seemed certain she would recover with no lasting effects. Even so, the physician had accepted the offer of a room for the night.

Elias shifted with a silent huff of amusement at that. He had caught the gruff old Scot glancing at the dowager duchess with a tenderness that had nothing to do with medicine. Elias would wager his favorite horse that the good doctor had fallen completely under the dowager's spell.

He leaned over the bed and pressed the backs of his fingers to Celia's forehead and couldn't help but smile. He too was helpless against the Hasterton women. Especially this one. Celia's cool, silken skin pleased him to no end. No fever meant no infection. Elias prayed it stayed that way.

The quietest scratching on the bedroom door drew his attention. After a glance at Celia's peaceful countenance, he went to the door and cracked it open.

Monty motioned for him to come out and join him in the sitting room.

"What is it?" Elias whispered. "When she awakes, I do not wish her to be alone." He opened the door wider and straddled the threshold to keep an ear tuned to his precious Celia.

"I have an idea." Monty's smug grin reminded Elias of when they were boys, and Monty was about to throw Father into a rage with his antics.

Elias folded his arms and leaned back against the doorframe, keeping an ear perked for any sounds from within. "An idea?" he prompted, almost dreading to hear the answer.

Monty rubbed his hands together as if he had just won a large sum at the tables. "We have a body now."

"What?" Elias blinked hard, trying to relieve the burning weariness plaguing his eyes and muddling his brain.

"Friedrich wanted to be a peer. I say we let him. He can be the murdered Duke of Hasterton." Monty's smug grin became a blinding smile. "And since the poor duke was pummeled and shot by highwaymen while rushing to his mother's side after learning of the attack on his sister by a nefarious blackguard outside Vauxhall Gardens, having his body laid out for viewing before the burial is out of the question." He arched both brows, as though so proud he was about to pop. "We can send for a funeral furnisher immediately." He cleared his throat and lowered his voice. "And pray do not take offense, but I took the liberty of having Henry and Reginald move Friedrich to a spare bedroom. After all, the funeral furnisher would not expect to find the body of a duke down in the root cellar."

Elias glanced back into the bedroom, eyed Celia long enough to ensure she was still resting peacefully, then quietly stepped fully into the sitting room and closed the door—firmly. He turned to his brother, still trying to process the mad scheme Monty had proposed. "Are you dicked in the nob?" he finally asked.

Monty hung his hands on his lapels as if slightly insulted. "I assure you I am quite sane, and if you think about it, this provides the perfect opportunity to hurry the patent before Parliament. If we propose the amending at the same time that the duke's death is announced and also ensure that the story of his murder, as well as Lady Cecilia's terrible attack, is properly spread through the *ton*, the amendment will pass quickly because of sympathy for the duchess and her daughter."

"And how are we to explain all this not only to the Bow

Street Runners but also to Dr. MacMaddenly? The more actors we include in this theatrical scheme, the greater the danger. Might I offer Friedrich's actions as a case in point?" Elias fixed his brother with a superior look, almost dreading what an extraordinarily illegal and immoral farce Monty might come up with next. Had his sibling always been this devious?

"Let me handle everything," Monty assured him. "I am thinking the less you know, the better." He took hold of Elias by the shoulders and aimed him at the bedroom door. "Back to your bride. Hurry, now. You don't wish her to awaken without you." He gently nudged his brother forward while easing open the door.

Elias cast a disgruntled look back at Monty, then decided he was too weary to fight it. If his brother believed the scheme would work, then perhaps it would. He was merely thankful Monty was an ally and not an enemy.

A weak "Elias?" made him toss those thoughts aside, and he rushed to Celia.

"My love," he said, then gently scooped up her hand and kissed it while trying not to jostle her.

She gave him a sleepy smile. "Why do I feel so very heavy and...slow?"

"Dr. MacMaddenly got a generous dose of laudanum down you before you completely blacked out. I am sure it's the effects of the drug. He said when you awoke, if the pain was too great to bear, you could have more. There is no need for you to suffer any more than you already have." He pulled his chair as close as he could and sat while still holding her hand. "Do you wish for another dose?"

She eyed him with a sleepy gaze, then the slightest pucker appeared between her brows. "No. I do not care for this feeling at all, and I can bear the pain so far." She slowly lifted her hand as though to touch her face but stopped partway and stared at the ring on her finger. "Oh my. It is so beautiful," she said in the softest whisper, then blessed him with a loving smile. "So marrying you wasn't just a dream?"

"It was not, Mrs. Raines." He reverently touched the small, round aquamarine gemstone surrounded by tiny pearls in the gold setting. "This was my mother's ring. Monty said it would bring us luck."

"I shall properly thank him when next I see him." She grimaced and shut her eyes tightly while slightly arching her back.

"Celia?" He jumped up and hovered over her, panic thrumming through him.

She eased in a deep breath and, just as carefully, let it ease back out before relaxing back into the pillows. She opened her eyes and looked surprised to see him hanging above her. "A shooting pain caught me off guard, but I think it's settled now, and I can bear it. Are you always going to be so dramatic?"

"I have the right to show ample concern about my wife." He settled back onto the edge of his seat, then huffed a disgruntled snort. "Dramatic. Indeed."

"And now you intend to pout?" She seemed to try a frown, but amusement still sparkled in her eyes. "I do not believe I have seen this side of you before."

Allowing himself a sheepish grin, he lifted her hand again and hugged it to his cheek. "I was so afraid I had lost you—again."

"I knew you would come," she said softly, then looked away. "Deep down, I wondered if I would ever fully trust you again." She turned back to him and smiled. "I now know that answer, without a doubt."

He stared at her, struck mute with thankfulness.

"Elias?"

"Yes, my love?"

"Come to bed, will you?" She gently touched his cheek and coaxed him with a faint smile. "After all, it is our wedding night, and you seem so very weary."

Elias swallowed hard and shamed himself for the sudden rush of need burning through him. Celia was in no condition for his company in her bed. "I do not wish to jostle you and cause you any pain."

"Move slow and careful," she told him, sounding like a patient nanny instructing a child. "I need you beside me, Elias. To feel your warmth. Have the safety of you here at my side. I want to breathe in your comforting, familiar scent with every breath. Please join me. You won't hurt me. I saw such terrible things while I slept. A twisted reliving of what happened." Her voice broke as she tugged on him. "And I dreamt you died. Please, Elias. Come to bed and hold me. I need to feel you with me while I sleep."

He kissed her, gently at first, and then carefully deepened the connection so she would know he would always protect her. "I am here for you, my love. Always and forever."

After shedding his boots and waistcoat, he rounded the bed and pulled back the covers.

"What about your shirt and pantaloons?" She squinted at him with a critical frown. "They are surely ruined with all those stains."

He decided it was best not to tell her that her blood had caused those stains. He peeled off his shirt and tossed it aside. "Mrs. Camp works miracles with stains."

"Pantaloons, my lord," she said as he started to climb into the bed.

"My lady," he said, leaning across the bed. "Your insistence that I be naked has altered me dramatically, and you are in no condition to relieve me of my state."

Her wicked smile nearly undid him. "I fear you have married a selfish woman, my lord. One greedy to behold all her husband has to offer, whether she can properly enjoy it or not." She smoothed her hand across the space beside her. "After all, I will not be mending forever."

"Indeed." What a deliciously uncomfortable defeat. Elias straightened, unbuttoned the garment in question, and shoved it down to the floor. As he slid into the bed beside her, he reveled in the way she wet her lips and drew in a quick breath. "You do realize I shall have to address your greediness once you are fully healed?"

"I sincerely hope so, dear husband, because I enjoyed our *betrothal* tryst in the garden immensely." She laced her fingers through his and held his hand tightly. "I wish I could lie on my side with my head on your chest, but I am afraid to try it."

"Do not, or I shall exit this bed immediately. You must lie still so as not to start the bleeding again." He kissed her hand, then pointedly placed their entwined arms down at their sides like a chaste barrier between them. "Close your eyes, my precious lioness. Rest and heal. We have the rest of our lives together."

"The rest of our lives," she repeated, worrying her delicate thumb back and forth across his as she held tightly to his hand.

Her sudden silence as she stared up at the canopy made him turn onto his side, prop himself on his elbow, and peer at her closer. "I said close your eyes and rest, my love. Not stare up into the night and fret about the future."

"But that is all I have ever done." She shifted to look at him. "And now I have dragged an honest man into my illegal legacy. I fear you will regret what you have done as much as I regret bringing you to your ruin."

"I am not ruined," he reassured her as he closed her eyes with a gentle touch, then stroked a fingertip over the curve of her cheeks, across the fullness of her lips, and along her jaw line. "Leave tomorrow's worries to tomorrow, my precious one. Sleep, my love, while the remnants of the laudanum help hold the brunt of your pain at bay."

"I never want to be alone again," she said in a drowsy whisper without opening her eyes.

"You never will be, dearest. Never again." He tickled his touch in slow circles across her forehead, along her cheeks, then back up again across her temples. "I am always with you," he murmured, smiling as her breathing slowed back to the steady rhythm of earlier while she slept.

"Elias," she uttered on an exhale.

"I am here, dear one." He kept up the methodical stroking of her face that mesmerized her into a relaxed state.

"Love…you."

"And I love you, Celia, with a never-ending fury."

CHAPTER SEVENTEEN

"H AS MADNESS TAKEN over this entire household?" Propped up in the bed among a multitude of pillows, her face flushed with the vibrancy of returning good health, Celia scowled at the three of them as though ready to pass judgment on their eternal souls.

Elias glanced over at his brother and Duchess Thea in a silent plea for help.

With a tug on his black armband of mourning, Monty cut an amused look back at him as though reveling in Elias's dilemma of handling his prickly wife.

Celia's mother, swathed in yards of black bombazine and crepe, blew out a high-pitched sigh and flexed her hands in their black lace, fingerless gloves atop the jeweled handle of her cane.

"Celia—" Elias decided on a different tactic to convince his stubborn new bride that Monty's somewhat elaborate plan actually held merit and, so far, had worked brilliantly.

The dowager duchess rapped her cane on the floor for silence and marched closer to her daughter.

He readily surrendered the floor to his mother-in-law, silently wishing her luck and Godspeed. As Celia had gotten stronger, her patience with remaining abed as the doctor ordered had lessened with each passing day. The devil himself couldn't get along with his fractious beauty, and Elias dared any brave demon to try.

He also secretly reveled in every minute of it. Her furious

temperament meant she was healing, and soon—very soon, he hoped—their marriage bed would serve for something much more enjoyable than sleeping.

"Celia," the dowager said with another sharp stamp of her cane. "The plan is already in motion and has been quite successful thus far. It is the answer to our dilemma."

"And has dear old Prinny already gobbled up our entailed lands now that he knows no one holds the title? Has he declared it extinct and asked for the accounts? What about our businesses? The people who depend upon us? Those things not covered by Charles's will?" Celia fisted her hands atop the bedcovers. "That is exactly why we didn't kill off my beloved brother in the first place, remember? So everything we worked for wouldn't end up in the hands of Prinny's favorites!"

"Cecilia Elizabeth! Keep your voice down and mind your tone!" Duchess Thea rapped her cane on the floor yet again, then turned and ordered Elias forward with a snap of her head. "Explain it to her, son-in-law. Details, if you please. It is the business side of her. She only listens to details."

"Facts," Celia said, her eyes flashing. "I understand facts, and as yet, all I have seen and heard goes against everything you ingrained in me since birth, Mama."

"The Hasterton estate, the entailments, and personal property of the duke will take some time to settle for two reasons, my love," Elias said. "First, thanks to the brilliance of you and your mother, the estate is vast and multilayered. Ample time in probate will prevent any nefarious disputes which might rear their ugly heads." Elias couldn't resist a smugness he rarely allowed himself. "And second, as the executor of the duke's will, I shall insist that the Prerogative Court of Canterbury here in London proves the terms are properly settled beyond a shadow of a doubt." He leaned down and kissed her cheek. "All this will give us time to get the original Hasterton letters patent amended. The announcement of the duke's untimely demise is in this morning's papers, as is the report of the dreadful attack on your person while you, Lady Sophie, and a gentleman whose name Lady Sophie refused to divulge strolled around Vauxhall Gardens."

"And I shall see to it that the motion for the amendment is brought to the floor next week," Monty said with a gloating hike of his brows that made Elias duck his head to hide a smile. His brother was enjoying this entirely too much.

"You shall soon be the Duchess of Hasterton, my lady love, and legally so." Elias braced himself. His lioness was still not happy, and was about to enlighten all of them on the error of their ways. He saw it in her eyes.

She stared straight ahead, her delicate nostrils flaring as she pulled in a deep breath. With her hands clasped so tightly in her lap that her knuckles turned white, she attempted a smile and failed. "Might I have a private word with my husband?" she forced through clenched teeth.

The dowager and Monty looked to him as if waiting for his last request before he went to the gallows.

After a tip of his head to release them, Elias resettled his stance and watched them file out and close the door softly behind them.

"This will never work. None of it!" Celia whipped her covers aside with a pained grimace, then gingerly rose from the bed.

Elias rushed to support her. "You were ordered to stay in bed, remember?"

"I am sick of that blasted bed!" With careful steps, she stayed the course until she reached the chaise longue beside the window. "Lying about is making me weaker. I can feel my energy ebbing like the tide going out."

There was no point arguing with her, and if she felt strong enough to be up and about, then more power to her. Elias doubted very much that old Dr. MacMaddenly could best her.

"How much did you have to pay the Bow Street Runners and Dr. MacMaddenly for their silence?" She winced as she lowered herself to the couch and leaned back among the pillows.

"They are honorable men who refused to take anything once

we explained the situation." Elias draped a light cover across her, then settled down beside her. "Elkins still loves your mother, and it appears old MacMaddenly is smitten with her as well. Portney has worked for me for years and is a family man. He knows what happens to women not properly provided for. England's laws about such things are reprehensible." He placed her feet in his lap and started massaging them, as a rather talented whore had once shown him after a long night of celebrating his cruel father's death.

"And your brother suggested this farce?" Shifting a pillow to better support herself, Celia eyed Elias with such an infuriated look that he laughed. She shook a finger at him. "This is not funny, Elias. Have you forgotten your reaction when I confessed my story to you? And yet here you accept your brother's escapade with open arms when his plot is a great deal weightier on the immoral and illegal side of things than mine was." She shook her head. "Using Friedrich's body as the duke's?" She gingerly clapped a hand on her chest. "For heaven's sake, they shall hang us all."

He ached to gather her in his arms and kiss away her frustrations but didn't dare—not as sore as she still seemed to be. "Monty's plan will set you and your mother free. *That* is why I accepted it with open arms."

"And you truly believe Parliament will pass the act amending the dukedom?" The way she bit her lip made him ache to find the words to console her as he brushed her tousled curls back from her face. She caught his hand and clutched it as though fearing he would abandon her. "What if they vote the amendment down? Then what will we do?"

He wished he could ease her worries but realized she had carried them with her all her life. His dear one didn't know any other way to feel. "At the very worst, my love, the entailed properties would be lost and the title would go extinct. But you know as well as I that with so much transferred to the Bening accounts, all of us could live quite comfortably—even without my earnings, which are nothing to dismiss, by the way."

"But what about *my* businesses? *My* investments? Have you any idea how many people depend on my help for their livelihoods?" Her lower lip quivered, and she clutched his hand tighter. "Mama and I worked so very hard to build an empire that not only helped us but helped others like us. Is all of it to be lost?"

"As I recall, the will has the executor take over their management." He knew she wouldn't like his next suggestion, but it was all he could offer her. "You could maintain your operations under my name." Another thought reared its ugly head. "Even after the letters patent is amended, the business dealings might have to be handled much as we have addressed them in the past. Through my office, and rather than *Charles's* signature—mine. Anything you attempt might not be taken seriously because you are a woman."

Celia released his hand and massaged her temples. A bitter huff escaped her. "I must be getting soft. All this talk is making my head pound."

"You were supposed to stay in bed, dear one. It has only been a few days since your attack."

"Do not chide. I am not in the mood to bear it and have not an ounce of politeness left within me." She leaned her head back against the pillows and closed her eyes. "I want to dress and sit in the gardens, since the sun has finally decided to shine once again." She cracked open an eye and glared at him, daring him to refuse her.

Fresh air would do his precious one a world of good. Dr. MacMaddenly could fuss all he wished. The man was not only paid well but had yet to vacate the guest room with which he had been provided. The old goat's excuses grew lamer with each passing day.

Elias rose and pressed a lingering kiss to Celia's forehead, breathing in the sweetness of her jasmine scent. "I shall fetch Berta immediately. Once she has you ready, I shall carry you down to the gardens, and when you tire of butterflies, bees, and sunshine, I shall carry you back upstairs. We shall have tea there. A delightful picnic. How does that sound?"

Celia lifted her head, her eyes brighter at the prospect. "What about Dr. MacMaddenly?"

"If necessary, I shall lock the bugger in his room."

She laughed, then cringed and caught her chest. "Do not make me laugh." But the pleasure in her tone softened the scolding. "I could probably make it down the stairs all right."

"Either I carry you both ways or you do not go to the garden at all." Elias waited for her to accept his non-negotiable terms.

"You have become a great deal more assertive since our vows." She eyed him with a teasing look he found immensely stirring. "I haven't decided if I like such assertiveness or not."

He leaned in for a slow, thorough kiss. When he drew back, he smiled at the high coloring on her cheeks. "I am merely being a good husband, my love."

Before he straightened, she caught hold of his shirt and pulled him in for another heated kiss, entwining her tongue with his. "I shall be glad when we can be good together," she said in a breathless whisper across his lips.

"I as well, my lioness." He cleared his throat and stepped back, struggling to regain control of the yearning that raged just below the surface, anxiously waiting to be unleashed. "I shall send in Berta and order our picnic."

Her coy smile inflamed him even more. "Yes, my love."

Celia luxuriated in Elias cradling her against his muscular chest as he carried her into the gardens—to the spot beside the waterfall where she had not only given him her virtue but also finally accepted his capture of her heart. Several blankets were spread on the ground. Carefully stacked piles of pillows created a pleasing lounge for two.

She arched a brow at him. "Really? You chose this very spot?"

"What better place, my love?" His attempt at appearing innocent failed miserably.

"Indeed." She couldn't resist a soft giggle. After he gently deposited her onto their pillowed nest, she smoothed out the folds of her black dress and frowned down at them. "I wonder if this would be considered an improper activity for those in mourning?"

"It is your private garden," he said. "What others think does not matter."

The servants had also somehow found a short legged table for setting in their midst. It was covered with a fine linen tablecloth embroidered with tiny roses and everything needed for the perfect picnic. A plentiful assortment of delicate finger sandwiches, sweetmeats, cakes, tea, and even a small decanter of pale golden brandy waited for them.

"Brandy or tea, my love?" Elias sat closest to the table and cut her off with a stern arch of his brow when she started to argue that she should be the one serving. "Brandy or tea, and which sandwiches and cakes do you prefer?"

"How did you know what I was going to say?" She nodded at the teapot. "And I shall start with tea, please, and perhaps a small slice of the lemon cake."

"I knew what you were going to say because your eyes not only show me your soul but also mirror your thoughts and feelings." He handed her the tea and cake, then served himself. "By the way, your brother's funeral was the day before yesterday. What with the summer heat and his condition after the highwaymen finished with him, it was better that it take place in a timely manner—even before the announcement hit the papers."

She took a sip of her tea, then frowned down at the delicate golden cake. Her appetite suddenly left her. "Poor Friedrich. In a grave marked with another man's name. Do you think he will haunt us?"

"Only our memories and nightmares." He offered her the

salver of sweetmeats, but she declined. "What is it, love? You have that look."

"Where were you on the night of my *attack* outside the Pleasure Gardens? Will people not ask about that, since I am now your wife? I do not wish you to appear to be a coward."

"I believe Monty covered that by saying you and I had a rather spirited disagreement that night, and you sent me packing, then off you went to the gardens with Lady Sophie just to spite me."

"Did I? How terribly foolish of me. No wonder I was attacked." Celia found the story mildly irritating. While she didn't wish him to be emasculated by the scheme, nor did she wish to be portrayed as a mindless ninny. "And then, I suppose, my injuries made us realize our undying love and marry immediately?"

"Something like that." He leaned in close and gently caressed her cheek. "The scheme has worked admirably, my love, and I see no reason why it should not continue. We must play this opportunity with all the grace and intelligence you and your mother commanded for so many years." The love in his eyes melted her worries away. "We can do this."

An exaggerated cough came to them through the hedges. Celia shifted among the pillows and called out, "Gransdon? Is that you?"

"Yes, my lady." The butler emerged from the leafy maze, his long face more sour than usual. "Lady Bournebridge and her daughter, Lady Temperance, would like to offer their condolences."

Celia turned to Elias. "When did you say the announcement was to hit the papers?"

His suspicious scowl mirrored her concerns. "This very morning," he said. "Could they not just leave a card?" Elias asked the butler.

"No, my lord." Gransdon's displeased pucker deepened. "They are in the drawing room. They vehemently insisted on seeing either yourself or Her Grace. Do forgive me, but I felt Her Grace should not be disturbed and that such an untimely meeting would be better handled by yourself, my lord."

"Quite correct, Gransdon. That cackling old hen and her daughter merely want to be the first to confirm the gossip." Elias rose.

"Surely, you do not mean to speak to them?" As far as Celia was concerned, the woman and her daughter could be swept out with the day's dirt.

"It is important that word spread through the *ton*, my love." He tipped his head in the exit's direction. "What better way could we ask for? And her brother-in-law also happens to be none other than the prime minister himself. We need Lord Liverpool and his cabinet on our side because they introduce all legislation. It is also my understanding that Lady Bournebridge is related to the speaker of the house as well. Monty brought it to my attention that the woman has more influential connections than I have hairs on my head. We must tread carefully with them. Lord Bournebridge and the prime minister both attended the funeral and offered their condolences. I am still not quite certain how Monty pulled that one off."

"I dislike this." Celia felt the same uncomfortable sense of something about to go very wrong that always guided her with choosing investments. Her intuition never led her astray. "There is more than gossip at stake here. I feel it." She tried to rise, but a stabbing pain when she tried to push herself up made her cry out and fall back among the pillows.

"Celia!" Elias dove back to her. "Lie still. Gransdon, fetch Dr. MacMaddenly immediately."

"Yes, my lord." The butler disappeared.

A harsh stinging set her chest on fire. Renewed throbbing at the deepest part of her wound forced her to sink back into the pillows and obey. "If that man lectures me, it will be his last," she warned, while curling on one side and holding her chest. Her bandages still appeared dry, thank heavens. At least the surly Scot couldn't complain she had torn open the wound and caused it to bleed.

After a few slow, steady breaths, she opened her eyes to Elias kneeling at her side. She patted his arm. "Go flatter Bournebridge and her daughter out of here. I shall behave while you are gone and be still as a statue until you return. I promise."

"I will not leave you like this." He hovered over her like a magnificent beast guarding its young. "The Bournebridges can sit there and gather dust, as far as I am concerned."

"My protective panther." She cradled his cheek in her hand and smiled. "I am fine. I simply moved too quickly." She had also been rash enough to move as though she had no wound at all. Quite a poor decision on her part. "Since you refuse to leave me, once Dr. MacMaddenly has seen to me, might I please accompany you to the parlor? You can help me get there. I cannot bear the thought of not hearing your conversation with those two firsthand, because I know you'll forget and leave out details I should know."

His scowl failed to give her much hope that he would agree. "You still do not trust me."

"No!" She pulled him closer. "I want to be there and hear what they say. Isolation in that damn bedroom of mine has been unbearable." He had no idea how frustrating it was to be cut off from everything.

"Damn bedroom?" he repeated with a grin. "Such language, my love."

"The situation demands it." The sound of hurried footsteps warned her she had little time to extricate a promise from her overly protective husband. "You can carry me into the parlor and have them visit us there rather than the drawing room. I can rest on the sofa just as easily as I can convalesce in bed. Please?"

"If Dr. MacMaddenly allows it—" Elias started before being cut off by the man himself.

"If Dr. MacMaddenly allows what?" The gruff Scot glared down at her in disapproval. "You were ordered to remain in your bed, Lady Cecilia."

"I have never done well with orders," Celia huffed. "You might as well learn that about me now. And how do you expect me to strengthen and recuperate if you weaken me by forced confinement to my bed?"

The doctor astonished her by chuckling. "Ye are a great deal like your mother, I see." His amusement disappeared as quickly as it came. "Can I trust ye to be honest, about whether or not ye feel the slightest dampness of your bandages?"

"Of course you can trust me. What sort of question is that?" She shot Elias a warning scowl to be quiet, then gently rested her hand on her chest. "The bandages are not wet. I have not torn the stitches nor restarted the bleeding. I simply moved too quickly and did not consider that I would need to rise in a different manner so as not to stir any more pain."

"Help her stand," Dr. MacMaddenly told Elias.

Determined to prove to both the doctor and her husband she was quite able to move about, Celia forced herself to take greater care. With Elias's arm around her, she faced down the doctor, daring him to defy her. "You see? I am a little weak, but with care and an appropriate amount of time free of my bed, I will become stronger."

The physician shook his head and clapped a hand on Elias's shoulder. "God help ye, man." He leveled a stern glare on Celia. "I shall grant ye your freedom, but know this: if ye overdo, ye will be right back where ye started—if not worse." He pointed at her. "Do not overdo, my lady. I shall check the wound later when we change your bandages, aye?"

"Yes, Dr. MacMaddenly."

"And I will thank ye not to spit out my name as though it tastes bad," he scolded, but his demeanor bordered on jovial. "Send for me if ye need me, m'lady. I shall be with your mother in her sitting room."

"In her sitting room," Celia repeated, finding the idea impossible to imagine.

"Aye." The doctor puffed out his chest and straightened his spectacles. "Her Grace has challenged me to a game of chess, and placed such a tempting wager on her winning that I canna refuse."

"And the wager is?" Celia asked even though she wasn't quite certain she wished to know.

Dr. MacMaddenly winked. "That is between your mother and me, m'lady." Then he strode away, quietly whistling a jaunty tune.

Celia turned to Elias, ready to scream because she didn't have the strength to run up to her mother's rooms and put a stop to such nonsense. "Surely, he does not mean…"

Elias steadied her, then gently pulled her into a hug. "What your mother does is none of our affair, my love." He kissed her forehead and smiled down at her. "Now, I must see to our influential guests that cannot be ignored. If you refuse to stay here or retire to your rooms, then allow me to help you to the parlor, and I shall have Lady Bournebridge and her daughter brought to you, so you might hear every word uttered."

"When my strength fully returns, you shall regret teasing me," she threatened while leaning closer to breathe in his strength and revel in it. Perhaps tonight, if they were extremely slow and careful…

An aching heat flooded through her at the prospect. She allowed him to wrap his arm around her waist but attempted to appear sternly displeased with him. "We will continue this conversation later."

"I look forward to it, my love. Shall I carry you?"

"No. I wish to try it on my own, thank you."

He walked slowly beside her, holding her steady and letting her draw from his quiet strength. As they neared the parlor, he brought them to a stop and whispered, "Remember—we need Lady Bournebridge's connections. Her support. If she is not pleased—neither her husband nor her brother-in-law will aid us in our cause."

She blew out a pained sigh. "I will try not to pull the old cat's tail."

He eyed her as though doubting her sincerity. "Swear it."

She couldn't help but roll her eyes and blow out another disgruntled huff. "I swear."

Elias slowly shook his head and continued on into the parlor. "Here on the sofa, I think. With a footstool to rest your feet on, and I shall sit beside you."

"To keep me properly behaved, I suppose?"

He laughed. "I would never attempt such a thing, my love." With a smoldering look, he added, "I rather enjoyed it the last time you misbehaved."

Another surge of heat rushed through her. She pressed her hands to her cheeks and prayed for them to cool as she settled into her seat. The ladies would surely wonder at the redness of her face.

With some dismay, she realized she was relieved to be sitting. To be so weary after such a short walk simply would not do. She needed to be a wife in every sense of the word—both for herself and Elias. She made a silent vow to build her strength with a great deal more walking. Dr. MacMaddenly and Elias both could either accept it or not. She would do what she would do.

As if reading her mind, Elias caught hold of her hands and kissed them. "Patience, Celia. We have the rest of our lives. Give yourself time to heal. I am here at your side and not going anywhere."

"Swear it," she whispered, allowing herself to sink into his gaze.

"With my life," he answered without hesitation. "And now I shall ring for Gransdon to bring in our guests."

"If you must." She dutifully folded her hands in her lap and waited, wiggling her feet to make sure her somber black dress fell into graceful folds all around her legs. *I must be nice,* she chanted to herself.

The unwanted women fluttered into the room, reminding

Celia of a pair of startled geese running along with their wings flapping. Both wore gowns of the palest yellow with white flowers embroidered on the skirts and puffed sleeves. Their white gloves and white bonnets were in stark contrast to the red mottling of their faces. They must have worked themselves into quite a state before being told someone would finally see them.

"Lady Cecelia—you poor, poor dear," Lady Bournebridge said in a long, drawn-out whine that nearly made Celia gag. "Temperance and I could not bring ourselves to believe the horrid reports from Lord Bournebridge and my sister's husband, Lord Liverpool. We thought them surely mistaken. But when we read the grim details in print, we could no longer turn our beliefs aside. Please, please accept our condolences."

"Yes, please do," Temperance added in her nasal whine. "Are you quite certain you are recovered enough for callers? We thought to see no one other than Lord Raines." Her pinch-faced gaze flitted to Elias then returned to Celia.

"I am still quite weak," Celia said, which wasn't a lie, but she loathed admitting it. She drew a handkerchief from her sleeve and dabbed it to her eyes, drying imaginary tears. "And my poor brother Charles is gone."

"Terrible loss," Lady Bournebridge said with a sad shake of her head. She squirmed in her chair like an overly excited child. "With no known heirs, whatever shall become of you and your mother?"

Biting the inside of her cheek to halt a sharp retort, Celia reached for Elias's hand. "Only time will tell, I fear. The future is almost too awful to bear. Thankfully, I have my husband to give me strength."

Both ladies perked like a pair of cats spotting a mouse. "Your *husband*?" Lady Bournebridge repeated. "We knew you to be betrothed but were not aware you had already married."

"By special license, I suppose?" Lady Temperance asked, sounding prickly with envy.

"Yes," Elias said. "We exchanged vows while she lay there

bleeding. They fetched me as soon as they brought her home. I feared she would leave me before we finished our vows."

Celia squeezed his hand, willing him to proceed with caution. The ladies were lapping up his every word. They would surely need to be burped when he finished.

"You thought her dying and wished to marry her before she left you." Lady Bournebridge clutched both hands to her ample bosom. She and Lady Temperance exhaled wistful sighs.

"So romantic," Lady Temperance added, her thin lips quivering and her eyes gleaming with tears.

"Please do spread the word about my awful attack," Celia said, trying to sound weak and fragile. "I would so hate for anyone else to suffer such a thing. It was so terrible, I cannot bear to even think about it, much less speak of it." She didn't need them to ask questions about the attack, since she did not know what wild embellishments Monty had claimed.

"Indeed, we will," Lady Bournebridge promised. She leaned forward, her hands still clasped to her chest. "Your mother—how is she faring?"

"She is with the doctor now," Celia managed to tell them without smiling. "Dr. MacMaddenly has been indispensable to us during this terrible time."

"We should go, Mother," Lady Temperance said quietly. "After all, the household is in deep mourning, and Lady Cecilia surely needs her rest."

"Quite right." Lady Bournebridge hefted herself to her feet and offered a solemn curtsy when Elias stood and bowed. "If there is anything at all we can do to make this trying time easier," she said, "please do not hesitate to send word, and it shall be done. I will see to it personally."

"Do forgive me for not rising." Celia weakly fanned herself. "I am still so weak. And thank you so much for coming by, Lady Bournebridge, Lady Temperance. Your thoughtfulness has brought us more comfort than you could ever know." Celia politely bowed her head at both ladies, while biting the inside of her cheek to keep from choking on the lie.

Both ladies preened beneath the praise, curtsied again, then took their leave.

Elias hurried to the window with his hand held high to signal the need for total silence. After a long moment of peering through a crack in the drawn draperies, he let it drop and turned to Celia with a smile. "Your concerned friends are gone, my love."

"Concerned friends, my foot." Celia wrinkled her nose. "The room reeks of them now. We must ask the maids to air it."

"In the meantime, my dear lady, shall I carry you to your sitting room, or do you wish to return to the garden? You have been up for a while now and even received visitors. Remember what the doctor said about overdoing it?"

"The garden." She needed the sun and fresh air. But most of all, she needed Elias beside her, assuring her everything would be all right.

"The garden it is." Elias scooped her up and settled her against his chest. "It will be all right, Celia," he said quietly as he curled her even closer and looked down into her eyes.

"As long as you are here with me," she whispered. "Never leave."

"I never will, my love. I swear it."

CHAPTER EIGHTEEN

CELIA'S SOFT SNORES sent a warm surge of joy and content-ment through Elias. Her head rested in the dip of his shoulder, and her arm lay across his chest. She had thrown the silkiness of her leg across his thighs, and her wondrous breasts shifted against him with her every intake of breath. Not a stitch of clothing existed between them, and never would whenever they were in bed, if Elias had his way about it. With the greatest of care and mindlessly superb ecstasy, they had, at last, after waiting two weeks for her wound to heal, consummated their vows—three times, in fact.

He stared up into the darkness, thankful he had not lost her—the first time because of his own idiocy and the second time to that murderous fiend Friedrich. Now their lives could settle into the routine of a happily married couple. An amused huff escaped him. Somehow, he doubted life with Celia would ever be dull or routine.

His thoughts turned somber, going from blissful thankfulness to worry. Monty's efforts to get the letters patent amended had not gone as smoothly nor as quickly as they had hoped. In fact, envious whisperings of opportunistic money-grabbing and jealous glances had become disturbingly regular—even from those in Elias's office. The amendment seemed to have stalled and kept getting pushed aside for other matters. Frustration made him blow out a heavy sigh.

"You insisted I not fret over the delays, yet you huff and puff like the bellows for a fire." Celia shifted with a deep yawn, then curled tighter against him. "I do not mind so much about the title or entailments anymore. My greatest worry is damage to the businesses." Her voice was raspy with sleepiness. She cleared her throat and blew out a heavy sigh. "So many families depend on us to help them keep their shops going until they can fully manage their accounts themselves." She lifted her head and gave him a worried frown. "If we cannot secure the dukedom, is there any way we can transfer what remains under the name of Hasterton to the Bening accounts—including the businesses?"

"I am afraid not, my love." Elias wouldn't lie to her. "With everything in probate, we can move nothing." He combed his fingers through her dark, silken curls, loving the way they tumbled across his chest. "But all is not lost yet. There is still hope for the amendment to be approved. Everything is astir right now because of Wellington's victory. Once things settle, I am sure we will persevere. Lady Bournebridge assured it. Remember?" He gently pulled her in for a long, slow kiss that stirred him to consider pursuing a fourth consummation of their vows. "At least now you and your mother are safe," he whispered across the suppleness of her mouth. "Everything else can be...*handled* however it needs to be."

"Handled," she repeated while sliding her hand downward. She cast a quick glance at the dwindling candle on the nightstand, then smiled. "Are we terribly wanton for doing this so many times in one night?"

"Terribly," he said with a groan as she artfully stroked his member with slow, teasing pulls that made it difficult to be patient and resist the temptation of rolling her over and sinking back inside her. "But if you think about it," he said, "we are making up for lost time. After all, we have been married for two weeks."

"Indeed," she said as she straddled him and rubbed her wetness against him with every excruciatingly perfect stroke. "Two weeks. Fourteen days. Once a day—or, say, twice—since we are newlyweds." She guided him in, encasing him in her hot slickness. As she slowly rocked her hips, she leaned forward, sliding her hands up his chest to nibble on his bottom lip. "That works out to be twenty-eight times. We have a great deal of catching up to do."

He filled his hands with her luscious bottom and helped her rock faster. "Your mathematics are exemplary."

"One can only strive to do one's best," she whispered as she guided his mouth to her breast while grinding against him harder.

With his mouth full, Elias could only groan in agreement.

Celia clutched him to her breasts, pulling him upright as she arched and threw back her head while filling their bedroom with her moans.

Patience could just be damned. He gently rolled her, ground in deeper, then pounded hard and long.

She met his every thrust, then shrieked as her shuttering spasms spurred him to hammer on to his own release with a hearty roar.

Trembling with the need to collapse on top of his precious love, Elias forced himself to shift and pull her back into his embrace at his side. While she might be strong enough for their loving, his weight on her would be far too much. He turned her face to his, lifted his head, and kissed her. "I love you, my precious lioness. More than you will ever know."

"I love you, dear husband—even though you irritated me into doing so." The light from the nearly spent candle sparkled in her eyes, making him catch his breath at the depth of love he saw there.

"I am glad I irritated you into loving me." Relaxing back on the pillow, he rested his cheek against the top of her head and pulled her hand to the center of his chest. "Feel that? My heart beats for you, Celia. It always will."

"I am glad," she whispered in a sleepy voice. "Now, sleep and restore yourself. We have to go twenty-four more times before we catch up to where we should be."

Elias couldn't resist a lazy chuckle. "And if we lose count, we shall have to start over again."

"Indeed."

EPILOGUE

Six months later
Hasterton House
London, England

"…AND FAILING THE heirs male of his body, all titles, entailments, and honors shall pass to his eldest daughter and the heirs male of her body." Monty lifted his glass of champagne higher. "Huzzah! The Hasterton duchy is amended!"

"Huzzah!" Celia steadied her glass while swiping at happy tears that insisted on rolling down her cheeks. "I cannot believe it is done."

"Nor can I, *Duchess* Cecilia," her mother said. After a sip of champagne, she handed her glass to Dr. MacMaddenly. "You see? I promised one sip, and one sip is all I took."

The old Scot rewarded her with a kiss on the cheek. "Well done, Mrs. MacMaddenly. Well done, indeed."

Celia's mother took his arm and hugged him closer. "*Mrs. MacMaddenly* sounds so much better than the old dowager duchess."

"I agree." He turned and lifted his glass to Celia and Elias. "Congratulations to ye both." Then he turned and lifted it to Monty. "And to the man who kept at it with the tenacity of a Scot. Are ye certain ye've no Scottish blood in ye?"

"None of which I am aware," Monty replied, laughing.

"I wish Sophie and Frannie were here to share in the news,"

235

Celia said as she handed her half-empty glass to Elias. "We shall have another celebration when they arrive in two weeks' time for Christmas."

"And which news shall we celebrate then?" Elias asked with a smug grin.

Celia tried to give him a warning nudge but couldn't help but smile. He was so proud and so excited. "Tell them, my love. I shan't make you wait any longer."

"Tell us what?" her mother demanded with a hopeful step toward them.

"You are to be a grandmother, Your Grace," Elias said. "Late spring or perhaps early summer, as near as we can calculate."

"Of course," Celia added with a wicked grin, "my mathematics are exemplary, but if the little one proves to inherit the stubbornness of the father—June."

"And late May if he or she possesses the impatience of his or her mother," Elias shot back. He set their champagne aside and pulled Celia into his arms. "But I wouldn't have you any other way, my duchess," he murmured, then kissed her so soundly, she became breathless. He lifted his head and whispered, "By the way, my love, what number are we on?"

With as innocent a look as she could manage in front of their family, she whispered back, "I fear I have lost count, my lord."

He swept her up into his arms and started for the stairs. Before exiting the drawing room, he turned back and smiled at Monty, Dr. MacMaddenly, and the dowager. "Do excuse us. It appears we must start over."

"Start what over?" Monty asked.

Celia buried her heated face in the crook of Elias's neck as he answered his brother with a hearty laugh, then strode forward and took the steps up to their bedroom two at a time.

About the Author

If you enjoyed TO STEAL A DUKE, please consider leaving a review on the site where you purchased your copy, or a reader site such as Goodreads, or BookBub.

If you'd like to receive my newsletter, here's the link to sign up:
maevegreyson.com/contact.html#newsletter

I love to hear from readers! Drop me a line at
maevegreyson@gmail.com

Or visit me on Facebook:
facebook.com/AuthorMaeveGreyson

Join my Facebook Group – Maeve's Corner:
facebook.com/groups/MaevesCorner

I'm also on Instagram:
maevegreyson

My website:
https://maevegreyson.com

Feel free to ask questions or leave some Reader Buzz on
bingebooks.com/author/maeve-greyson

Goodreads:
goodreads.com/maevegreyson

Follow me on these sites to get notifications about new releases, sales, and special deals:

Amazon:
amazon.com/Maeve-Greyson/e/B004PE9T9U

BookBub:
bookbub.com/authors/maeve-greyson

Many thanks and may your life always be filled with good books!
Maeve